THE SPY RING

CAKE LOVE Series Book 4

Elizabeth Lynx

For information contact:
lynxelizabeth1@gmail.com
http://www.elizabeth-lynx.com

Book and Cover design by Elizabeth Lynx
Photography by ikostudio
Formatting template by Derek Murphy of Creativindie Design
ISBN-13: 978-0-9992799-1-5

DEDICATION

To all the loving and devoted parents of the little superheroes in the world...their special needs children.

Table of Contents

THE SPY RING 1

DEDICATION 3

TABLE OF CONTENTS 4

ONE 6

TWO 12

THREE 18

FOUR 25

FIVE 31

SIX 37

SEVEN 44

EIGHT 51

NINE 58

TEN 65

ELEVEN 71

TWELVE 77

THIRTEEN 83

FOURTEEN 90

FIFTEEN 96

SIXTEEN 103

SEVENTEEN 110

EIGHTEEN 117

NINETEEN 123

TWENTY 129

TWENTY-ONE 136

TWENTY-TWO 142

TWENTY-THREE 148

TWENTY-FOUR 155

TWENTY-FIVE 162

TWENTY-SIX 169

TWENTY-SEVEN 174

TWENTY-EIGHT 180

TWENTY-NINE 187

THIRTY 194

THIRTY-ONE 201

THIRTY-TWO 207

THIRTY-THREE 215

EPILOGUE 224

BEHIND THE SCENES 231

ABOUT THE AUTHOR 234

THANK YOU 235

ONE

Tiffany

"He's flipping married?"

I whisper screamed as I fisted the thick, smooth band of gold.

It had weight. It's funny how I noticed that little tidbit instantly but never realized the man I slept with last night was married.

At least, I think we had sex. My stomach began to churn as I tried to recall anything from the night before. Nothing but throbbing head pain and something about a whiskey sour sucker punched my brain.

Ugh, I couldn't even remember the guy's face.

Wow, Tiffany, you can't even do your first one-night stand right.

I shook my head and glanced around the stranger's hotel room. It was a much bigger version of my room. The same soothing lavender and gray color scheme but somehow knowing this guy had bank in order to afford this big suite in Las Vegas did nothing to appease my nausea. Or my guilt.

Was it my imagination or was the ring burning an *O* into my palm? *O* for odious because that's how I felt and, lifting my arm to take a whiff under my pit, that's definitely how I smelled. Flipping the ring over, the inscription made all thoughts of the big *O* disappear as my throat tightened. *Honor always. Protect fully. Love forever.*

"What a crock of gobbledygook," I said giving the ring the stink eye.

The hot hands of remorse spread boney fingers around my neck and across my chest.

"I'm not the one that cheated," I said to the ring.

The burning guilt had to end.

Stop blaming yourself, Tiffany. He's the one that cheated, not you. You don't have a husband anymore, remember?

I dropped the wedding band and it made a clanking sound, bouncing on the wood of the coffee table. The stabbing behind my right eye grew in strength from the joke he obviously believed his marriage to be. The pun where I played the fool to satisfy his needs.

A woman placed this beautiful ring on his finger believing him to be her savior, her true love, and the man who would never deceive her. And that meant nothing to him.

I'm done. Bile inched up my throat, making me desperate to find my clothes so I could get out of this den of sin before the guy got out of the shower. It was nice to feel some relief this morning knowing he was in the bathroom when I woke. I was thankful I never had to put a face to my shame.

All my friends, except for Evaleen, told me I needed to get laid. Since my husband was gone, I haven't been able to find the time or the heart, to be with another man.

It had been too long. That's why when I came to Las Vegas for the weekend with my friends, I thought it was the perfect time to have a no-strings-attached fling.

Wrong.

They were wrong. I was wrong.

The only thing the night left me with was nausea, terrible remorse, and breath so bad it could be used to bring down a small elephant.

As much as I needed a drink of water and a hot shower to clean off my regret, I had to find my clothes.

One of my red leather heels was under the coffee table and after further inspection, I found the other behind the lavender couch. After a few minutes of hunting, I had gathered all my clothes, even my green lace undies that were wrapped around the telephone.

I dressed quickly—if not clumsily—and thought maybe I should be glad I couldn't remember anything.

As I closed the door to his room behind me and stumbled my way toward the elevator, I considered turning back to leave a note. But then I imagined what I would write in my current mental state.

Hey You,

Yeah, you know who you are so let's not play that game where I impress you with my ability to recall your name. I'm the one you had sex with last night. I'd like to say it was great but since I was blackout drunk, I won't comment on what I don't know.

And that brings me to a very important point . . . Why did YOU take advantage of an obviously drunk woman? Were you blackout drunk yourself? I am hoping you were because if you ever see me again, like walking down the street, I wish upon all the wishes in the world that you don't recognize me. That way last night can turn into a forgotten memory.

All the Best,

Tiffany

P.S. I don't really want to give you my last name for fear you might look me up. I have a kid, and I don't want him finding out that his mom had blackout sex with a stranger.

In the end, I figured the letter wouldn't make anyone happy. He might have remembered me and been disappointed I didn't.

What if he found me in the lobby of the hotel and explained what had gone down? I might not like what I heard or, even more disconcerting and probable, I could throw up on him while screaming about forsaking his vows to his wife.

Therefore, I felt the note wasn't necessary but a shower and tooth brushing certainly were.

Once I went down two floors and made it to my room, I came inside and leaned back on the cool metal door in relief.

"Oh good, you're back. Can I borrow a shirt? I threw up on all mine," Evaleen said as she popped her head around the corner with a queasy smile on her face.

The lingering stench of vomit in the room had me running to the bathroom before I could answer her question.

After upchucking liquid orange and wondering what I drank last night, I sat on the cool white tiles of the bathroom.

"We're a pair. Maybe we should take a bet and see who can make it through the plane ride back to Chicago without barfing," Evaleen said as she stood over me in a stained blue T-shirt and sweatpants.

Her usually perfect blond chignon was disheveled with some strands of hair sticking to her face. She held out her hand to assist me and I took it. I put my other hand on the toilet seat to get up, thinking I was helping but realizing too late it only worsened the situation.

Having forgotten I lifted the seat to empty my stomach, I shrieked at the cold, clammy toilet rim. My arm flew back from shock and I smacked it on the counter.

Evaleen almost fell when I pulled too hard on her hand but managed to catch herself by twisting her foot. By the time I finally stood, both of us were out of breath. I was nursing a swollen finger and she was rubbing her pained ankle.

"I'll take that bet and add, whoever makes it back puke free *and* without any broken bones, wins," I said.

She laughed. I laughed. We sounded more like geese dying.

"I need a shower," I said pulling at my gross dress as it stuck to me.

I hated feeling sticky.

"And I need a shirt. It seems you have something to give and I have something to give. Maybe we can work out a deal?" Evaleen smirked and tilted her head toward me.

"What do you have to give me?"

"Privacy."

I shook my head and walked over to the shower, turning on the hot water.

"Just take a shirt from my suitcase. I always over pack just for occasions such as this," I said as I held my hand under the warming spray.

"You prepare for a pukepocalypse?"

Once I assessed the temperature was a soothing, scalding degree, I turned to Evaleen and helped her out the door. "Of course. I'm a mother." Then I closed the bathroom door behind her.

Peeling off my disgusting used clothes, I stepped behind the curtain and into a gorgeous hell of skin flaying water.

This must be what heaven felt like, minus the nausea.

As I worked the shampoo into my long, chestnut hair, I tried to recollect how last night happened. Morgana, Aria, and I went to the hotel bar last night. The bartender gave me a drink that a man across the bar had bought me.

But that's it. I barely remember what the bartender looked like. Was the drink spiked?

It must have been.

How stupid could I be? I'm a mother; I shouldn't have put myself at risk like that. What if I had gone to bed with a man that wanted to kidnap or murder me? Who would take care of David?

My son was only twelve and with his physical and verbal disabilities, he needed someone to be with him. Someone to make sure he got the treatment and care his body needed, and the love his heart deserved.

It's terrible enough that the same thing that took his might, also took his father.

He's finally started to gain that strength back and is becoming independent for the first time in his life. I don't think there's a parent prouder of their child than I was of my son. And what do I do to show him how pleased I was, putting my own life at risk so that he could grow up without a father *and* a mother.

I shut off the water after washing and stepped out of the shower. While drying off, brushing my teeth, and finally putting on a clean gray T-shirt and jeans, I made several decisions.

My son needed a father. If something happened to me, even beyond my control, I had to know he would be taken care of. I needed a man that could protect my son and make sure he got the care he needed.

Another decision, there had to be a better way of finding a man—and future father to my son—than a drunken one-night stand.

The little band of gold that caused all this grief inspired my next decision. I had to, above everything else, make sure the man I chose would honor me. There would be no way I wanted to end up with some fool that would cheat on me like the drunken sleaze I stupidly slept with last night.

And finally, he must love the both of us. I am a woman, I may crave affection from a man from time to time, but I'm also a mother. If that man couldn't understand the deep love I had for my son, then he wasn't the man for my family.

There was a knock on the door as I finished pulling my hair back into a ponytail.

"Yes?" I said raising my voice so Evaleen could hear me.

"You ready to catch a plane back home? Morgana's here. It's time to leave," Evaleen said from the other side.

I smiled for the first time today. Excited, I was going to see my son in a few hours.

As I opened the door to the steamy room, I nodded at Evaleen who had miraculously transformed into her perfectly coiffed self with the help of my pink T-shirt.

"Yes, I'm ready to go home."

I felt strong in my decisions, knowing they would be good for my son and me.

TWO

Jagger

"Take a Chance . . . on me." Tennessee bent over in his swivel chair with a full belly laugh.

My eyes slid to my partner. He was wiping the tears from the corner of his eyes. His breath was coming in gasps as his laughter dulled.

"Oh, man, that joke never gets old," he said with a stammer still trying to ease back the chuckle.

"It's definitely old," I said trying to finish the paperwork so I could leave a little early.

I had tickets to an improv show at IO theater in Wrigleyville with Cate. Good old Cate. I smiled at the thought of making my fuck buddy come on my cock in her office above the theater.

The great thing about Cate, she was boring. I don't mean her personality but her life. A squeaky-clean history and no outstanding debt.

There was no way she could be bribed and give me away. Not that she knew anything about me. I told her once I worked downtown and that's all she cared to hear.

Bonus points to her for not wanting a relationship. In the line of work I did, a relationship just brought desk duty.

And who wanted that? I didn't. Sure, it sounded nice to one day have someone to come home to or discuss problems with, maybe binge-watch a television series. But I worked over a decade to get where I was in the government. That love stuff could wait.

Besides, relationships, even family, weren't always what you hoped they'd be. I learned people were selfish from my job, giving up on their loved ones when things got tough.

"Here, I have a good one you might like," Tenn said as I tapped away on my keyboard and continued to ignore him. "Why was everyone so tired of April first?"

He's not going to stop until I acknowledge him. That was the thing about Tenn, he craved attention. He should be up on that stage tonight trying to be funny with how much he performed for everyone. Of course, Tenn wasn't adult funny. He's five-year-old funny. Perhaps he should perform for kids' birthday parties like a clown or a pony.

"Because it isn't funny?" I asked.

Like that joke he was telling. But that didn't stop him. I could almost smell his eagerness. There was a gleam at the corner of his mouth, and I wondered if it was drool.

"No. Because they had just finished a March of thirty-one days!" He dissolved into laughter before he could get out the last word, his blond hair falling onto his face.

The door to our shared office opened, and a petite woman with short graying black hair and the boxiest looking jacket I had ever seen stood in the doorway.

I felt both fear and relief at the same time.

"Chance, I need to see you in my office. Now." Katlin Chester's deep voice clattered the window on our door before she turned and walked off.

"Uh oh, is there a *chance* you're in trouble with the boss." Tenn chuckled but stopped once I glared at him.

I stood and turned to him before I left. "You know Jagger Chance isn't my real name. Just as Tennessee Golden isn't your real name. The government gave us all aliases when we started working at the Inter-Terrorism Agency, yet you keep making fun of what they gave me. Why?"

He shrugged. "Because you're my partner. I always joke around with people I like. My therapist tells me it's a defense mechanism. I don't let people close to me and keep them at a distance with my jokes."

"Personal or Randy?" I asked.

"Personal."

Everyone here had to meet once a month with our in-house psychologist, Dr. Randy Tenner. Randy worked for the government to make sure the stress of the job hadn't gotten to us and we could still do our missions.

"Tell your therapist to try to work with you on better jokes," I said before turning to leave.

After walking across the cheap brown carpet to the corner office, I knocked once before I heard my boss, Katlin Chester, yell back to come inside.

I took a seat in the small black pleather chair across from her as she leaned back and stared at me.

"What is this, Chance?" Katlin said just before her lips pursed into a hard line holding up a piece of paper.

I swallowed hard before clasping my hands on my lap. "A marriage certificate, ma'am." I willed my eyes to stay on her steel gray stare but faltered.

Not good.

"I know what it is. What I am asking, agent, is why your name is on it?"

My head raced with possible replies. Confess everything—tell her I drank on the job and let this happen—or lie through my teeth. Blame it on Tennessee. Make it into one of his stupid pranks.

"Surprise," I waved my hands in the air like a magician, "I'm married."

Her thin lips frowned. I should have known better not to make a joke about it. Katlin Chester did not help create the newly formed ITA, Inter-Terrorism Agency, a specialized go-between of the CIA and FBI, because she had a sense of humor.

This place was so secret that most people in the CIA and FBI didn't know of its existence. A person doesn't get asked to help form a new government agency because they were good at cracking jokes.

Katlin sat in her government-issued black chair and focused on the certificate. "It says here this was in Nevada three weeks ago, back in June. I seem to recall you being on a reconnaissance mission to gather info on the Jewel, Emma Hawthorne, in Las Vegas in June. You got lucky when she spilled everything and you had the opportunity to bring her in."

Despite the smirk on her face, I knew her words were no compliment. She had already congratulated me a few weeks ago when I brought back the criminal, we nicknamed the Jewel, that we had been targeting for over a year. Emma Hawthorne was planning to infiltrate the government with her family and friends and destroy it like ice in a cement crack.

Despite the takedown, I fucked up. I made one very big mistake that I hoped my boss wouldn't find out about. I don't know which was worse, believing my boss—who had access to every piece of information about every government employee—wouldn't find out I got married, or, that I never did anything about getting a divorce.

"Did you decide that would be a great time to bring your fiancée along and have a cheap wedding on the government's dime?"

My jaw ticked. "No."

She placed the paper on her brown particle board desk and leaned forward. I tensed knowing this was far from over as she placed her elbows on the arms of her chair and steepled her fingers to her lips.

"I never realized you were engaged, agent. Why did you never say anything? Did you have an engagement party? I figured you would have invited someone from the department. I don't recall anyone mentioning it. Your partner, Golden, never said a word."

Crap, that was the second time she called me *agent*. I was in some deep shit now.

"I was drunk," I mumbled.

She cupped her ear. "I'm sorry, agent, I don't believe I heard you."

I rolled my head back staring at the drop ceiling. "I was trailing some of her son's friends who happened to be at the hotel bar. I thought it would be a perfect opportunity to gather some intelligence and they bought me a drink."

Katlin held up her hand. "Wait, they bought you a drink? Did you even test the contents? Were you drugged?"

This wasn't going well.

Why did I let my dick do my thinking that night?

Oh, I know. Because the woman was beautiful and funny and sweet. There was something about flirting and spending time with her that felt wonderful. I missed it. Being a government spy for eight years in the CIA and then the past two years in ITA, I missed being a normal guy hitting on a woman in a bar.

There were too many steps I had to take just to consider having sex with a woman. Background checks, credit checks, pulling up files on her friends and family. And after all that, I'm only allowed to sleep with them, nothing more.

Technically, I'm allowed to have a relationship with someone, but that would mean I had to lie to them on a regular basis. Never tell them the truth about me. Something about all that felt wrong.

My life could be lonely but at least I had Cate. I liked Cate, well, I liked her body. I rubbed my chest. There was an odd sensation that made me frown when I thought of Cate.

That never happened before.

"No, I wasn't drugged."

I remember everything perfectly clear.

"You realize you compromised the mission, yourself, and the agency?"

I nodded.

"Where is this," Katlin looked down at the certificate before continuing, "Tiffany Blackburn now? Has she signed the divorce papers?"

As much as I dreaded telling my boss I was married, I loathed having to explain I haven't seen or spoken to Tiffany since that night in Vegas.

"Maybe a divorce isn't necessary. What is a divorce anyway but a slip of paper?" I stood and walked over to the window in the office that overlooked the Chicago River. "Technically, she didn't really marry me. She married Jagger Chance. Maybe I should get a new identity, social security card, and—"

"Agent Chance!" Katlin stood, bringing her fist down on her desk with a loud *thwack*. "The United States Government does not give out identities like pieces of gum on a playground. According to your record, you are now legally married to Mrs. Tiffany Blackburn. I suggest you rectify this or your clearance and job will be taken away from you."

"Yes, ma'am," I said as I turned to leave.

"Oh, and Chance?" Katlin said just before I crossed the threshold.

I kept my back to her. "Yes?"

"Remember what happened to Agent Snow? She disobeyed orders and it cost her, her life. Take care of this as soon as possible. Now close the door behind you."

"But what about Agent Hack or Grey?" I asked.

"They aren't agents anymore, are they?"

I nodded. Both of them left the agency. Grey moved out west and Hack owned some kid's sporting center or something with his wife just outside of Chicago. But, they chose love and marriage over their jobs.

I swallowed and did as she requested.

Snow was a great agent. They still used her missions as teaching tools for new recruits. But then, she let her heart do the thinking for her.

Katlin was right. I had to end this marriage, and quick. Too much was at stake.

THREE

Tiffany

*"**David John Blackburn!**"* I yelled down the hallway.

Nothing. No sound. No movement.

"Okay, I guess I have to come find you," I said in an even louder tone.

That's when I heard his voice and some banging.

"Mom. Wait. Getting dressed," David said with a crack in his voice.

I stood about twenty feet from his room and smiled. It was just six months ago that he couldn't speak more than fifty words, often garbled so that only I could understand. Though he had trouble speaking the words, he understood tens of thousands, which was typical for a twelve-year-old.

Earlier this year, he also wouldn't have been able to dress himself or walk to me. It may take him longer than other boys his age to do all those things, but he could accomplish them by himself now. And I couldn't help the large grin on my face every time I witnessed him doing the most mundane tasks on his own.

"Hurry up because your new physical therapist is going to be here any minute," I said and placed my hands on my cheeks trying to will back the tears.

For it's those mundane things that brought me the most joy. David always had a smile on his face and loved life, appreciating everything. But, there were times when he didn't think I was looking, when I saw him stare at his friend Matt.

Matt could walk.

They met at the therapy center several years ago. Matt had difficulty with communication and issues with social skills. They both had different speech therapists but the same appointment time. Sometimes they were in the same room, working on tasks together. Their therapists quickly learned that Matt and David challenged each other to work harder.

Though they went to different schools and Matt lived in a different neighborhood, those two were inseparable. That was, until last year when Matt moved to Virginia. He hasn't seen David since before the operation.

Matt had never seen David walk.

"I think I heard the buzzer. That should be the therapist," I said and turned toward the front door.

I pressed the intercom. "Hello?"

There was some crackling and static but I heard a male voice say Blackburn, so I pushed the open button for the front door of the building. I made a mental note to contact the landlord again about fixing the intercom so I could hear the visitors more clearly.

Just this morning I read in the paper about a thief pretending to be a visitor of a residential building nearby, but the intercom was broken so he was easily buzzed inside. Luckily, the tenant was unharmed, but the thief did steal some valuables.

What if that happened while David was here? We lived in a high-rise that overlooked Lake Michigan because we needed a building with an elevator. How quickly could we escape from someone out to do us harm?

The rent in this building was pricey enough despite the iffy neighborhood. The landlord needed to stay on top of safety. I was thankful my good friend and David's godfather, Henrik Payne, helped me out with the rent, but I refused to take more than was necessary.

We met the night of the accident. The same accident that killed my husband and left my son disabled, killed Henrik's parents and sister. Henrik blamed himself for the accident, but how could he have known that his mother was too drunk to drive that night? He wasn't anywhere near his parents that night.

We grew close in our grief. In a way, he had helped David not just by making sure he got the best care but being the father figure that David craved.

But now that Henrik's getting married I feared he wouldn't be in David's life as much. That made me more determined to find a man who could be a good father to David.

I walked over to the door when I heard a knock and glanced through the peephole. My breath caught at what I saw.

The man on the other side of my door didn't appear to be a robber, but he also didn't seem like a physical therapist, either.

Once I opened the door my eyes swept his long, muscular body. Something seized in my chest, and I rubbed at the spot wondering if it was disappointment or something much different causing the ache. Logically I knew that it required strength to help a twelve-year-old boy that had some difficulty with walking and bending and lifting. But my mind wasn't going there. It was on the opposite side of the logical planet.

All my thoughts involved heat and touching and groping. As if I left stable Earth to land on the steamy, sexy party planet of Venus.

I frowned and shook my head trying to focus on the reason this guy was in my doorway. But when he smiled and the twinkle of his jade eyes sent a shiver throughout my body to my fingertips, I had to hold onto the door to steady myself.

The only thing that brought me back down to earth was his clothing. Particularly, his white button-up shirt, navy dress pants, and dress shoes. If this were a meeting in an office, he would be dressed appropriately, but it's a physical therapy session.

He ran his hands through his shaggy brown hair as his eyes darted to the floor and I licked my lips. He must have realized he was overdressed.

"You must be the PT. I'm Tiffany, David's mom." I held out my hand and forced a smile that didn't appear too lecherous.

His eyes shot up to mine and widened. But that was it. He didn't shake my hand or say a word. The man stood there staring at me.

"And you are?" I asked tilting my head.

He blinked but still no sound.

"Okay, then. Please, come inside. David is getting dressed. He will be out in a minute. I can explain his history while we wait." I moved and waved him inside.

He hesitated but after a minute decided it was safe to come into my apartment. We walked past my small galley kitchen to the right and straight into my living room. As he lowered himself onto my brown suede chair I had to pry my eyes away from his ass. The man had a nice butt but I reminded myself it wasn't for staring at while I sat on the pale green sofa.

"I'm afraid I don't know your name. I am sure I wrote it down somewhere but can't seem to find it," I said.

"Jagger. My name is Jagger," he finally spoke.

The hairs on the back of my neck rose as he told me his name. There was something about his voice which was unexpected. Maybe it was because he refused to speak when he was at the door that I anticipated his words to be whisper-quiet.

They certainly weren't soft. In fact, they were the opposite. Hard with a dark edge that pricked at my skin. But there was something else, too. My heart beat a little faster as if I knew him.

"It's nice to meet you, Jagger. Now about my son," I said as I put my instructional face on. "He was in a car accident when he was two that left him unable to develop at the same pace as his peers in regard to motor skills. He is twelve now, will be turning thirteen in a few weeks, and this year he took his first steps."

I found that when speaking with professionals about my son's history, it's easier to remove the emotional element. Like reading from a textbook, just the facts.

Jagger's brow creased. He appeared uneasy but let me continue.

"The accident affected his primary motor cortex. This past winter he had a fairly new procedure to try and reverse what the accident had done to him. It worked. He can now speak and walk and do most of the stuff a kid his age can do."

"What's the PT for?" Jagger asked.

Wait . . . What? Was he serious?

"Why wouldn't my son need physical therapy?"

Jagger's face lit up with merriment mixed with surprise. "Oh, physical therapy. You think I'm a physical—"

He was cut off as my son entered the room.

I got up and walked to David. He was my height, not so little anymore. Now that he could tell me anything he wanted, he decided he had to let his hair grow. The boy who stood in front of me was tall, skinny, and had a big brown mop of hair.

"Hey." David's blue eyes stayed focused on the floor.

"David, this is Jagger. He will be your new physical therapist." I took David's hand and helped him onto the couch.

"As you can see, while David can now walk," my smile widened as I gazed at my son's reddening face, "he is still building his strength and coordination. That's where you come in."

Jagger's eyes bounced between my son and me with a strange expression on his face. The best way to describe it was that he appeared to be holding in a fart.

The man stayed silent. Was this how it was going to be with him? Am I going to have to show him how to do his job?

"David. Is there anything you would like to ask Mr. Jagger?"

"No," my son said as his eyes stared at the gray block-patterned rug.

I was so happy when I found out my new insurance would cover most of the cost of home visits from a physical therapist. Who knew that I would end up with the worst PT in the world. Maybe I could request a new one from the group I contacted.

"Is there anything you would like to ask me, Mr. Jagger?"

"Yes, I mean no." He paused and held his breath. I expected him to continue but he didn't.

"We do have a room with some equipment in it. Perhaps you would like to see it, and then you can get started with David."

I stood and helped David up. As we moved toward the hallway, I turned my head to find Jagger still in the leather chair

"Mr. Jagger. Are you coming?"

His jaw tightened as he stood and it seemed painful for him to answer, "Yes."

Once we stepped into what used to be the master bedroom, David leaned against a wall as I waved my hand around.

"As you can see, we have a bucket of various sized medicine balls, hand and foot weights, foam rollers, a few PT bars, a balance board, the three steps in the corner with a handrail," I moved to the larger equipment, "and our newest item, the treadmill."

"Wow. You're really serious about all this." Jagger chuckled and gazed around the room.

What was wrong with him?

"Yes, I take my son's health very seriously, Mr. Jagger."

"It's Chance."

"What?" I asked.

"My name. It's Jagger Chance. So, I would be Mr. Chance. But feel free to call me Jagger."

I was about to call him a few other names too, but Jagger decided now would be the best time to finally start talking.

"This stuff is awesome. You're one lucky kid, David." Jagger winked at my son.

Lucky? He had the audacity to call my son *lucky*? Did he really think my son was lucky to have an idiot for a therapist?

My jaw fell open. I was in such shock that I couldn't even form words.

"Huh?" David said, and I was grateful my son was confused.

"Imagine all the sick moves you can learn with this stuff. I bet you know some cool ninja moves." Jagger went over and grabbed a blue foam roller, placing it on the black mat that covered our beige carpet.

He then took a red PT bar and swung it around between his arms. Finally, he rolled his body over the foam and hopped back up as if he were in a movie battle.

"Cool," David said and walked over to him.

Jagger gave him the red bar, and David tried to imitate his moves but the bar quickly fell from his hands.

"Let me break it down for you. It took me a while to learn this, too." Jagger bent down to pick up the stick.

"You're a ninja?" David said with wide eyes.

"Not quite, but I did learn tae kwon do and parkour. Which is what you need if you ever decide to be a ninja."

"I don't know if that's appropriate for David. He's still building his strength and core muscles." I crossed my arms, worried that this would be too much on my son.

But the look in David's eyes had me doubting myself. I was used to protecting him; it's my job as a mom. But he wasn't a little boy anymore.

"Mom, please," David said with a tone filled with worry bordering on desperation.

I stood there staring at my son and realized for the first time that my job had changed. It still included protecting him, but the job description grew to include letting him take risks so he could learn to be a man.

I let my arms fall as I faced Jagger's mossy green eyes. "All right. As long as you make sure he doesn't get hurt."

"I'll make sure everything I do with him is safe. When I'm done with him, he won't need protection from the most evil of villains," Jagger said with a wink.

I could feel the heat in my cheeks and wondered if it was because there would be a day when my son no longer needed me.

Or, perhaps, it was the tall man with the strong arms watching me for slightly longer than he should.

FOUR

Jagger

"You're a ninja?" Tenn laughed so hard he splashed his coffee on the small round table.

"Come on, Tenn. It's not that funny," I said as my eyes swept the café out of habit.

A few people sitting at small, square, wooden tables turned in our direction due to the volume of Tenn's chuckles.

"Oh, it's funny. You ask me to take our lunch break here at Wake Up Joe's and then drop bomb after bomb after bomb on me. Each one funnier than the last." He shook his head and started to lift his coffee cup before stopping mid-rise.

"We should start an act. Tenn and the Ninja. You could do your moves around me while I tell jokes." He snorted.

"That's not even funny. How is that funny?" I leaned forward and turned my head from prying eyes.

"Think about it." He tapped the side of his head.

I sighed as I knew I had to battle Tenn's laughter and sad jokes in order to get his help. When I went to Tiffany's place on Friday, I had forgotten about her son. When I read her file before I went off to Vegas over a month ago, I skimmed the part about her son—probably where it mentioned he required some special help.

That was sloppy work on my part. It seemed when I took a step toward the idea of family, even an accidental one, I became careless. Another reason to end this and stay away from close relationships of any kind.

"Does he have Cerebral Palsy?" Tenn turned serious.

"No, I don't think so. I looked up physical disabilities and if a child has Cerebral Palsy, they had damage to the brain before, during, or just after birth. From what Tiffany told me, David was two when he was in the car accident."

"My aunt has CP. She had lots of therapists. Maybe I can call her and get you some information for your role as a physical therapist," Tenn said before leaning back in our corner booth and taking a sip of coffee.

The memory of my cousin popped into my head. He was my best friend despite how my family told me to keep my distance. I wish they had been more open to him like Tenn's family was to his aunt.

"No. The reason I told you all this is to help me get out of it. I didn't mean to pretend to be her son's PT—"

"Look at you already getting into the role! You sound legit using the acronym like a pro." He smiled and finally picked up some napkins to wipe up the spill he made earlier.

I groaned. Dealing with Tenn was like dealing with a talented athlete who was still in high school. Yeah, the athlete was gifted, but they made ignorant life decisions and had the mental agility of a teenager.

"I told you, I don't want to be the physical therapist. I went there to give her papers for the divorce. I had them folded up in my back pocket, ready to break them out the moment we were alone. But she started talking about her son's accident and then her son walked out. I felt like . . ."

"An asshole," Tenn added.

I thinned my lips. "No, dick. I felt terrible, like I took advantage of this good woman trying to do right by her son. Fuck." I ran my fingers through my hair. "The worst part was she didn't recognize me. I thought when I walked up to her at the bar in Vegas she was sober, but maybe she had already had a few drinks."

"Or, maybe she took one look at you two days ago and thought it was best to play dumb for fear you might try to kiss her."

I balled up a paper napkin and flung it at him. He grabbed it out of the air, balled up a few more napkins, and began to juggle.

"Why are you an agent? Shouldn't you be performing at the circus?"

"They wouldn't take me. So, I entered the government instead."

I stared at him in silence. For once, Tenn wasn't joking.

"Putting that scary thought aside, I do need your opinion on how to get out of this."

"You never want my opinion. Why now?" He kept on tossing the balls of napkins in the air until one finally fell.

"You're my partner. We work together."

His eyes narrowed. "That's news to me. Usually, you take control of a mission and delegate all the communication and paperwork to me. I'm at home keeping everything clean while you gallivant across the country."

"That's not true," I said and tried to come up with an example.

Nothing came to mind.

"What about Plastic? You had me research his family history and place wire tapes in his house. While you got to trail him to New York and Miami."

I held up my finger. "But, it was what we got from the wiretaps that brought him down. And the same with Emma Hawthorne. Didn't you fly to Vegas to put in the tap?"

"Nebraska. The warehouse was in Big Springs, Nebraska. Woo hoo! I had the best time because you know, what happens in Big Springs, stays in Big Springs," Tenn said without inflection as his lips thinned.

I held up my hands. "Okay, I get it. Maybe you should call the shots for a while. The next big case that comes up, I'll stay back working on things here."

"Really?" His brows shot up but he nodded. "Sounds good. I'll help you get out of it. Now, show me what Tiffany looks like."

I was about to ask why he needed to see her picture but grew tired of trying to figure out Tenn's mind. Somehow, I knew that if he explained it, I would end up more confused.

Bringing up the pictures on my phone, I showed him some of the shots I took as we walked the streets of Vegas.

"Which one, the redhead or the brunette?" He swiped his finger across my phone.

"The brunette."

The corner of his mouth curved. "You must have had a good night."

I did. For the first time in over a decade, I stopped being an agent for the government and chose to be a guy out for the night. I drank. I danced. I kissed a beautiful woman. And, finally, I got married.

That last one might not be what an average guy does during a night of drinking, but even with that, I had fun. And if I had to get married to anyone, I didn't mind it being Tiffany. She had a smile that did things to my heart and a body that made it very hard not to have sex with her that night.

She was drunk and knowing that, I couldn't do something she wasn't in her right mind to say yes to. Even when she played hide-n-seek with her clothes, I had to bribe her with a ring. Since it was a quick wedding, she really wanted one of those candy lollipop rings. The kind that's plastic but had the candy jewel on top. I told her I would get it first thing in the morning if she got under the covers.

I left her in bed and slept on the couch. Not the best sleep, and I worried I would wake her when I got up early to take a long, muscle relaxing, hot shower. Apparently, I did wake her as she was gone when I came out.

"It was intel," I said as I stared at my fingers, curled around my coffee cup.

"You were really thorough on the information you gathered, I see. How did marrying Tiffany help you capture Emma Hawthorne?"

I reached over and grabbed my phone from his hands. "I made a mistake. That's why I'm here. You said you could help me if you saw what she looked like."

"No, I didn't. What I said was I wanted to see what she looked like. Then I told you I would help you get out of this. I never said one had to do with the other."

Gritting my teeth, I willed my hands not to wrap around Tenn's throat. "Okay, so help."

"Just tell her you aren't a physical therapist."

"Why didn't I think of that!" I slapped my hand on the table and glared at Tenn.

"What's the worst she could do? Run off? Then you never have to see her again."

"But I need her to sign the divorce papers."

He nodded. "Right. Forgot about that. Can you hire someone to hand them to her?"

"I thought about that. What happens when she looks me up? She'll realize I'm her son's PT. She might even go to the police. I can't have this getting out. That might cause the government to reassign me."

"Reassignment, fuck no." Tenn shook his head.

He knew what reassignment really meant.

Tenn's face lit up with a wide smile as he nodded his head. He had something and a part of me, foolishly, hoped it was something solid— the answer to my dilemma.

"I know. Rip the bandage off with Tiffany. Confront her and explain you aren't a physical therapist. Remind her that you met her in Vegas, accidentally married her, and now you need a divorce. She may be mad but if she does anything . . ." Tenn leaned forward but said nothing.

"And?"

"If she does anything have Chester get you a new identity. Problem solved." Tenn sat back. He had a look on his face that told me if he was a cat, he would be licking the cream off his paws.

"Can't happen."

Tenn's eyes widened. "What?"

"I asked Chester already for a new identity. She said no."

He shrugged. "Then I can't help you. I tried. Anyway, I have to get back to work. Mondays, am I right?" Tenn chuckled as he got up.

Left at the table gripping a cold cup of coffee the same thoughts swirled around in my head. What's so bad about being married if both people, in this case, one person, doesn't know about it. If Tiffany ever decided to settle down with a man in the future, she would realize she got drunk and married in Vegas. By the time she contacts me, I could claim I had no idea too.

We would get divorced and move on with our lives.

As easy as that idea seemed, I couldn't shake the uncomfortable feeling it left behind. It wasn't fair to her. Realizing I was going to have to tell her the truth and risk my job, I began to turn in my seat but a voice stopped me.

"If it isn't Agent Dick-punch."

Glancing up, I saw a pair of gray eyes settle on me like steel.

"If it isn't Edgar Mimir. And how are your nuts?"

FIVE

Tiffany

Early as usual.

Every Thursday my friends and I meet for drinks at a bar. We've been doing this for about six months now. We call it SWIM Meet, which is an acronym for Smart Women with Idiot Men.

It was started by Morgana Drake, who had a thing for her boss and my good friend, Henrik Payne. And her best friend, Aria Dixon, joined along with Morgana's coworker at the time, Evaleen Bechmann.

They all had troubles with the men they were dating, hence the name of the group. I was the odd one out because I wasn't dating anyone or hadn't since college, over a decade ago.

I started coming around the time of David's surgery. It gave me a break from the ups and downs of wondering if he would come out of the coma he was in for a week after surgery, and the stress of not knowing if the surgery even worked.

It was a low time in my life, and these ladies helped me make it through by letting me talk, cry, and get a little tipsy from time to time.

Now, it gave me something to do that was just for me. Up until earlier this year, my life consisted of working on graphic design projects for clients and taking care of my son. Running to David's doctor appointments, specialists, therapists, bathing him, feeding him, making sure the medical equipment arrived on time, and countless other tasks.

I never had time to go to the movies with friends or do all the things single women at thirty-two do. Now that David had some independence from the operation, everything had changed.

"Here's your whiskey sour." The waiter placed it on the round wooden table in front of me.

"Thank you," I said.

It's funny, but I never used to drink whiskey sours. For some reason over the past month, whenever I came to SWIM Meet, I craved one.

"What a day." Morgana appeared as I was taking a sip of my drink.

She threw her purse on the table, removed her jewel green blazer, and plopped down on the dark leather booth seat opposite me. Her fiery hair pulled back into a long ponytail.

"Busy at work?" I asked.

"You'd think Armageddon was about to happen if we changed the color of our logo from blue to green." Morgana pulled at the band holding her ponytail in place and shook out her hair.

"Can Henrik help? I know he used to do that." I smiled, trying my best to help my stressed friend.

"Ugh, no. As much as I would love to be able to ask for his opinion from time to time, when I do ask for help, he proceeds to explain the entire history of Mimir and how marketing the past thirty years has changed drastically. If I wanted lectures, I would go to college again."

Morgana lifted her arm, signaling our waiter and placed her drink order when he arrived.

"I heard from Aria and Evaleen. They are both running a little late."

"I bet they are." Morgana smirked.

"What does that mean?"

"Aria works from home—painting—and Evaleen now spends her day writing from home. I know for a fact that Edgar left early today. I think they are being held back, so to speak, by their men."

I felt the blood rush to my cheeks and tried to cover it up by tilting my head forward to drink through the little red straw in my glass. Some tendrils that fell out of my braid fluttered around my face, shielding the embarrassing blush.

Despite knowing these women for six months, I still felt like an outsider. Morgana's wedding was coming up in just over a month, and I had a terrible feeling I was going to be the single woman at the reception that every relative and friend in attendance would try to set up with any "perfect man" they knew.

Maybe I could hire an escort for the wedding, just to ward them off. I've heard some crazy stuff about Morgana's family, especially her grandmother. Best to be prepared with a male shield.

The waiter arrived with Morgana's white wine.

"I wanted to discuss with you about David having a part in the wedding," Morgana said as she placed her glass down.

"Of course. I think he would love that." I smiled but wondered what she would expect of him.

Maybe she wanted David to draw something creative for their program. He's been getting into comics and dabbling with creating a special hero for a comic book he wants to write. He won't let me see anything, but if it's anything like the digital drawings he did for art in school, it's going to be amazing.

"Henrik would like David to be one of his groomsmen."

I stared at Morgana, her round hazel eyes full of hope. She didn't realize, even Henrik was naïve at times, when it came to David. My son couldn't stand for long periods of time—especially, through a wedding ceremony.

"Would he be allowed to sit or maybe use a cane?"

I added the cane as an option but knew David would hate that. With his new ability to walk, he did everything he could not to use a walker or cane. Even when he took his first steps earlier this past spring, the therapist tried to get him to use a walker but he said he'd rather fall than use one.

The boy that spent most of his life reliant on medical equipment to get around and live and never wanted to look back.

Her eyes widened as she frowned. "Oh, well, I guess we hadn't discussed that. Henrik mentioned how strong David had become this year and he thought David might like to be included with the guys. He's getting older—"

I held up my hands. "It's your wedding Morgana and I don't want to put limitations on it. That's not my place but as strong as my son has become, he wouldn't be able to stand through the ceremony without some help. Perhaps he can help design the program or even be an usher."

Morgana nodded and turned her sight to the growing after-work crowd in the sports bar. Her brow wrinkled as she tilted her head. "That guy is staring at you. He looks really familiar."

I glanced in the direction Morgana was staring at to find Jagger across the room, in a corner booth by the hallway to the bathrooms.

My head whipped back as I cupped the side of my face so he couldn't see me. "Oh no. That's David's new physical therapist. He's an idiot. I'm guessing that David is the very first client he's ever had as the man doesn't know what he's doing."

Morgana's face brightened as her smile grew. "Really. He may be an idiot, but he's a mega-hot idiot."

She wiggled her eyebrows as she stared at me.

"No. Just, no. I'm done with one-night stands. After what happened in Vegas, I don't ever want to go down that road again. Who knows, next time I might wake up next to a serial killer."

"You wouldn't wake up if he was a serial killer."

"Exactly," I said.

Morgana tilted her head. "It's really weird about that night. I can't remember anything other than meeting you and Aria at the bar. Some guy bought you a drink. I tested it with my special nail polish to see if it was drugged, but it wasn't. Then I ordered my drink after Aria left and that was it."

What Morgana said didn't sit well with me. I thought I had too much to drink in Vegas but if Morgana can't remember anything either, then perhaps it was something else. She tested the drink to see if it was drugged, so that wasn't it. What could have happened?

I was about to discuss this further with Morgana when a familiar deep voice called out my name.

"Tiffany," Jagger said as he appeared in front of our table.

He was taller than I remember, but that might be because I was currently sitting. His disheveled brown hair wasn't as annoying as it was last week. Perhaps it was his dark T-shirt and fitted jeans that complemented his features as to why I didn't find it as off-putting as I did last week.

"Hello, Jagger." My smile not so forced.

"Funny running into you here," he said as his eyes slid to Morgana before quickly turning back to me.

He seemed nervous. He seemed nervous when he came to my apartment. Maybe he was the type of guy who always appeared on edge.

"Yes. I guess we will see each other at five o'clock tomorrow for the session," I said as I widened my smile trying to give him the hint that he could leave.

I wasn't usually this rude to people, but how he acted at the session last week still made me question his ability to help my son. After he left I mentioned to David that I wanted to contact the PT group to find another therapist, but David begged me not to. As much as I disliked Jagger, my son loved him. I gave into David because he would be the one working with Jagger, not me.

"Of course. Yes. Now about that, is there somewhere we could talk?" Jagger asked as his eyes flickered back to Morgana.

"Hi, I'm Morgana. It's nice to meet you." Morgana stood and shot out her hand to him.

His eyes widened and he grew silent, staring at her hand. Jagger had the same fearful, confused gleam in his eyes when I answered the door last week.

"Hello, Morgana. I'm Jagger," he mumbled and shook her hand once before pulling his hands behind his back.

"I have to use the restroom so you two can talk while I'm gone." Morgana turned and bounced happily toward the back of the room.

I frowned as I watched her leave but as I turned my attention back to Jagger, I caught him watching me.

"Please, sit." I waved at the booth seat Morgana had recently vacated. "Now, what did you want to discuss?"

Just as he took a seat, the waiter appeared and Jagger waved him off.

"Perhaps I wanted a drink," I said.

"I'm sorry, I didn't realize. I saw your glass and just assumed . . ." He waved his hand at my mostly full glass of whiskey sour.

"I usually like to have two drinks at a time. You know, double fisted," I said as I glared at him.

That was a lie. The truth was, I rarely drank. Only during SWIM Meet did I allow myself one drink, on occasion, two. Having a drunk driver kill my husband made drinking something I refused to let hurt me any more than it had. That was until Vegas. I hadn't planned to drink a lot, even in Sin City. Yet, I must have as I blacked out. I wish I could remember what happened.

I had no idea why I said that to Jagger. Maybe because he assumed a lot of things. Assumed I would tell him how to do his job. Assumed I wouldn't need to place an order.

Assumed I found him attractive.

Whoa. Where did that come from?

"I can call him back?" He began to raise his hand but I reached over and pulled his arm down.

Heat traveled up my arm and my skin tickled with the most curious yet exciting sensation. I snapped my arm back, and as I gazed up at him, his emerald eyes darkened.

"I was only joking, haha." My weak laugh wasn't fooling him. "What did you want to talk with me about?"

I shoved my hands under the table and crossed my fingers, hoping he was here to tell me he couldn't be my son's physical therapist anymore.

"I'm not who you think I am," Jagger said as he pulled some folded papers from his back pocket.

SIX

Jagger

"You're not Jagger?" Tiffany's cute little forehead crinkled.

I kept glancing back to see if her friend, Morgana, was about to return but she hadn't appeared. I didn't know whether to be relieved or disappointed that she wasn't coming back yet.

"Yes, I'm Jagger Chance. I mean, not exactly. Shit, I shouldn't have said that." I ran my hand through my hair.

This was much harder than anything I had ever done. Infiltrating the Luciano family and learning Italian in less than two weeks was easier than telling Tiffany I was her husband.

"How could you be and not be Jagger Chance? That doesn't make sense. Did you change your name?" Tiffany said but right after she spoke her eyes widened.

She straightened her back, and I realized she was remembering. What happened in Vegas was finally coming back to her. But how much? Because I said some things when I was drunk that I shouldn't have. Thankfully, Katlin can't get reports on that, unless Tiffany tells someone—specifically, someone in the government.

Shit.

"Yes, I did, but that's not what I came here to talk to you about. As I can tell from your expression, you are starting to figure it out. Now, in my defense, I had a little too much to drink. I'm sorry. But that's why I'm here, to rectify it," I said as I lifted the papers in the air.

"I don't care if you were inebriated. That's no excuse." Tiffany scowled and pressed back into the leather booth seat.

"Look, if we could go somewhere private to talk, I could explain what happened." I reached for her arm, trying to push out the memory of how her earlier touch sent a shiver straight to my cock.

She stumbled to her feet but stretched over the table to grab her purse before stepping back. "No, we cannot go anywhere to talk. Why would I want to be alone with someone like you? Did you think you could trick me, too? When you showed up at my door, ready to do what you do best, you felt a little sympathy for the single mom with a kid that required extra help? I guess you think I should be thankful for that?"

"No, I mean, I was there to—"

"Save it." Tiffany held up her arm. "I'm going to leave right now and call the police, so no one has to be hurt by you ever again."

I began to stand and stop her but as I did, I saw two women come through the front door of the bar. Both women had the power to make this so much worse than it already was.

My heart picked up speed and my training kicked in. I appraised the room to find an out. Unfortunately, the only other way out was through the back hallway that led to the bathrooms and the kitchen—the same hallway Morgana was now exiting.

I was trapped.

My only alternative was to find the less dangerous of the two escapes and take that route. At least, for some reason I couldn't understand, Morgana didn't remember me from Vegas, either. We all drank at the bar, walked around the strip, and eventually ended up at the chapel together. Morgana was the witness that signed the marriage certificate.

Yet, both women didn't remember me. They hadn't appeared drunk when I met them at the bar that night, but I guess they both were drinking for a while before I came.

I turned toward the Morgana escape route and made my way toward the back.

"Are you all done speaking with Tiffany?" Morgana asked as she met me just outside the hallway by the corner of the bar.

"Yes. And I wanted to discuss something with you, but I don't want Tiffany to find out. Do you mind if we move back here to talk?" I pointed toward the hallway from where she came.

"Okay." She tilted her head in confusion.

As I leaned against the wall between the men's and women's bathroom, I looked down at Morgana with a serious expression. "Tiffany told me what you two had been discussing."

This was one of the tricks I learned as an agent. If you wanted information out of people, pretend as if you were included in their secrets and discussions. If a person felt safe with you, they would reveal everything.

"Really? Well, I guess if you are David's physical therapist it makes sense she would talk to you about it."

Nodding, I rubbed my chin. "Of course, it does. That's why I'm here. What do you think about it, in regard to David, of course."

She shrugged. "Tiffany would know her son better than anyone, but Henrik, my fiancé, felt he would be able to stand throughout the ceremony. I don't think Henrik would have thought of forcing David to stand throughout the ceremony, as a groomsman, if he didn't think he could handle it."

"Tiffany doesn't think David could stand as a groomsman during the course of the ceremony because of his strength?" I asked just to be clear I understood.

"Yeah. I've met David a few times, and he was so happy for Henrik when he found out we were getting married. He loves Henrik so much and Henrik loves him. We thought it would be a great way to include him. He's family to Henrik."

My jaw tightened and I tried to keep my features calm, but it was hard. Tiffany seemed like a good mother, but now I wasn't so sure as she sheltered her son like that. Sometimes too much of a good thing can turn horribly bad.

"I know he has the strength. I may have only had one session with him, but that boy is stronger than she realizes." I blinked and wondered for that brief moment if David and my cousin would have been friends.

Ben was David's age when he died.

"That's what Henrik thought too. Maybe since you're his therapist, you can talk to Tiffany. We don't want to ask David until we have Tiffany's blessing." Morgana reached her hand out, laying it on my arm.

It was funny, when Morgana touched me there was no spark. Morgana was beautiful, but Tiffany was the one that dazzled.

I nodded. "Yes, I'll talk to her."

"She's a great mom. Tiffany loves that boy. I'm sure if she knew your opinion, she would see how far he's come in the last six months."

Why didn't her friends see that Tiffany was holding David back? Maybe they didn't want to see. As much as I had to get this divorce and rectify the PT situation, maybe one more session with David was necessary to convince Tiffany that her son had more strength than she realized.

"I'm heading back to the table. It was nice to meet you, Jagger." Morgana patted me on the shoulder and walked out of the hallway.

I nodded and waved, lost in thought of how I was going to fix everything with Tiffany. Based on Tiffany's reaction at the booth, she realized I was the man she married. Would she even let me into her home again?

At least now that she knew, I could easily get her to sign the divorce papers. But how do I convince her that her son had enough strength to stand in a wedding ceremony?

I may not be a family type of man but I liked David. He reminded me how I felt at his age. All I wanted to do when I was young was be a spy. I watched every spy movie ever made, no matter how unrealistic they were.

Scenes of agents sitting at desks filling out endless paperwork don't make for intriguing storylines.

David appeared to be obsessed in the same way I was, but with ninjas. He needed extra help from me to do the moves that required a lot of strength, but I knew with time and training, he could do them on his own.

If just last year he wasn't even able to walk and now he can get up and down from crouching positions with some effort, then I am positive that boy could one day do ninja moves. And he would definitely be able to stand in a wedding ceremony.

Just as I was about to move closer to the bar to see if Tiffany had left I ran into a woman, close to my height, with blond hair.

"Excuse me," I said and was about to move around her when I realized who she was.

"Agent Jagger. When Edgar told me he ran into you a few days ago, I almost didn't believe him. Considering all you have done for us, I wonder why he hates you so much?" Evaleen Bechmann said as her bright blue eyes flickered between me and the hallway.

She had the sense of an agent. I tried to convince her over a month ago to consider joining the government, but she gave me a knowing smile before telling me no. I was disappointed but understood.

"Edgar and I have a misunderstanding. I'm sure he'll get over it in time, I know I have."

She nodded, and I knew only the most trained psychologist would be able to decipher what she was thinking. "Why are you here?"

"It's government business," I said.

Her lips thinned as she shook her head. "You've upset Tiffany, haven't you?"

My eyes widened. Dammit, she was good.

"Did Tiffany tell you?"

She smirked. "No, but you just did."

I couldn't believe I fell for that. These past few weeks I've been struggling to avoid mishaps and focus on work. Making careless mistakes like drinking and getting a quickie wedding, then avoiding seeking the divorce, and now easily giving in to a pedestrian question was now becoming the norm.

Something like that would never have happened to me a few months ago.

"Did she leave?"

Evaleen nodded. "Yes, and before she did Tiffany warned us to stay away from a tall man in a navy T-shirt with unkempt brown hair."

I groaned. "She told you about the marriage then."

That was all my fault. If I had taken care of it three weeks ago when I got back from out west, none of this would be happening.

As I stood there beating myself up inside and digging my nails into my scalp to let out some of my stress, Evaleen folded her arms and stared at me.

Her eyes narrowed as her lips curved slightly at the corners.

"Tiffany didn't tell you, did she? Fuck."

I wondered how I managed to make it all these years as an agent.

"No. She told us to keep an eye out for a thief. A man, fitting your description, who breaks into people's homes while they are there and steals their stuff. That the thief almost tricked her but took pity on her and David, so he pretended to be the physical therapist instead."

"What? How did she assume that? I never said anything about being a thief. It was a mistake. She assumed I was the PT and when I realized how big of a mistake I made back in Vegas, I was . . . It doesn't matter. I came here tonight to fix everything." I shook my head at what had occurred.

"Instead you made it worse," Evaleen said as she leaned back against the hallway wall to let a woman through that was heading toward the restroom.

She bit her lip as her eyes sized me up. Her agent brain was hard at work, and I feared what Evaleen would come up with.

"I was grateful for what you did to help me, my mom, and Edgar last month. I don't know what would have happened if you hadn't arrived," she said.

"It was my job."

"Regardless, I feel like I owe you. How about I help you with Tiffany? But, in order to do that, I will need you to be honest with me. Explain what happened in Vegas. She is my friend after all, and a wonderful mother to her son."

How can I tell this woman? She wasn't a government agent, tested and scrutinized to make sure secrets would always remain secrets.

"Fine, but I can only tell you on one condition," I said.

SEVEN

Tiffany

"Eww. Who farted?" I said as my hand flew to my face to cover the stench.

Two arms raised from the couch.

"I did," David said with pride.

"No, I did," Henrik said as he jokingly elbowed my son in the side.

"This isn't a contest." I moved toward the hallway entrance to avoid the gas cloud.

"Yes, it is," my son corrected me.

Henrik smiled as he turned his head from the direction of the television that sat on a dark brown bookcase against the wall.

"We just made it up to pass the time. Whoever wins gets to claim the title of *fart master*. So far, your son's in the lead."

I rolled my eyes. "I've never been prouder. When are you two leaving?"

"The Cubs game doesn't start until seven tonight, but I'm taking him out to dinner first," Henrik said just before I heard a squeak escape from underneath him.

His grin grew. "One more point for me."

I glanced at the clock on the microwave in the kitchen. It was a little after five o'clock.

"Where's the PT?" David asked.

Henrik glanced up at me. He knew. I called him last night when I got home. He was livid. Henrik wanted to hunt the guy down and make sure he was never able to walk into a building again.

I called the police this morning and an officer stopped by to get my information, but David wasn't here. He was with my neighbor, Celia. Her kids had grown, and we would invite her over for dinner on occasion. There were times I asked her to watch David for an hour or two, this morning was one of those times. I didn't want David to worry about what happened.

To take David's mind off of not having a ninja teacher—as he called Jagger—Henrik promised to take him to the Cubs game.

"He can't make it anymore. I'm afraid you are getting a new physical therapist. She should be here Monday."

When I contacted the PT group, they apologized for the mistake. It wasn't their fault Jagger showed up and I mistook him for the therapist, but I was never contacted about the real PT that never came. They promised that the new PT was one of their best and would be here promptly at four o'clock Monday afternoon.

David's large, azure eyes softened as his smile fell. Watching the disappointment on my son's face hurt worse than Jagger wanting to steal from me. I would give up all my possessions if it meant my boy was happy and healthy.

If I ever see that man again, Henrik won't have to lift a finger. I'd make sure Jagger would need PT for the rest of his life.

"But I liked Jagger. He's badass."

"He's an ass all right," I mumbled.

"What?" David asked.

I cleared my throat. "You know, I could teach you some ninja moves."

"You?" Both of them said at the same time.

"Yes. I might be an undercover spy for all you two know." I threw my hands up.

Henrik stood and began to chuckle. "When did this happen?"

Folding my arms, I walked toward the kitchen. "I would tell you, but then I'd have to kill you."

I heard laughter behind me as I began to wipe down the kitchen counter with a rag by the sink.

"I don't think Morgana would be happy with a dead fiancé," Henrik said.

Turning to glare at him, I put my hand on my hip. "She may not like it, but I'm sure she'd understand."

At that moment, the intercom buzzer went off. Creasing my brow, I pointed to Henrik. "Did you order food?"

"No," he said, and we both glanced at my son who was shaking his head.

I went over and pushed the answer button. "Hello?"

As clear as day, I heard a familiar voice. "Hey, Tiffany. It's me, Evaleen. Can I come up?"

I answered her with a push of the open button. Perhaps the police visit today spooked my landlord into finally fixing the intercom.

"Did you invite Evaleen over?" I asked Henrik as the two were finally on speaking terms.

"No." Henrik shook his head.

It wasn't long before we heard a knock at the door. I glanced through the peephole to see Evaleen standing there.

"Hey. What are you doing here?" I asked after I opened the door.

Evaleen's blond hair was back in a long braid. She usually wore her hair up in a restrictive bun, and the braided look softened her. She had on jeans and an oversized gray T-shirt that bunched at the sides.

She peered over my shoulder and frowned. "Crap. What's Payne doing here?"

"Henrik is here to take David to the baseball game. They should be leaving soon if you need to speak with me in private."

"Nice to see you too, Evaleen," Henrik shouted from behind.

She groaned. "Okay, if this is going to happen then I need to tell you both something before I even step into your apartment."

"You can tell me anything, Evaleen," I said and stepped closer but she held up her hands to stop me.

"Stay right there. After I tell you there will be no hugging, we all agree to stay exactly where we are," she said and then leaned to the side to glare at Henrik.

"Yes, if that's what you want." I was worried. Evaleen was a tough woman, and she never acted strangely like this. I hoped nothing was wrong with her or her mother.

"I promise," Henrik yelled.

She took a deep breath and glanced to her side before lifting her eyes to me. "I'm pregnant."

"Aaaah! I'm so happy for you." I jumped up and down and began to move toward her to give a big hug.

"Stop. You promised not to move," she said holding up her hand.

I nodded. "Yes, of course. Sorry, I forgot."

Despite her serious expression, I had a huge smile on my face. No wonder she was acting strangely. I've heard that sometimes pregnant women can become overly sensitive to sound or smell and even touch. That's probably why she doesn't want us near her.

I remember when I was pregnant with David becoming nauseous every time I heard a Beatles song. And I normally loved listening to the Beatles.

"Congratulations, Evaleen! Is Edgar pooping his pants." Henrik laughed and I heard my son giggle too.

"No, he isn't shit—" Evaleen started to speak before I cut her off.

"Language," I said in a straight tone.

"I mean, pooping himself. He couldn't be happier." Evaleen narrowed her eyes at Henrik. "Anyway, there's a reason I am telling you this now instead of a week from now when I planned to announce it to everyone."

I noticed she twisted her fingers together as if she was gathering strength. Perhaps she felt nauseous. I wish she would come inside so I could have her sit and rest.

"I brought someone with me. Someone who needs to explain something to you, Tiffany. There was a misunderstanding but when you see this person, you will not react well. So, I am here to moderate, to make sure you listen," Evaleen said.

I was about to ask her to clarify as I was confused to what she was referring to when my ears burned and my hands had the sudden urge to wrap around a neck.

"Jagger. You came." I heard David behind me as he saw Evaleen pull Jagger next to her. He must have been standing on the other side of the wall this whole time.

He took advantage of me and now he was using my friend!

"You dingleberry!" I said as I reached for Evaleen to pull her away.

Evaleen held up her hands. "I would advise both of you not to push, pull, or jostle me in any manner. As I mentioned, I'm pregnant."

She stood in front of Jagger like a shield.

Henrik moved next to me. "You son of a bitch—"

"Language, Henrik," I said.

He groaned. "David, go to your room."

"What? But—" David said.

"Just go, David. Henrik will take you soon." I turned and went over to my son, helping him up from the sofa. He walked slowly, reluctantly, toward his room.

Once we heard the door close from the hallway, Henrik let it all out. "You fucking piece of shit. Once Evaleen moves and your coward ass is unprotected, I'm going to make sure you won't be able to walk out of here. You like pretending to be a physical therapist? Why don't I make it so you have to be surrounded by them for the rest of your life."

"I'm not a thief, I promise," Jagger said, holding up his hands.

"Is that what you told Evaleen? What lie did you feed her so she would protect you?" I asked and hated that my body was heating with a mix anger and attraction. The anger part felt normal, given what Jagger had done, but the attraction. That part needed to leave and never come back, much like the man standing in my building hallway.

"Nothing. I told her the truth. That I'm a government agent and I came here last week to get Tiffany to sign some documents," Jagger said as he pulled some papers from his back pocket.

"Right. Sure. I'm just supposed to believe you work for the government." I folded my arms forcing my eyes to stay on his and not slide down his body.

He pulled out a black leather wallet. Flipping it open, he produced an ID card with his picture.

"How am I supposed to know that isn't fake?" Henrik asked.

Jagger pushed it toward Henrik. "Here, take it. Go call it in. You can look up the department of defense website and there should be a phone number. They won't acknowledge my name, but the verification code changes daily. Today it's blue. Agents use it to check in. My boss knows I'm here, so if I call from here to check in, it will be accepted."

Henrik took the badge and picked up my cell phone that was on the kitchen counter. He took a minute looking up the DOD's website and number before finally calling it.

"Blue," Henrik said.

I watched as his eyes widened and he removed the phone, handing it to Jagger.

"Yes, ma'am. I'll have the report on Monday," Jagger said before he tapped on the phone and handed it back to Henrik.

We stared at Jagger. Evaleen moved from in front of him.

"It looks like my work here is done," she said and turned to Jagger. "We are even now."

As she started to make her way toward the elevator, Jagger shouted, "Monday, first thing."

"As promised," Evaleen yelled back.

Jagger laughed and turned back to face Henrik. "Can I have my ID back?"

Henrik blinked before realizing what Jagger was asking for. "Right. Of course." He gave Jagger back the wallet containing his identification.

We stood in silence and I realized we were all still standing in the doorway.

"Why don't you come inside." Henrik and I moved aside to let Jagger through.

I directed him to the couch. Henrik stumbled back toward the bedrooms down the hall. "I'm going to get David now. Take him to dinner so you two can discuss whatever you need to."

He was about to turn but stopped. "Excuse me, Jagger, but since I know the verification code is blue, what's to stop me from getting information from the government with that code?"

Jagger sat back and smiled, his arm lazily dripping over the back of the couch. "You could try but that code, once used, is no longer relevant. Each agent gets a unique code daily. If you did try to use it, you would discover federal agents showing up at your door within minutes. I'm sure they wouldn't detain you *that* long. You might make it out in time for your wedding."

"My wedding isn't for another month."

"I know," Jagger said.

Henrik's eyes widened and the usual stoic man shrunk back and scurried down the hall.

"Agent Jagger. Why would you need me to sign papers?" I asked as I sat on the other end of my sofa.

EIGHT

Jagger

"You're my husband?" Tiffany's voice rose with every syllable.

Before Henrik and David left a few minutes ago, I apologized to David for pretending to be his physical therapist. He was disheartened but more so that I wouldn't be there to teach him ninja moves. His disappointment only intensified my own. It was fun last week showing him moves I had learned over the years. Not only that, but my heart beat with a new challenge. I was invigorated when I left our session. Something I hadn't felt in a long time.

The rush I used to get at the climax of a large operation like bringing down a criminal organization or capturing a terrorist was better than any drug. Over the years I felt less and less satisfied, as if it wasn't enough.

I was happy to keep this country safe, but growing increasingly unfulfilled with what I did for a living. Or was it what my job did to me?

"Technically, yes," I said and pushed the wrinkled divorce papers toward her on the coffee table.

She didn't reach for them. Tiffany only stared at me.

"Then we met before. When?"

"In Las Vegas. In the hotel bar where you were staying. I bought you a drink. Then came over to talk to you and Morgana."

The sun was still high in the sky as it was mid-summer and the light reflected off her dark hair, turning some pieces golden. Tiffany was beautiful. As foolish as it was to marry her, I couldn't blame my drunken self for so easily falling for her sweet charm and succulent lips.

Thoughts of how she tasted dotted my memories causing my tongue to reach for them. Tiffany was saying something but flickers of her naked body as she raced through the hotel room hiding her clothes kept blocking out her words.

"What?" I realized too late that Tiffany expected me to respond.

"I said, neither Morgana nor I remember that night. You were there last night. She doesn't remember you." She tilted her head, concern etched in her features.

"Okay."

"Okay?" Her chocolate eyes widened as she pushed to the edge of the couch, gripping the seat cushion. "Did you do that on purpose? Drug us so we wouldn't remember you?"

I sat up straight. "No, of course not. I was only observing you. Well, I was supposed to only observe you but it ended up being more than that."

Her nose flared, causing a slight indent in her chin. The blush that filled her face produced a question in my head that I would never give voice to—is that what she would look like if I climbed her body and sunk inside?

"Then how can neither of us remember you?" Tiffany asked after she took a breath, grabbing her braid and tossing it over her shoulder.

"Weren't you two drinking before I came over?"

"No. The drink you bought me was the first one I had that night. And it wasn't like I had an empty stomach. Morgana and I went to the buffet for dinner. I remember because we were going to go straight to the bar after but I told her I needed to check on Evaleen, who wasn't feeling well at the time . . . Wait, I can't believe I didn't figure that out." Tiffany smiled as she shook her head.

"Figure what out?"

"That Evaleen was pregnant. Of course, now I know because she just told me. That's why she was sick in Vegas. I thought she had the flu. And Aria knew!" She smacked her hand on the table. "That's why Aria told me when I was concerned I would catch whatever illness Evaleen had, that I already had it. But why would Evaleen tell Aria and not anyone else?"

I threw my hands in the air. "What are you even talking about? We started on how you and Morgana couldn't remember me and ended up discussing Aria's feelings on Evaleen's pregnancy."

"Not her feelings, but how she knew." Tiffany pursed her lips.

"Whatever. Can we get back on topic?"

"Yes, what were we talking about?"

Taking a calming breath, I was thankful to be divorcing this woman. She may be beautiful and kind and—despite my reservations with her not letting her son do more—a good mother. But, I had a feeling if I spent any time with her I would end up going mad. I had even more respect for David now, having lived with this woman.

"About both you and Morgana not remembering me," I said before rubbing my hands in irritation across my face.

"Right. I'm going to get something. Would you like some tea or candy?" She stood up and walked past the couch and into the kitchen.

I watched her from over my shoulder but turned completely around in amazement at what was in the cabinet.

"Wow, that's a lot of candy. I guess your son likes the sweet stuff." I stood, moving to the other side of the beige, granite island that separated the living room from the kitchen.

"Actually, most of this is mine. I have a bit of a sweet tooth. Especially when it comes to hard candy."

"Did you buy out the candy aisle at the Jewel Osco?" I gazed in wonder as all four shelves were overflowing with various bags of candy. The two upper shelves had boxes of the stuff. She must have bought them online because I don't think they sell bags of candy by the box at the grocery store.

"I have a subscription." Tiffany frowned. "It's called Candy Gram and I have the VIP subscription."

"No wonder you stripped," I said without thinking of the consequences of my words.

She dropped the green lollipop that was in her hand with a small *thwack*. Her face had lost all its color.

"I was a stripper in Las Vegas? Oh no. I must have been drugged. You have to believe me, I would never have done that otherwise."

I came over and put my hands on her shoulders. "No, that came out wrong. You didn't become a stripper. It was something that happened in the hotel room. You kept saying you needed a wedding ring and only a candy ring would do. I thought it strange but figured you had too much to drink."

Due to her surprise and horror at thinking she stripped in front of strangers, I felt it best to leave out the part where she did strip for me.

"Oh, thank goodness." Her head fell into her hand.

My thumbs rubbed circles around her shoulders to give her relief but I felt she might need more so I pulled her into an embrace. Tiffany melted into me as my arms circled her back. She was warm, soft, and it seemed right.

She felt amazing.

And her hair—it was soft and smelled as sweet as that lollipop. It was only natural when my hands slipped lower. Moving without thought or hesitation to the part of her back that dipped and then curved just before it separated into two plump cheeks. I shuddered with every twist of her body.

Tiffany pushed back. "What are you doing?"

"I'm sorry. I got, uh, carried away."

Leaning against the counter, I shoved my hands into my pockets to disguise the growing bulge in my jeans.

An awkwardness fell over the room like something sticky and thoroughly unwanted. She didn't step away but her head turned in every direction that didn't include me.

"You had sex with me," she whispered. Her hands clasped in front of her and for a moment she was too delicate to touch. As if a brush of my finger across Tiffany's shoulder would shatter her completely.

"No, we didn't. I would never have done that with someone who was drunk," I said.

That was a fact. I wanted to have sex with her. But as inebriated as I was, I had enough sense to keep her safe.

Her eyes peered up at me, wide but still uncertain. "But I woke up naked? In your hotel room. Wait. Was that your hotel room?"

Tiffany was shrinking again.

"Yes, that was my hotel room. I was in the shower when you left." I paused and gathered the courage to explain what happened. "Maybe I will take that tea."

My smile was weak but she nodded. I walked back to the living room and sat on the couch. In a few minutes, she came over placing a dark blue mug with a red crab on it that said, Got Crabs, in front of me on the coffee table.

"Here's some cream and sugar if you take that." She sat on the other end of the couch and waved at the small white porcelain container of creamer, shaped like a pitcher, and a bowl holding loose sugar.

I took a sip of the bitter tea and decided to drink it straight.

"You were naked because you insisted on taking off all your clothes," I said and took a second to gauge her reaction.

She had one leg folded, resting on the couch, while the other leg dangled over the edge. Her eyes weren't looking at me, but at something in the distance.

"I know it doesn't sound believable but it's true. I would never take advantage of someone while they were drunk. Even if you didn't have anything to drink before we met, you did afterward. At one point, I told the bartender to stop giving you anything."

I chuckled and placed the mug on the table. "That's when you got mad at me. You and Morgana stormed out of the hotel and I followed you to make sure you two were safe. We all walked for a while. That's when you proposed to me. You told me you needed someone to help take care of your family."

"I proposed to you? Oh no." Tiffany put her hand over her eyes, shaking her head.

"Yes, and being drunk myself, I accepted. We found a church and I decided to use my father's ring." I pulled the long gold chain from around my neck that hid under my shirt. Dangling at the end was a thick gold ring. "He passed away a few years ago and left me this ring. I always have it on me so that's what I used."

Her hand fell as she stared at the it. "May I see the ring?"

I took it off and handed it to her. Tiffany was searching for something and when she found it, she shook her head. "I feel like a doodoo butt."

She frowned and as uneasy as this was, I couldn't help but smile at her adorableness.

"Morgana insisted you use her engagement ring but after we were married she took it back for fear that Henrik would be mad. But I promised to buy you that candy pop ring in the morning. Obviously, that didn't happen."

We sat in silence for a minute before Tiffany picked up the divorce papers. She reached over to a side table and pulled out a small drawer, lifting a pen.

"Where do I sign?" she asked.

That was it. All the chaos and uncertainty of the past few weeks gone after a few strokes from a pen. I hesitated for a moment. Something in me wanted to shake my head. To take the pen away from her and stay married. Just for a little longer. To be normal for a few minutes more.

I quickly pushed that insane part of me away and pointed to the bottom of three different pages she had to sign.

"And initial here," I said.

She did.

Sighing, I took the papers and forced a smile. We got up and she walked me to the door.

"Well, Tiffany, it was nice being married to you these past many weeks even if you didn't know about it." I chuckled.

She laughed as she leaned against the open door. "Yeah, I guess."

I turned to leave but only made it two steps before she stopped me.

"How did my clothes in the hotel room end up in such odd places?"

Shit. I had to tell her.

I refused to turn and look at her as I spoke, "You took off each piece and hid them around the room. You said that if I found them you would give me a treat."

"Where were you when this happened?" she asked, her voice soft but I heard her clearly.

"I was watching you."

NINE

Tiffany

"Of course, cake," Aria said as if it was the most obvious answer. She spread her arms back on the bench, shaking out her platinum blond hair to enjoy the breeze.

It had been almost a week since Jagger dropped the bomb of us being married and the almost equally embarrassing bomb, of me stripping for him.

I had refused to step outside my apartment since then until David begged to go to the skate park. I said I would go with him if he promised not to actually use his skateboard inside the park.

Henrik thought it would be a wonderful gift to give my boy—who was still working on building his strength—a gift of a skateboard.

I almost punched Henrik. But I said David could practice standing, gaining his balance, and in time, learn to do a trick. That it might help him build his core and leg muscles.

"I asked if Morgana could marry anyone else, who would it be?" Grace said as she pushed her short black hair behind her ear.

I invited the ladies to join me. Only Aria and our latest recruit to the group, Grace Jensen, could come. She was the receptionist at Mimir and apparently, Henrik was scared of her. She had a crush on him and he didn't know how to deal with it.

Aria and her boyfriend, Alex, had run into her in Vegas back in June. There was some problem with all of them trying to get home, so they decided to drive cross-country together. That's when they grew close to Grace.

We all sat on a bench in the park and I watched my son move toward the skate park. The heat of the last few days had gone away, leaving a beautiful, warm, summer day.

"And she answered the question. Ask her yourself if you don't believe me." Aria waved her hand at Grace.

I giggled at Morgana's deep love of cake.

"Has she decided on what cake she wants for the wedding?" I asked.

"Yes, but she wants it to be a surprise," Aria said but shook her head. "As her maid of honor, I feel I need to know these things. Especially, considering the location of the wedding and reception."

"Edgar is in charge of the flowers," Grace said holding her hand over her eyes to shield the sun.

"Why would Edgar be in charge of the flowers? Isn't he the best man?" I asked.

Aria nodded. "Yes, but he told Henrik he knows of a great florist."

"Okay," I said but didn't ask any more questions because I got the feeling someone was watching me.

"That guy is staring at you, Tiffany," Aria said and I turned to look in the direction of where her head was turned.

I gasped as I realized she was right. A guy in dark gray running shorts that hit mid-thigh and a form fitting bright blue T-shirt leaned against a tree near the bike trail watching me.

"That man is cut." Aria continued her impressed assessment of his body.

He pushed off the tree and began to jog in our direction. All of us quickly whipped our heads around, taking our eyes off the approaching man.

"Looks like Tiffany might have a hot date tonight," Aria singsonged.

"I don't think he's about to ask me out. Besides, who goes up to a stranger in a park to ask them out on a date?" I said rolling my eyes.

"That's how I got my date," Grace said.

"What? You never told me you had a date." Aria leaned forward, placing her hand on Grace's shoulder.

"Last week I decided to go for a walk after work. I eventually found a bench that looked out over the lake. Some guy came up and sat. We got to talking and he asked for my number. We're going out on Friday."

"All right, Grace! You just might have a date for the wedding." Aria lifted her hand for a high-five and Grace, with blushing cheeks, slapped it.

"Hello, ladies," a familiar deep voice said.

I lifted my hand to block the sun and realized the runner with the cut body was Jagger. His legs and arms glistened with sweat but that only seemed to enhance the curves of his muscles. Placing his arms behind his back, he waited as my eyes lingered on the blue fabric that appeared to have melted onto his chest.

"Jagger. I didn't realize you lived in Chicago," Aria said.

That caught me off guard and I turned to Aria. "You know Jagger?"

"Yes, we met him on our way back to Chicago," Aria said and then abruptly began to cough.

Grace patted her on her back, but Aria couldn't stop.

"I think I need to go back home," Aria rasped and pulled Grace with her.

They waved and I watched them, noticing Aria's coughing stopped once they reached the sidewalk.

"That was weird," I said.

"What do you expect from an artist." Jagger made himself comfortable next to me.

"I guess," I said still unsure as to what just happened.

"Nice day." Jagger turned to face the skate park, waving at David.

My boy was standing on his skateboard just outside the gate that separated the skaters from the observers. A few boys were talking to him.

"I'm glad he's making friends," I said putting my thoughts to words.

"You sound like he's five," Jagger said.

"What?"

He sighed and turned his body so his arm was propped on the back of the bench causing me to stare at the muscles in his upper arm. Normally, I wasn't into that sort of thing—men with lots of muscles like athletes or models, but I swear it seemed like Jagger was flaunting them at me. Wearing T-shirts that hug his chest or shorts that bared his legs.

Looking around I noticed all of the men, and women for that matter, were wearing similar items but on Jagger they appeared provocative. He might as well have had a giant neon sign pointing to his body that said, "This man has a body made for licking."

And that's another thing. When did I get into licking? The mother in me knew that licking anything, even bodies, could lead to illness. But the woman in me that had Jagger in her line of vision seemed to think licking might be fun.

"Doesn't David have friends?" he asked.

"Of course, but only one. There was a boy, Matt, but he moved away last year. There's another boy that's in our building, Walker, who comes over to play video games every so often, even before David had the operation."

I turned to find David standing and playing with his board with one foot, talking to some kids. "David had a special communication device and we adapted the game controller so he could invite people over to play with him. He's liked to play games with Walker, but I think Walker only liked David for the games he had and nothing else. At least, that's what I heard him tell Henrik a few weeks ago."

It wasn't easy for a boy that had difficulty communicating, even with a speaking device, to make friends with kids.

"I feel sorry for that kid."

I narrowed my eyes at Jagger. "Don't feel sorry for David. He's done more in his twelve years on this planet than most people do their entire life."

"I didn't mean David . . . I meant Walker."

"Oh." I shrugged. "I just think their personalities didn't match up."

At least, that's what I told myself even when I noticed Walker would always make excuses when David invited him to his birthday party. Every year.

We sat quietly, enjoying the weather and watching my son laugh with his new friends. Unwittingly, my throat tightened and a few unsolicited tears fell from my eyes.

"Darn," I whispered and turned my head, brushing the tears away with my fingers.

"Allergies?" Jagger asked before handing over a tissue that I hoped came from his pocket.

I wanted to let it all out. To sob and scream and jump for joy. But this wasn't the time or the place. Not in front of my son and his new friends. Not in front of the handsome man that worked hard to defend this country.

Only alone, in my room, with a pillow to help me relieve my years of stress, of fears, of hope.

"Something like that." I pretended to laugh as I pushed the corners of my lips up into what I hoped to be a believable smile taking the tissue.

I glanced over at Jagger and noticed he was watching me. His brow creased in uncertainty. Finally, he turned to look out over the park and watched the people go by.

"They don't know and that's too bad." Jagger sighed waving his hand at all the people around us. "They walk around the world, ignorant to what is real. Their eyes never seeing the invisible beauty. Searching for answers that are there. Always there, if only they stopped running to find them. Because sometimes it's too late when we see . . . and that's the biggest heartbreak."

His hand moved over mine and Jagger turned his head, his green eyes full of something I worried was being reflected back at him. "It's okay, Tiffany, because I know. You and me, we know."

I couldn't stop them. The tears. They came and when I tried to speak, only rough breaths escaped. He pulled me close and let my eyes dampen his shirt. It felt good and I didn't care. He was a man and I needed that right now. It had been too long.

His arms were firm, giving me the comfort and support I craved. Jagger never said a word because he didn't need to. He knew it was his touch I required the most.

We would have stayed like that for a while if loud voices from the skate park hadn't made me look up. I saw David on the ground and a group of boys around him yelling. Before it registered what was happening, Jagger had hopped up and was running over to the boys.

"I need everyone to get back," Jagger demanded, his tone loud and authoritative.

The boys listened and a few ran away. One of the boys, a kid with black hair, was helping David up.

"What happened?" I crouched down and assessed his face, his arms, his legs.

He didn't appear to be hurt but that didn't mean he wasn't.

"I fell," David said. He folded his arms and refused to look at me.

The kid with raven hair tapped me on my arm. "The boys who ran off tried to steal his skateboard. We were talking, me and David, and they came over wanting his skateboard. They pulled it out from under him, that's how he fell over."

"Thank you for telling me. What's your name?" I asked.

"Diego."

Jagger moved beside me as I stood.

"Hey, Diego. Would you like to learn how to be a ninja?" Jagger asked.

The boy's dark eyes rounded as his mouth fell open. There were a few gasps and "no way's" from the boys around us.

"It's just, I've been teaching David here, how to be a ninja." Jagger turned to David, and with a serious tone he said, "You didn't use any of the moves on those boys, did you? Because those moves are deadly and not to be used on anyone."

My son shook his head as he stared up at Jagger.

The agent nodded, scratching his chin with his fingers. "Good. You still need some practice. Why don't you give Diego your info and we can all set up a time to discuss more ninja training?"

"Yeah," both boys said at once.

"Is that all right with you?" Jagger turned to me, doubt lining his features.

I gazed at my son's face. So much hope in his while mine filled with worry.

"Yes, it's all right with me," I said as the boys cheered.

TEN

Jagger

"It's ninja time!" Tenn crouched down and sliced the air with his hands.

Grabbing my partner's arm, I yanked him back up. People eyed Tenn in suspicion as they curved around us on the sidewalk.

"Come on, I don't want to be late," I said studying their faces out of habit, but mostly due to embarrassment.

"Can I come and help?"

It had been a few days since I volunteered my services to David as a ninja instructor. I felt good when I left the park that day. Helping some kids be able to defend themselves gave me that high that's been absent these past months.

Instead of hurting the bad guys, I was helping the good ones. It was different but something about it made my heart full.

Then I walked into the office the next day and gazed into Katlin's cold eyes. She was relieved I obtained the signature for the divorce, but warned me to stay away from anyone related to Emma Hawthorne's case.

I confided in Tenn. He promised to keep my secret but suggested I not tell anyone else.

"No, I don't want to get you involved. It's one thing to put my job on the line but I don't want to risk yours too."

He nodded but as we walked toward Tiffany's building, I realized my partner was unusually quiet.

"What is it?"

Tenn shrugged. "I don't know why you're doing this—risking the case like this. You know if this gets out and Emma Hawthorne or her lawyer find out, it doesn't look good for us."

My throat tightened. "Yeah, I know. Just this one time and I'll explain I can't do it anymore. One time shouldn't be a problem. I mean, I already fucked up marrying the woman. At least Katlin can work her magic to make sure that doesn't get out."

"I guess." Tenn paused and looked at me. "What happened to you, Jag? You've been different lately."

Shoving my hands into the front pockets of my jeans, I turned my head toward the street. "Don't you ever want to be like them?" I removed a hand and waved it toward the people around us.

"What? Naïve? Boring? No, thank you." Tenn laughed.

"Sure, they're innocent of the evil people that we fight so hard to protect them from, but if I'm going to be honest, I'm jealous of them. I want to be blissfully unaware sometimes. Hang out with my friends and go to a bar on a Friday night. Maybe date a woman without having to search her background and the backgrounds of her friends and family."

"What happened to Cate?"

"She's dating some guy. He has a regular job downtown doing finance or something. When I saw her last that's what she told me. No more hookups for me."

His hand came to rest on my shoulder with a hard smack. "Sorry, man. She was hot. I'm sure you'll find another fuck. Someone with a clean record that only wants sex."

Maybe I want more than a fuck.

"Perhaps you're right. Looks like I'm here. Thanks for walking with me. And good luck on your lunch date. Hope you get lucky," I said just outside Tiffany's building.

"Hopefully she lets me into her inner circle." Tenn winked before he continued on his way.

I used to be like that. Find some woman, have a casual fling, and not feel like I was the loneliest man in the world.

Tenn usually bragged about the women he was about to hook up with, but he didn't tell me anything about this one. Maybe he wanted more than sex, too.

Pushing the buzzer to Tiffany's apartment, I forced myself to get out of this funk I was in. Making the country safe, that was more important than some woman to come home to at night.

"Yes?" Tiffany's garbled voice came through the speaker.

"It's Jagger."

The door buzzed and I pushed through. I took the elevator to the eighth floor, moving thirty feet down the hall and came to stop in front of door 803. I knocked.

The door opened as the smell of garlic and spices wafted past me. Tiffany stood there with her thick hair cascading around her face and over her shoulders. Her smile inviting and curved with a pale red.

"Great. You're here. David's been talking all day about the lessons. Come in."

She moved to the side as I stepped past her. Her frilly, heart-dotted apron wrapped over her green blouse and jeans had my eyes momentarily fixed on two hearts in particular. I swallowed as I pried my eyes away from her chest.

"Do you like garlic?" Tiffany asked as she brushed past me and into the kitchen.

"Of course. But why would—"

"Good." She cut me off as she moved gracefully around the kitchen. "I'm making a lemon garlic pasta and salad for dinner. And I use garlic in my salad dressing."

My head jerked. "You make your own dressing?"

The servants made the food in the house I grew up in. I may have only been six when my mother died, but I remember she never cooked. As for my dad, he refused to even eat in the same room as me.

As she stirred whatever was in the metal pan with a wooden spoon, she turned her head. "Of course. I'm not a fan of the bottled dressings. My mom used to make her own dressing before she died. Luckily, she taught it to me before I went off to college. I guess she thought I might need it because of all the salad college students eat."

Tiffany snorted at her own joke.

"I forgot about your mom," I said and realized too late at what I revealed.

"What?" Tiffany put down the spoon and turned to face me.

"I mean, I'm sorry about your mom," I said as I leaned against the counter to appear casual as my heart pounded in my ear.

She hesitated but shook her head before turning back to the stove.

"It was right after I met John, my late husband. He was a senior at Northwestern and I was a sophomore. We had only been dating a few weeks and then, my mom had a heart attack." She pushed the pan off the burner and turned off the heat.

Tiffany stood there, staring at the pan like a statue frozen in a memory. She sighed. "She was a great cook. A little too good. I think all the fattening food she loved to eat and the toll of being a single mom finally got to her. There's a part of me that still regrets not being there when she died. Not holding her hand and telling her I loved her. She had done that for me a thousand times, but when she needed it the most from me, I was at some party at school. The music too loud to hear my phone."

Coming up behind Tiffany, I put my hand on her shoulder. She turned and without a thought but loaded with emotion, I embraced her. Her pain was my pain. Not because I loved her. How could I? I barely knew the woman. No, it was because my life had been battered by that same regret. When I was too young to understand and when I was older and knew better.

Regret like that forces a person to make lonely decisions and unhappy mistakes.

Her arms came around my back, tightening. A fluttery soft sensation made circles on my back as Tiffany comforted me as much as I was trying to console her.

Tilting my head, I brushed my lips over the top of her head, inhaling. She smelled like garlic and flowers. Two scents that should work against each other, but for some reason, I had never smelled anything so amazing in my life. My hand lifted into her hair. So thick, that when my fingers curled, I wondered if she even felt it.

Her fingers stopped. It's what they did next that caused my head to lower until my lips were brushing hers. Tiffany moved her hands to my ass. Nothing subtle. No light movements that could be mistaken for an accident.

They cupped my cheeks and dug in.

"Mom?"

Tiffany's hands moved from my backside to my front in seconds, pushing me away from her. I grasped the granite counter so I wouldn't fall to the floor. For a petite woman, she had some strength.

"Yes, David?" Tiffany said as she turned her back to me, to her son, and resumed cooking.

I glanced over at David as he moved closer to the kitchen. His eyes remained on his mother, refusing to even turn my way.

"Is it okay if Diego and I have dinner in my bedroom?" David asked as his voice cracked halfway through talking.

"Sure. Sure. Just eat at your desk."

"Good. Uh, hi." David finally turned his head toward me. His eyes remained glued to the floor, but at least I knew he was speaking to me.

"Hi, David. It's nice to see you again. I guess we're getting started after dinner." My eyes bounced between him and his mom.

"Yes. In fact, if you take a seat over at the dining room table, I can bring you your plate," Tiffany said.

I turned back to her and was surprised to find several bowls filled with pasta as she was grating a hard cheese over top.

"Why don't you get something to drink for you and Diego, David."

I suddenly felt out of place. David knew what to do and helped his mother without her having to say a word. Just before he was ready to leave with two cans of soda in his hand, she turned to kiss his cheek.

"Mom," he groaned as his eyes flickered to me before shuffling out of the kitchen.

"What can I do to help?" I asked.

"Just bring these plates back to the boys. Thank you." She handed me two large plates with salad, forks, and a bowl full of pasta on them.

I easily found David's room from the sounds of explosions and gun fire. The boys leaped up as I placed the plates on his desk. They awkwardly thanked me before shoveling some angel hair pasta into their mouth.

Once I came back out to the main area, Tiffany had already placed our plates on the dining room table.

As she came over I tried my best to pull out her seat in time, but she waved me off.

"I've gotten used to doing everything myself. It feels weird when someone tries to help. I guess I'm just not used to it," Tiffany said as I insisted on helping to push her chair in before I took my seat.

"Being alone for a long time will do that to a person." I smiled at her as the aroma of the food made my mouth water.

The small, round wooden table caused my knees to bump into hers. A jolt of electricity seemed to make me sit up a little straighter.

"I'm not used to this sort of thing either," I said.

And I wasn't. The past twenty minutes felt nothing like a ninja session and everything like a date. It caused my neck to burn with doubt and my heart to surge with wonder.

ELEVEN

Tiffany

"Your mother's sweet," I said before shoving a fork full of chicken into my mouth. Trying to fill it so I wouldn't have to talk anymore.

Greg smiled and turned toward his mom, taking her hand in his.

"She makes sure every woman I go out with is good enough for me. She's the perfect judge of character," he said.

I almost threw up the dry chicken I had swallowed.

"My little Greggy never told me how you two met?" the robust woman with a black, protruding mole on her cheek asked.

The mole matched her short, curly hair, which matched her son's hairstyle as well. Even their outfits—plaid button-up shirts and khaki pants—appeared to be planned to coordinate.

"Through a dating app. It helps single men and women find locals with similar interests," I said and forced another piece of chicken in my mouth.

Despite my dinner being a bit overdone with very little flavor, I had to distract myself from this abysmal date.

After what almost happened between Jagger and me four days ago, I knew I had to do something, and quickly. I liked Jagger, but I was looking for someone that valued safety and support for my family.

While I knew very little about Jagger's job—other than it was secret and he worked for the government—I knew even less about the man himself. I thought he would tell me something about his life over dinner the other night, but he only wanted to know about me. Every time I asked about his past, he would change the subject or explain there wasn't anything to discuss. Everyone has a past, yet he acted like he didn't.

And when I asked anything about his job, his response was, *I'm not at liberty to discuss that with you.*

I had no doubt that Jagger was good at what he did but was it dangerous? I had a feeling it was, and I'm not about to put David or me at risk because Jagger had a tight butt. Or that he had the ability to see into my soul and made me weep in the park last week. Or that my heart melted when he helped David out with those bullies when they tried to steal his skateboard.

No, that wasn't important. Safety, that's what counted. There's been too much trauma in my life, too many losses. I don't believe I could handle anything like that again.

"An app? Greg, you told me you two met while volunteering at the children's hospital," his mother said with a frown that accentuated her mole.

"Oh, he didn't tell you?" I said, trying to hold back my smile.

Perhaps this morsel of information, which was much juicier than my chicken, would be the knife that killed our date. I felt very little guilt that Greg was breaking out into a sweat and his plaid shirt was sticking to his chest.

His dating profile was completely misleading. Everything, except his photograph, was a lie. I wasn't disappointed when I saw him tonight. He's not a bad looking man—slim with handsome features. The frustration came when he led me to a table with his mom. And that wasn't the worst.

"Tell me what?" his mom asked.

Greg shook his head, pure fear creating lines on his face.

"He's a doctor. Your son doesn't volunteer at the hospital. He's a doctor. Isn't that right, Greg?"

I knew he wasn't. My son spent most of his life in and out of that hospital. If Greg worked there, I would have come across him at least enough times to recognize him.

"Greg, you're not a doctor. You're the assistant accounting manager at RT Mitchell. Why would you lie to Tiffany? Or to me, your mother?"

We both kept our attention on Greg waiting for an answer, but nothing came. His eyes flickered back and forth between the mother that wondered what happened to her perfect man-child, and me, the date that just wanted to spend a few hours with a normal guy.

"What's that over there?" Greg pointed to something behind me.

I glanced back but only saw the other patrons enjoying their meals at matching round tables covered in green linen. When I turned back, Greg was maneuvering through the tables, bumping into one and almost knocking it over, on his way toward the front of the restaurant.

"Greg," his mother yelled as she stood and went after him.

I sat there for a few minutes expecting one of them to come back, but they didn't.

"Would you like anything else, ma'am?" the waiter asked, who was dressed better than my date in a blue button-up shirt, gray tie, and dark slacks.

"No. I guess I'll take the check," I grumbled and made a mental note to punch Greg if I ever see him walking down the street.

After the waiter left, I leaned back in my chair and I wondered if I had been spoiled with men. I met my husband in college; John wasn't perfect but he was a good man—a wonderful and amazing dad, which was all that mattered.

I remember once I threatened divorce if he didn't pick up his socks and put them in the hamper. But those were superficial problems. He was incredible where it counted, with his heart.

"The bill has been paid, ma'am," the waiter said upon returning.

"It has? By whom?"

Maybe Greg redeemed himself a little by paying the bill before he ran off.

"The gentleman at the bar." He pointed to the long bar that hugged the front of the restaurant.

When I gazed over, there was a fluttering in my heart. My hand cupped my chest, trying to push back the exhilaration. It was just a man after all. Someone I knew, but not a person that I should be having that reaction toward despite his simmering stare.

He stood, his eyes shone and homed in on me as he moved closer.

"Jagger. Thank you for dinner," I said and only just noticed the waiter had left.

I thought it odd that I hadn't even realized he was gone. My surprise at discovering Jagger here and staring too long at his hips as he walked over to me must have made me forget there were other people in the room.

"I felt obligated," Jagger said as he pointed to Greg's abandoned chair.

I nodded and he took a seat. He looked good, but Jagger always seemed to be wearing something that caught my eye. Tonight, it was a dark navy suit, and it fit him perfectly.

"For what?"

"For the show. I have to admit when I came here tonight to have a drink at the bar, I never expected there would be a comedy show." The corner of his mouth ticked up.

I gasped and was about to let him have it but when I opened my mouth, laughter spilled out. And the more I laughed, the more his green eyes sparkled. Which finally killed my merriment, replacing it with a meandering heat that settled between my legs.

"I suppose you're right. The mother and son show was ridiculous. That's the last time I use the dating app Morgana suggested. I don't care if it was, as she put it, 'scary accurate' when she used it." I gave another chuckle.

"No, those apps can't be trusted. In fact," Jagger leaned closer, lowering his voice, "most men can't be trusted."

I angled near so his warm breath slipped down my neck causing my turquoise blouse to flutter around my chest. "Can you?"

His stare fell to my lips, and the ambient noise of the room dimmed to the point I wondered if we had floated away. It took a few moments but Jagger finally answered my question, "No."

A shiver sparked by the heat of his breath and the chill of his voice ran down my body.

I watched him study me, perhaps memorizing my nose, my cheeks, and my lips. Knowing it was wiser and by his admittance, safer, to have pulled away but I didn't.

There was something in him that seemed to heave open a door I bolted shut a long time ago. And I was having a terrible time trying to close it again.

"Then you'll hurt me?" I asked. The anticipation of his answer had me wetting my lips with my tongue.

Jagger scooted forward so his cheek was only an inch away. His body heat became mine. When he tilted his head, I felt the scrape of his stubble.

"I would never hurt you, Tiffany. There are many things I dream of doing to you but nothing that would ever cause you pain."

His breath was sharp, laced with whiskey, and when he pulled back just enough his lips hovered over mine. If I gasped or shuddered or did anything that caused my head to shift, I knew his lips would be on mine.

There was a tickle in the back of my chest that grew with each passing second. That itch turned into something I knew no amount of clawing from my fingers would appease. Having spent so much time alone and reading every article ever written on love, relationships, and dating, or at least it felt like every article, I understood what that thing in my chest meant. And how much it took to satisfy.

It made me uneasy to stare at his lips knowing they were the cure.

It's with that thought I got up.

"Thank you again, Jagger, for the food. It's getting late, and I need to relieve Evaleen of her babysitting duties."

Grabbing my small black leather clutch, I moved toward the front door.

"Please, do come again," the hostess said as I briskly strolled past her station near the door.

Turning my head, I smiled and nodded at her, not wanting to be rude. As I reached my arm out to where I thought the door was, nothing but warm air remained.

I turned my head back to the front and found Jagger had sneaked past me and was now holding open the door like a gentleman. Ugh, why did he have to be so polite? It was annoyingly alluring.

Just about everything Jagger did had caught me off guard. Sometimes with irritation but more often than not, with pleasant surprise.

"Thank you," I grumbled as I scurried up the street.

The restaurant was near my building so I could easily walk home which was a good thing. The bad thing was Jagger knew where I lived and walked with me.

"You don't have to see me back home. I'm only two more blocks away." I pointed up the street.

"It's a nice evening. Besides, it's not safe to walk alone."

"I'm pretty sure nothing is going to happen to me in the one minute I have left in my walk. It's summer, there's plenty of light left. I think I'll be okay."

During our conversation, I picked up my pace but couldn't outmaneuver him. I guess when he trained to work for the government he was taught power walking as well.

"Well, I'm here." I pushed open the door to my building, but he grabbed my arm before I could escape.

"You trying to pull a Gregger?" Jagger asked.

That stopped me and I turned. "You joking about my date?"

"Yeah, how he jetted out." He chuckled.

I tiled my head. "But I never told you his name . . ."

TWELVE

Jagger

"You've been spying on her?" Tenn said.

I thought he would laugh. That was the sort of thing my partner got a kick out of—as awful as it was—since he had a childish sense of humor.

"I had to make sure she was safe. Being with her, in her life, was putting her at risk," I said accentuating my point by sawing my hands in the air.

It made sense. I didn't want anything to happen to Tiffany or her son. What better person to make sure no one hurt them than me, a government agent.

"Then stop having her in your life! Like I talked to you about last week when you swore you were going to end things."

"I was. I meant to but . . ." I drifted off not wanting to finish. Luckily, I had a cup of coffee in front of me to bring to my lips.

We were back at Wake Up Joe's taking a break from work. I was trying to get him on my side, make him understand why I still needed to see Tiffany and David.

"But what?"

"Tiffany grabbed my ass. And I sniffed her hair." With each explanation, Tenn's eyes grew wider. "Then after spying on her date three days ago, I almost kissed her."

Tenn sat back in the booth with a curious look on his face.

"But that's all that happened. I swear." I held my hands up.

"Does she know?"

"No. She started to figure something out when I mentioned her date's name, and she had never told it to me. But I quickly recovered by telling her I heard his mom yell out his name before they left the restaurant. That was close." I scratched the back of my neck as it was really itchy since we got here.

Tenn's eyes widened before shaking his head. "And how were you spying on her?"

"Hmm." I brought the cup to my lips again turning my gaze to the other people in the café.

"I know you heard me, Jagger."

"Oh, you know." I shrugged and blew air past my lips which made a ridiculous farting sound.

I was hoping if I dodged Tenn's question enough then he would drop it.

"No, I don't, Jagger. I'm your partner. What you are doing doesn't just affect Tiffany . . . it affects me, the agency, and even the government. This is the shit that gets agents thrown in jail. The best-case scenario in all this would be losing your job."

I guess he's not going to drop it.

"This time I'm going to end things. I swear!" I held up my hand as if I had the other on a bible in a courtroom.

He shook his head and wouldn't look at me.

I scratched at my neck again. "What? I am. Besides I got rid of the listening devices after her date. It felt weird doing that. It's just going—"

"It's not that, Jagger. It's the Jewel, Emma Hawthorne. She's saying that you framed her. That everything you did this past year, was a setup. She says she isn't the one who planned this out. It was someone else, and you're helping to protect that person," Tenn said as he finally turned to me, his eyes burrowing into mine.

I sat up straighter.

"What the fuck? Who does she think I'm protecting?"

That woman was a piece of work. She had all the money in the world and a good son. Instead of being a doting mother, she manipulated her son since he was a little boy so she could get back at the men who had hurt her.

To do that, she tried to force her loving son to marry into a political dynasty. Emma wanted her son to run for public office and one day become President of the United States. All so she could use his status and his name to take revenge on the men she despised.

Not only was she evil, but she was also petty.

"Emma Hawthorne is saying her daughter, Grace, influenced her. That she was so grateful to have found her long-lost daughter, that when Grace started to talk about getting back at the men who took her away, she promised Grace she would do anything to make her daughter happy. She claims she was just a mother being protective of her daughter."

"That's still a crime. I'm sure her lawyers have told her that. Mrs. Hawthorne may think she can manipulate her lawyers, but she can't screw the federal government," I said.

Tenn nodded but shrugged as if everything he was saying made sense. "She understands she played a part. But that part has less jail time. She said when she felt it was going too far she came to you because she was worried about her daughter. That you told her to play along to catch Grace. She agreed and only said those things at the warehouse to trick everyone into catching her daughter."

I shook my head. "But that doesn't make sense. Grace, wasn't even at the warehouse. She was with me. Why would Emma Hawthorne say all those things to incriminate herself at the warehouse if her daughter, Grace, wasn't even there?"

"Apparently, the judge is reviewing everything with her lawyers. In the meantime, the boss wants you off the case. I'm to take it over now."

This was all messed up. Emma was blaming her own daughter for the crimes she committed. Her daughter, Grace, didn't even know she had a mother until earlier this year when Emma tracked her down.

The case was complicated. Grace thought she was getting to know her real mother, not being framed for her mother's crime. I reached out to Grace earlier this year when I knew she had contact with Mrs. Hawthorne. Grace quickly learned her mother wasn't the sweet woman she hoped she would be.

Grace even helped me take her down.

"But Emma Hawthorne is lying. Even Katlin has to know that." I leaned forward as if getting closer would help change everything.

"It doesn't matter, Jagger. You're going to have to step off the case. When they go forward with her allegations, it will all come out in court. Maybe something else will arise in regard to Emma before the court date and all this will be forgotten."

"I guess," I said as my thoughts drifted to everything about Emma Hawthorne's case.

I analyzed anything that might be questionable in my head as I sat in that café. There were a few things I had to do in order not to blow my cover but nothing that would lend truth to her words.

"I got to get back. You coming?" Tenn got up and threw his thumb toward the door.

"No, I'm going to be here for a while. I'll see you later."

He nodded and turned to leave the café.

Something wasn't right. Why all of a sudden, almost two months after Emma Hawthorne got caught, does she come up with the allegation that she's being framed?

Tenn was right, I had to walk away from Tiffany and her son, no matter how hard it was going to be. I couldn't let anything jeopardize this case. As much as I wanted to watch Tiffany melt as I made her come on my fingers, on my mouth, and on my cock, I had to walk away.

I got out my phone and texted Tiffany to tell her I needed to discuss something with her in person. After a few minutes, my phone vibrated letting me know she responded.

Tiffany: *I'm here now. You can stop by. David's here, he wants to ask you something.*

Me: *I'll be there in fifteen minutes.*

Damn it. I forgot about David. I can't give him ninja lessons anymore. I only gave him and his friend lessons once, after Tiffany made that amazing dinner, but I had a great time. I'm usually around intense and emotionally closed off government agents, so it was refreshing to goof around with some kids.

I left the café. As I made my way farther south toward Tiffany's building in a taxi, I tried to come up with an explanation that wouldn't break that boy's heart.

By the time I was in front of her building I realized I had thought up every excuse but nothing was going to prevent me from letting him down. He reminded me so much of my cousin, Ben, which made this worse. With Ben, I could be angry at his mother, and especially my father, for doing what they did, but with David, I'm the one abandoning him.

Tiffany buzzed me inside and I took my time getting to her door. I wanted to prolong the inevitable forever but knew that couldn't happen.

The door swung open before I even brought my hand to knock.

"Jagger!" A shining pair of blue eyes with a mop of dark hair greeted me.

"Hi, David. Is your mom here?" I didn't have to force the smile on my face. That boy was always alight with life, even when he was unsure and awkward like the first couple of times I was around him.

"Yeah." He held onto the door as he stepped back, stumbling slightly.

He was still working on his balance, which I noticed when I taught him some tae kwon do. I decided to give him extra core strengthening exercises to help him better master the moves I was teaching him.

"Before you talk to Mom," David said as I followed him into their living room, "can I ask you something?"

I helped him onto the couch and took a seat next to him. "Shoot."

"I'm having a party on Saturday. It's my birthday," he said as his eyes darted to the carpet and his cheeks turned pink.

"Happy early birthday. How old?"

"Thirteen."

"How does your mom feel about you becoming a teenager?" I laughed, making light of it but David frowned.

"She still thinks I'm a three-year-old. I'm surprised she's even letting me have a party."

I hated to admit it, but I agreed with David. Tiffany was a little too protective of that boy.

"Where's the party?"

A smile broke out and his face glowed with happiness. "At Kart One in Buffalo Grove. They have kart racing. It's going to be cool."

I took a big gulp of air to brace myself and tell him why I couldn't be at his party. Why I couldn't be in his life anymore.

"The thing is, David. I am going to—"

"Oh, you're here. Did you ask him, David?" Tiffany's voice came from behind.

I turned upon hearing Tiffany. The back of my neck already tickled as electric awareness grew the closer she came.

Her hair was down. Most of the times I had seen her, her thick mass of chocolate waves was pulled back in a ponytail or braid. The few times I had seen her with her hair down, it captivated me. But this time it framed her face bringing to life the red of her lips and the soft pink of her cheeks. I even noticed a dusting of freckles on the bridge of her nose.

I stared. It was obvious, but I wasn't going to hide it. If this was going to be the last time I saw Tiffany, I wanted to memorize everything. Even how the corner of her right lip lifted a little higher when she smiled. As if her lips contained knowledge only the luckiest members of the human race were privy too.

But when I got to her eyes, there was something there that had me wondering something I shouldn't. And as I wondered, my heart pounded. I knew there were going to be people upset with what I was about to do, but I wasn't trained for how she affected my heart.

"Yes, he did. I'd love to come to his party," I said and didn't regret it for a second.

THIRTEEN

Tiffany

"Crush them, sexy!" Aria yelled at her boyfriend who was currently whipping around a small indoor racetrack in a red electric kart.

I think it was her boyfriend Alexander. Everyone had helmets on, and I couldn't tell who was who. I even lost David in the crowd of testosterone that filled that track. Except for Morgana—she was the lone female of the racers.

"There are kids out there, Aria. I wouldn't encourage a six-foot-three man to crush them while racing around in metal vehicles." I pointed to the red and black blurs going around and around.

It was David's birthday party, and everyone was having a great time at the kart racing center. Several kids that David got to know through Diego were here, including Diego. Even Matt and his mom flew in to visit.

Matt was excited to see David walking. It was like no time had passed as they caught up with each other. Matt had sensory sensitivities, so he stood on the sidelines and watched everyone race around. Every so often, David would stop racing and come over to hang out with his old friend.

"When does he get here," Evaleen mumbled between bites of her hot dog.

I pointed to the corner of her mouth. "You've got a little mustard right there."

She wiped at the glob. "Answer the question, Blackburn."

"Who do you mean?" I asked as I turned my attention back to the track.

Of course, the SWIM Meet gals showed with their men. Evaleen and Aria were sitting with me at a table filled with hot dogs, French fries, and pickles. Evaleen was eating most of the food.

"Is it Jagger Chance?" she asked.

That made my spine straighten.

"Jagger? Why would Jagger come to David's party?" Aria asked appearing just as uneasy as I felt.

Evaleen leaned a little closer to Aria, dripping some of the mustard from the hot dog on her arm. "Because they have the hots for each other."

"We do not," I lied.

I was a healthy woman that may have been celibate for a decade—not by choice—but that doesn't mean my libido had shriveled up and turned into a tiny little raisin. Jagger had the body of a cross between a Greek god and a lumberjack. At least, that's what I imagined in my head when I pictured him naked. If he were a model in New York City, I'm sure he would be rolling in cash.

But he isn't a model, he's a secret government agent. I don't even know his real name. It could be Gerald or Gavin or Griffin. Why can't I think of anything but names that begin with a G?

"Stop lying to yourself, Blackburn. If anyone needs to get laid, it's you," Evaleen said.

"I one hundred percent agree with that statement." Aria balled up the paper napkin she used to wipe up her arm.

"What does me needing to get laid have to do with whether or not Jagger wants me or not? Or that I might want him?" I shrugged but wouldn't look into Evaleen's defense breaking blue eyes.

"Oh, well, if it doesn't matter then you won't care that he's heading right this way," she said before popping a fry into her mouth.

You know that moment when you feel a sudden charge in the air. In that second, no, less than a second, that nanosecond, you know everything will change. That's how I felt when I turned my eyes toward the front of Kart One, formerly a Skate-O-Rama that went out of business in the late 90s. The roller rink expanded and turned into a race track.

I don't know if it was the smell of the burned rubber or Evaleen's hot dog, but I felt nauseous and exhilarated all at the same time.

Evaleen was right. I had the hots for Jagger. I didn't like that I desired him like a warm bag of nuts at a World Series game, but I did.

He was sexy, great with David, and was kind to me. But I shouldn't have those feelings. Not for Jagger. He was the opposite of safe.

I know that, logically, he's not someone I should consider for myself especially with me having a son. I guess that's why my heart wasn't my brain and my brain certainly didn't feel like my heart.

"Hello, ladies," Jagger said as he approached the table.

"Agent Chance." Evaleen nodded before wiping her mouth with another napkin.

"Hi, Jagger. It's great to see you again," Aria said but stared at me the entire time.

"Jagger, glad you could make it. I know David will be excited to see you," I said as I waved for him to sit on the red plastic seat at our white linoleum table.

Aria began to cough. She got up and waved Evaleen to follow her.

"Looks like Dixon needs water. See you later." Evaleen got up but brought the red plastic basket of fries with her.

"Looks like everyone is having fun on the track," Jagger said.

"Yup. Sure does," I said as I felt the electricity devolve into awkwardness. The kind of awkwardness that crept up under your armpits and decided to go swimming by creating a pool.

"It's hot in here," I said flapping my arms and pulling at my white and green flower-patterned blouse.

I slid my eyes to the side and noticed Jagger tug at the neckline of his blue T-shirt.

"I thought it was just me. Maybe I can speak to the manager about turning up the air conditioning." He looked around and gasped just before his eyes widened.

Waving his hand in the air, I turned to see a man about ten years older than us wave back.

"I know him. We used to work together."

The man was coming toward us. Maybe I could find out something about Jagger other than he was a secret agent.

Jagger stood and opened his arms. "If it isn't Hack! What are you doing here?"

The guy, wearing a red button-up dress shirt and black slacks, hugged Jagger.

"I own this place. And it isn't Hack anymore. I can use my real name now—Tom Martinez."

They pulled back and Tom gazed over at me, nodding.

I stood and held my hand out to him. "Hi, I'm Tiffany. My son, David, is having his birthday party here today."

He gave a firm shake and then pointed to the track mentioning he wished David a happy birthday before he got into the kart. He talked about kart racing for a while before he asked about me.

"So, Tiffany, how do you know Jagger?"

I frowned and glanced at Jagger who didn't appear any happier at the question.

"We're married," I said because what could I do? I'm not going to lie to the man.

If Jagger needed to lie, he could do that himself. We both messed up getting married in Vegas, but I was drugged, or at least I think I was, so I didn't really have control over my actions. Jagger admitted he was drunk, but not so drunk that he couldn't remember. Not so drunk that he had no control.

"Married? You finally settled down. How'd they take that at the agency? I'm sure you're not in the field any more then."

Jagger was rubbing the back of his neck. His face red. "I'm still in the field."

Tom's brow creased. "But that's risky. When I met Nina, I knew she was it. I made a decision I had to take a desk job at the agency or leave. Since I hate paperwork, I chose to leave. Best decision I ever made."

He waved his hands around him, proud of his business.

"That's sweet you gave up your career for the woman you love. That's risky too. You could have grown to miss it and regret giving it up," I said.

"No, I knew it was time. I had that uneasy itch for a while."

"Uneasy itch?" Jagger asked.

Scratching the back of his neck, he gave a slight chuckle as if remembering a joke. "It was crazy. I kept asking to do more and more dangerous assignments. Is Katlin still there?"

Jagger nodded.

Tom sighed. "She knew. One day she sat me down and talked to me about burnout. It's not an easy life, and most agents don't do it long-term for a reason. I thought it odd after our talk that she invited me to a barbeque she was having that weekend."

"Katlin Chester? The walking, talking, government robot. She invited you to a party at her place?" Jagger asked with wide eyes.

"I know, crazy. I didn't even realize she owned a home. I just thought she slept at the office. The woman is all work and zero emotion. Anyway, I go to the barbeque and that's where I meet Nina. After dating her for a few months, I knew it was time to walk away."

"I guess when you two met, you were ready for something new, both professionally and personally," I said.

"Not so much new. More like, I was ready to face my fears and open my heart."

We stood for a moment in silence. I smiled up at Tom. His gaze flipped between Jagger and me before he slapped him on the shoulder. "I've got to get back. I'm glad you found happiness, Jagger."

Once he left, Jagger turned and as his eyes landed on me, it all came back at once. The heat. The electricity. And all that intensity seemed to drown out the noise and melt away the people around us.

"I need to talk to you, Tiffany. I meant to tell you three days ago when I came over and David invited me here."

Something propelled me forward, away from him. I needed the sounds and the lights and the zip of the karts as they raced by. Anything to ground me. To hold me up as I knew Jagger was about to knock me down.

I stood at the edge of the track. A hard, thick, white plastic fence kept the speeding vehicles from plowing into me. Something about that was thrilling and terrifying at the same time. And yet, I'd rather feel that, be dangerously close to that edge, than hear what Jagger had to say.

"Okay, so talk." I forced the words out.

He was going to leave us. What Tom had to say made it obvious. It was too dangerous for him to be close to David and me. I should be happy about that. It's what I wanted.

Why would I rather be hit by a speeding kart than hear his last words to me?

"It's about the ninja lessons and me coming over to your place," he said.

I closed my eyes to steel against the impending blow. This was going to devastate David. He talked about Jagger all the time.

"What about that?"

I could barely breathe as I forced the tears back. He wasn't right for my family, but that didn't stop me from caring about him. This was for the best. I just had to tell myself that over and over again until I believed it.

"I can't be David's ninja instructor anymore. I only came here today to wish David a happy birthday, drop off his gift, and give you something. Then, I'm afraid, I can't see you anymore."

I nodded. My eyes burned but I couldn't look at him.

"I'll leave David's gifts with the others," he said, and I glanced over at the table full of presents against the wall. "But this one, it's for you.

Please understand, we can't happen. As much as I want . . . never mind. We just can't."

I felt his hand on mine and when I looked down, I noticed a gift bag hanging from my curled fingers. When I turned around, he was gone. Glancing toward the front of the building, I saw the door closing and a tall figure leaving.

Sitting, I opened the bag. There was a note which I ignored. I knew what he had to say in it and I didn't want to read that right now. So, I opened the box. It was a candy bracelet. My lips curled into a sad smile.

Taking a breath, I got the courage to pick up the note.

You're like this candy bracelet, Tiffany. A never-ending loop of sweetness and joy. And I don't want to spoil your goodness with my bitter life. I'll never forget you. - Jagger

FOURTEEN

<u>Jagger</u>

"Four agonizing days," I said.

It's only been four days since I ended everything with Tiffany and it's felt like four hundred. I knew this would be hard but the lack of sleep and everything reminding me of her surprised me.

"And how does that make you feel?" Dr. Randy Tenner asked.

I rolled my eyes. That's all the man did, asked how anything made me feel. He got all that schooling to obtain a degree so he could ask people how they felt.

"Terrible. But it was the right thing to do."

"Interesting." He nibbled on the tip of his pen before he pushed it to the pad of paper in his lap, scribbling something down.

"It put the case at risk, not to mention Tiffany and David." I curled my fingers into the arms of the black leather chair. He must have bought this himself because I couldn't fathom the government forking over money for a nice piece of furniture like this.

"And that concerns you? Putting those two at risk."

"Of course. I'm not an unfeeling monster. It was my mistake, and they shouldn't have to pay for it," I said letting go of the arm of the chair and running my fingers through my hair.

"And besides, it's not like I'm in love with Tiffany. It hasn't even been a month since I've gotten to know her—"

"What about Las Vegas?" The doctor cut me off. "Didn't you get to know her then too? That was almost two months ago."

"That doesn't count." I waved my hand at him, blowing air through my lips.

"But you married her. How do you marry someone, even if you just met, without some kind of spark? Knowing something about them that makes you decide to spend the rest of your life with them."

Now he suddenly puts his degree to use. Not that I wanted him to. He should be jumping up and shaking my hand. Explaining that he must go tell my boss that I should be honored for my courage. How I put this agency first instead of my heart.

Why can't he just tell me what I want to hear?

"She told me some things about her. But I think I married her because I was drunk," I said picking at a piece of thread protruding from the seam of my pant leg.

"You weren't drunk enough to not remember. You told me she blacked out, but you remember everything. Even how you felt when she put your father's ring on your finger," he said flipping back a few pages in his notepad.

I should have known it was a bad omen to use that ring. Nothing good ever came from that man.

"Yes, I remember it, but that doesn't mean I fully grasped the severity of the situation."

"Perhaps not, but you knew the risk of getting involved with a woman to that degree. Maybe, deep down, you really wanted to be married," he said.

I stopped fidgeting. My eyes lifted to the round government issued clock above Dr. Tenner's head on the sterile white wall behind him.

"Oh look, my time is up. Thank you, Dr. Tenner, for your help. You will make a note in my report to Ms. Chester that I am no longer in Tiffany and David Blackburn's life."

I stood and glanced down at his notes hoping to see what he wrote. But he flipped over the cover and tossed it onto the small table between us before I could see.

I almost made it to the door before he said, "Yes, I will. But Agent Chance, if I could say one thing before you go . . ."

Sighing, I turned toward him and nodded.

"Who will be there to hold your hand when you are in the hospital? Tiffany . . . or this job?"

"What makes you think I will be in the hospital?" I asked, confused by the morbid turn of his words.

"It's hypothetical. If or when you need to be in the hospital, who would be there for you. I don't think a job can hold your hand or make you soup when you are sick. But a person who cares for you can."

He had a point, but it was a point that was too sharp for me to stand at the moment.

"But a job can pay the hospital bills." I tried to smile but it turned more lopsided than I wanted.

I left and went to the elevator as quickly as I could, not wanting any more of Dr. Randy's hypotheticals.

When I arrived on my floor, I heard someone call my name. The voice made me uneasy. For a moment, I wished I hadn't left Dr. Randy's office so soon.

"Agent Chance. I need to speak with you in my office." Katlin's booming voice rattled the hall and my head.

Katlin Chester had two volumes, loud and glass shattering. When she broke out her crushing voice you knew something terrible was about to happen. Based on her volume just now, I assumed the world around me was about to fall to pieces.

I swiftly made my way into her office and took a seat before her head lifted from what she was writing on her desk.

"I suspect you know why I called you in here?" she said with a glare so sharp it could have sliced me in two.

Did Dr. Randy call her? If he did, then she knew I severed all ties with Tiffany. That's a good thing.

"I'm sure you approve. I know it took me a little longer than I anticipated but—"

"Approve?" Katlin's voice hit notes I didn't realize could go that high. "Of using government-issued listening devices to eavesdrop on a citizen that may potentially affect the outcome of a case?"

Oh, that. Dammit Tenn and his big mouth.

"Actually, I bought the devices myself. They aren't government property."

"I don't care if a genie from a bottle gifted you those devices as one of your three wishes, what did you think you were doing, Agent Chance?" She rose to her feet and leaned over, putting her fist on the desk.

"Good question."

She blinked waiting for more. The trouble was I didn't want to expand on it. But I knew I had to. And as awful as it was going to be to give the details of this to my boss, what would most likely happen after would be much worse.

"I'm waiting, agent."

"I thought I was protecting Mrs. Blackburn and her son. By marrying her, I put her at risk. I only wanted to make sure they were safe."

"Why didn't you run this by me? We could have put an agent on her. Kept watch on her for a while," she said, her voice coming back to normal.

"But I was already there and I had the devices, so I just figured . . ." I shrugged and began to pick at the thread on my leg again.

Katlin sat and watched me work the black fiber as if I was on the verge of discovering one of the great mysteries of life like the Bermuda Triangle or slow drivers.

"Did you remove the listening devices?"

"Yes, I did. After the date she had a week and a half ago."

Katlin took a breath. "She doesn't know you were spying on her?"

"No. It was stupid, ma'am, I know that. I'm sorry. You're right, I should have come to you. I was worried you wouldn't approve it."

I didn't mention that I couldn't find one of the devices I planted in her kitchen. It must have fallen onto the floor and gotten swept up and thrown away. When I went to check on the device on my end, there wasn't any sound coming from it. I wasn't worried, sometimes that happened.

"You put this case at risk, Agent Chance. If your partner, Agent Golden, hadn't told me what happened, there would be no way of rectifying it before Emma Hawthorne's lawyers found out."

"*If* they found out," I said.

Her fist pounded the desk. "They are looking at you with a fine-tooth comb right now. Since Mrs. Hawthorne has implicated you, along with her daughter, they are trying to find anything that may look like you screwed up. And you know what this thing with Tiffany Blackburn looks like to me?"

I ran my fingers through my hair. "That I screwed up."

"That you more than screwed up. That you made a big, fat, screw-the-fuck-up sundae and slathered it in messed-up sauce before topping it with a I-don't-know-what-I'm-doing cherry."

"Tell me how you really feel." The laugh died on my lips as she stood again.

"This is funny, Agent Chance? Your partner may make silly jokes, but at least he hasn't screwed up any cases he's been on. The government has had an eye on Emma Hawthorne for a few years. When this agency formed three years ago, I worked hard to make the Hawthorne case something the higher-ups would give us the okay on. This case was supposed to be the jewel in our crown, hence why I gave Emma Hawthorne the name Jewel."

She took a breath and sat back down. Katlin's face was no longer a dark salmon color, and I felt the worst was over. She berated me, which I deserved, and got it out of her system.

"I don't think this is funny. It's best I'm off the case now and Tenn's taking over. Perhaps something new will help me to focus again. I got too involved in that assignment and let things go to my head," I said and hoped she didn't call me in here to reassign me.

Katlin nodded and clasped her hands in front of her on the desk. "I'm glad you feel that way." She reached to the side of the desk and pulled something out of the drawer, throwing it on the desk near me. "This isn't about reassignment."

I sighed in relief. Reassignment meant being moved to some nowhere town and only allowed to do paperwork, most likely in the basement of an old building. Working with government workers that only want to complain about their job and how they long for retirement.

I visited one of those places once and felt my skin crawl from mundane hopelessness. Nothing was worse than reassignment.

Katlin continued, "As of today, you are no longer an agent with the United States government. Please hand over your identification and any firearms registered to you from the ITA."

FIFTEEN

Tiffany

"You're okay then?" I asked for the third time tonight.

Holding my cell phone up to my ear, I could hear David groan on the other end.

"Yeah. I told you that an hour ago. Mom! Please stop calling. It's embarrassing. I'll be home in the morning."

There were some muffled voices in the background and I could hear laughter.

"All right. I'll stop. But please, call or text if you need me. Even during the night. I won't—"

David hung up.

David was at his very first sleepover. I assumed most parents first experience this when their kids were in elementary school, not when their kid was a teenager.

I'm nervous and happy for him. This was everything I dreamed of for David. He had friends and was getting to do fun things with them.

But now that he had what he wanted—to be just an average teenager—where did that leave me?

A year ago, I did so much for him and it felt like with a snap of a finger, I did almost nothing now. It's uncomfortable, like a sweater that looked soft but when you tried it on you realized it was suffocating and itchy.

I'm here, alone in my apartment for the night for the first time since the car accident ten years ago. And even then, I rarely came home, preferring to sleep at the hospital with my son.

I gazed around my living room and discovered a rare thought, I was bored. Weird. I didn't like it. Boredom was something I hadn't felt since before David was born.

I chuckled to myself as I sat on my couch remembering how I envied people with nothing to do. Now here I was. I'm sure there's someone out there envious of my time now.

Still felt scratchy.

My phone lit up next to me on the couch and I grabbed it, answering in a rush.

"David, what's wrong?" My heart raced so fast I thought it might explode out of my chest.

"Uh, is this Tiffany?" a man's voice I didn't recognize responded.

"Yes, who is this?"

"I have a Jagger here who needs to speak to you. Hold one second."

My heart, which had settled down the moment I realized David wasn't on the phone, began to pick up the pace again. Why would Jagger be calling me? He made it clear he wanted nothing to do with us on Saturday.

I made sure to keep that information from David until the next day. I wanted him to enjoy his birthday. He was hurt but loved the Ninja Boy comics Jagger bought him for his birthday gift.

As for me, I cried a bit. Like a dork, I put the candy bracelet he got me under my pillow. It kept making weird crunching noises when I moved so I ended up cradling it next to my chest. Succumbing to the sugary smell, I chewed half of it. I fell asleep with bits of candy stuck to my lips and chin. When I woke in the morning, I realized it was too tempting having the thing in my bed.

It now sits on my dresser like a broken dream.

There were loud scraping noises and a boom before I heard Jagger's voice.

"I got it, Benson. I got it." There was a pause before he started to speak again, "It's not Benson, then what's your name? Leo? I've been calling you Benson the whole time!"

Jagger started to laugh. I wondered if he realized I was still on the phone.

"Jagger?" I said.

"Tiffany! Oh, sweet Tiffany. It's so good to hear your voice."

"Nice to hear from you. Is there something you needed?"

"You. I need to tell you something. But not here. This place is too grimy," Jagger said and I heard some yelling in the background. "Sorry, Benson. Right, I mean Leo."

This back and forth had to stop. It was hard to say goodbye to him. I admit the warmth in my body upon hearing his voice made me a little eager but was this just another goodbye? Did he need to have me sign another document only to walk away again?

"I'm coming over," Jagger said.

"That's really not necessary. Can't you—"

He hung up.

I stood and went into the bathroom, inspecting my appearance. Running my fingers through my hair, I wondered if I should put it up. Maybe a little makeup or a skirt?

Leaning my hands on the gray marble countertop, I sighed. What was I doing? Jagger's job was everything to him. I can't expect to come along and make him risk that, even if he wanted to. It was selfish to expect him to risk so much for me.

The buzzer went off.

"Wow, that was quick," I mumbled to myself.

I did one last once-over before leaving the bathroom and headed to the front door. Pressing the call button, I said, "Hello?"

"Sweet Tiffany." I heard Jagger with clarity and trepidation.

Buzzing him inside the building, I waited. My hands fumbled with my fingers. My hair chose that moment to settle stray strands onto my cheek, then my nose, and every second I was pushing away another tickly wisp.

I needed to do something so I went to my cabinet of delight in the kitchen and grabbed a lollipop. It was cherry and I could barely taste it thanks to my nerves.

Finally, there came a knock on my door.

Taking a deep breath and a hard suck, I made my way to the door and opened it. Jagger stood there, with his hands bracing the doorframe and his head hanging forward. When he lifted his head, I noticed the normally disheveled brown hair was in even more disarray.

Even his red T-shirt had stains on it. There was a laziness to his eyes and when he let go of the doorframe, he stumbled forward, into me.

"Sorry. I'm sorry," Jagger said as he clumsily worked himself out of our embrace.

That's when I smelled him.

"Are you drunk?" I asked.

He stood straight, but swayed. He brought his finger and thumb together in front of us to pinch the air. "A lot. I'm a whole lotta drunk."

Wonderful. Now I have to deal with a drunk man in my home.

"Is there someone I could call for you, Jagger? A friend or relative."

He shook his head like a toddler, making his hair fly in all different directions. "No, my family is gone. The ones I care about and who care about me. The others can go fuck themselves because they know what they did."

His voice grew and I wondered if he might punch a wall. It broke my heart to hear him talk of his family like that. What sort of life did Jagger have? I wished I knew and that he could tell me.

"How about friends? Can I call anyone?" I asked and helped him farther into my place, guiding him to the couch in my living room.

He flopped back on the mint green sofa and melted back like it was made for his huge body.

I sat on the end, closest to his feet. I realized his eyes almost matched my couch but they were a little darker. Where the sofa was comfortable, how he stared was not. There was an intensity in him and he directed that intensity straight at me.

"Your friends?" I asked again.

"Don't have any," he said

I frowned but he laughed.

"Isn't that funny, Tiffany? I gave up everything for that place. I had no life other than work, and this is what happens." He waved his hands between us.

"I'm sure there's someone who you could call?"

He needed someone who was close to him and since I knew absolutely nothing about him, that person wasn't me.

"There are only two people I could remotely consider friends. One was Tenn, my partner at work. But based on the pile of papers I signed today, I'm pretty sure I can't have any contact with him for a long time."

"But why wouldn't you be able to have contact with your work partner? What happens when you go to work?"

I was confused. Did that have anything to do with us? Did being with me get him assigned to something else? I wish I knew what exactly he did so I could help him. I hated sitting here like an idiot and not being able to help someone in need.

"Because I got fired. I'm no longer working for the Federal Government. I'm unemployed, Tiffany. All because of my penis."

My eyes widened. "Oh no, Jagger, I'm so sorry."

I reached out and put my hand on his knee. He was lying in such a way that it was as close as I could get to him. He pushed himself up and scooted closer to me. Taking my hand in his, he gazed into my eyes.

"Which do you like better? Penis or cock?"

My head went back. "What? Uh, what, uh, why would you ask that?"

He ignored my question. "I like that you cook," he grabbed the sticky lollipop from my free hand and placed it back into my mouth, "and I really like watching you suck on this."

Jagger leaned forward so his lips were next to my ear. I could feel his hot, alcohol-soured breath drift down my neck. It felt good but he was drunk. As much as I still wanted him, nothing could come of it tonight.

His fingers drifted to my neck, cupping it as he said, "I have an idea. While you whip up a batch of cookies and continue sucking on that lollipop, I'll be hard at work making sure my cock keeps you hungry for more."

I was angry. Yes, mad that the idea of baking was turning him on. Like I was some 1950s housewife. But was I really annoyed at him or how I was reacting to his words? Because what was happening between my thighs was heated and tight and made me squirm.

His hand began to drift, lower from my neck to my collarbone, over my shoulder and curved around. It hovered just above my nipple. And I ached for him to continue, knowing that wasn't right. He was drunk and upset at his job loss. I would be taking advantage of that.

But it had been so long since I had been touched like that by a man. Maybe once wouldn't do any harm. Then I could put him to bed in David's room after making sure he drank a glass of Pedialyte I had in the refrigerator from when David was sick with the flu this past spring.

His forehead leaned on my shoulder but his hand remained still. He smelled of alcohol and something spicy that was most likely his shampoo or aftershave, but I wanted to believe was uniquely Jagger.

And he sounded . . . wait, he sounded like he was snoring. I pushed back on Jagger and realized he had passed out. So much for a little boob action.

I pushed him back until he was lying down and pulled his legs up on the couch. After taking off his shoes, I grabbed an extra blanket from the hall closet. I made sure he was lying on his side—in case he got sick during the night—and set a small wastebasket below him and a glass of water on the coffee table.

He looked so peaceful. The hard lines on his face that always seemed to be there vanished. His life couldn't be easy with what he did, and I wondered how much of a toll it took on him mentally.

I brushed my hand over his hair, pushing some strands that had fallen over his eyes, when he surprised me by grabbing my wrist.

I gasped as his eyes opened.

"I'm not Jagger anymore. You can call me Geoffrey," he said before his eyes closed and the snoring started again.

SIXTEEN

~~Jagger~~

Geoffrey

"Must you sing," I said as I hugged the cool, granite counter.

It felt refreshing despite the off-key rendition of "Single Ladies" being earsplittingly lacerated to a bloody demise by the most beautiful woman in the world, Tiffany.

"Drink this." She pushed a glass of cloudy green liquid at me.

With tremendous effort, I lifted my head and closed one eyelid to ease the dagger that was hacking away behind it. That's when I made the terrible decision to stand. Everything that hurt in my body, in my head, felt like it was about to explode.

"Will it kill me?" I asked.

"No." Her plump lips curved in that sexy way that normally drove me crazy but it only made me sad right now.

Unhappy because I couldn't enjoy it. My body wouldn't let me relish anything right now.

"What if I wanted it to? You could, you know. I'm sure no one would miss me."

The curve of her mouth turned down and I didn't like that. I was in terrible pain, but I would bear it if I could make her unhappiness disappear.

"I'd miss you and I know David would," she said before turning back to the stove to continue torturing me with that delicious smell permeating from the pan. Tiffany poked at it with a spatula.

For a moment, the pain dissipated and all I could feel was my heart filling my chest, in fear of choking me with happiness. The aroma, her pity for me, and how she had been puttering around me since I woke to ease my hangover.

She didn't realize her sour musical stylings were the things that woke me up on Tiffany's couch ten minutes ago. Or maybe she did, and this was to make up for her tremendous lack of talent. But if that were true, she would stop singing and she won't. No matter what I say.

Despite all that, I smiled as I watched her. So, I did as she commanded and lifted the repulsive looking liquid to my lips. It's weird apple flavor wetting my cottony mouth.

"Don't drink too much at once," Tiffany paused her melody to warn me as she continued cooking, "or you might get sick. Take it easy on your stomach today."

"Okay, Mom." I chuckled as I put the glass down and scooted onto the stool.

After a minute, she turned around with a plate of scrambled eggs with whole wheat toast.

"Wow, this looks great," I said with the sudden realization of how hungry I was.

"Here's some oatmeal, and honey for your toast." Tiffany moved around the kitchen, grabbing a bowl that she must have made earlier and the glass jar of honey.

It was all so much. I haven't had anyone take care of me—not like this—since I was a little boy. It was something I never really thought I needed. I believed that being strong and independent meant taking care of yourself, even when things were bad.

I stared at the food in front of me trying to find the words to tell this wonderful woman how much it meant but what I got out was, "Thank you."

"You're welcome. I'm used to it. I'm just glad I had some Pedialyte left over." She came around the counter while taking sips from her mug that had a picture of a coffee pot on it with the words Pot Head underneath.

She sat on the stool next to me with a funny look. "Are you going to eat or just stare?"

I was still in shock that she was taking care of me when I had done nothing but lie and spy on her. Ugh, I don't know what felt worse, this hangover or my guilt?

"Yeah, of course." I lifted a forkful of the fluffy eggs to my mouth.

They had to be the best eggs I had ever had. That added to the guilt. And the toast and oatmeal. Everything was delicious. Who knew toast could be satisfying? Tiffany must have done something to make it extra delicious.

The meal was so wonderful that I was done in a matter of minutes. Damn, I needed that.

Patting my belly, I turned to her to smile. I meant to compliment her but what came out was an extra loud, extra long burp.

Her hand went to her chest. Tiffany laughed and it was melodic. Her cheeks flushed and that smile was worth suffering through a thousand hangovers.

Her eyebrow rose as her laughter subsided. "I'm assuming you liked the food?"

"God, yes. How do you make toast taste like heaven?"

"I'm pretty sure the bees do that." She took a sip from her cup, never taking her eyes off me.

Fuck, she was sexy when she drank coffee. And cooked. And laughed. And stood there doing nothing.

"The bees?"

"They made the honey that gave the toast the sweetness."

No, I'm pretty sure it was you that gave it that sweetness.

"I almost forgot." She stood and disappeared down the hall.

My gaze drifted around the room. Her place, decorated in soft colors, looked like a comfortable home. Nothing about it stood out, but at the same time, it drew me in like a warm blanket on a cold winter day.

I smiled at the thought of how much her place reflected her. There's only one thing missing to make this room perfect. And as I comprehended that thought, that one thing strolled into the room.

"Aleve. It's all I got but it works great on headaches." Tiffany jiggled a small blue and white bottle.

She placed it in front of me on the counter. I stared at the plastic bottle as a war raged inside me. This time the battle involved guilt fighting attraction. Tiffany was like the sexiest nurse to never wear a uniform. One more fantasy for me to fuck my hand with tonight.

My hand and I had been getting to know each other a lot these past several weeks.

I threw the pills into my mouth but realized I had no water and had long since finished my Pedialyte. Instead of walking into the kitchen and getting some water, I made my way down the hall to the bathroom.

I locked the door behind me. After getting enough water from the sink to swallow the pills, I gazed at myself in the mirror. I looked like crap. Physically, I was starting to feel better—her food helped. But what I felt was reflected in that mirror.

I had lied to Tiffany for so long. First about being her son's PT, then not letting her know about our marriage, and finally, spying on her. At least I explained that I wasn't her son's therapist and finally came clean about the marriage. But I still haven't told her about the spying and it was screwing with my head. I took the devices away, the ones I could find. It was a stupid move. I'm glad they fired me because I deserved it.

After splashing water on my face, using some of her mouthwash, and washing my hands, I decided to go back out there and be honest with her. I may never see her again after that, but at least I won't feel so much like a scumbag.

As I emerged from the bathroom and slowly walked down the hall like a man making his way to the electric chair, I hesitated as I entered the living room. She was standing there waiting for me. Did she know I was about to admit to being an appalling excuse of a human being?

She frowned and it was the confirmation I needed. Tiffany must know.

"So, uh, what do I call you?" she asked.

"Asshole maybe, or how about turd-blossom? I always liked that insult for some reason." I tried to laugh it off, but she wasn't having it.

"Why would I insult you? I just want to know if I should call you Jagger or Geoffrey?"

My stomach did that thing when it wanted to try out for the Olympics by doing a half summersault followed by a backflip.

"My name? Did I tell you that last night or do you remember what I told you in Vegas?"

For so long I feared she would start to remember me telling her my real name in Las Vegas. Now, it didn't matter. It's not like the government could fire me again.

I don't remember much from last night. The most I could recall was buzzing her building. After that, it was a blank.

"Last night. I still can't recall anything from Vegas."

"I'm so used to Jagger now, it almost doesn't feel right to be called Geoffrey."

She paused and bit her lip. "I'll say both names and you see how it feels."

I nodded and took a step closer to her.

"Geoffrey."

Everything sounded lovely coming out of her mouth, but I didn't have much of a reaction to the name. I waved my hand for her to continue.

"Jagger."

Did she deepen her voice when she said that? Like she was trying to sound seductive. I took another step toward her with only a foot between us.

"Say it again," I said.

"Jagger." Her voice distinctly softened. Her chocolate eyes dipped to my lips as I took one more step toward her.

I was right in front of her. When I exhaled the wisps from her braid fluttered around her face. I reached for one that landed on her cheek, sliding my finger back until I traced a curl around her ear.

She shivered and I felt the vibration move with warmth and vigor up my arm. My finger never left her skin. Like a pencil to paper, I traced the beating line down her neck until I found the thin ridges of her collarbone.

Her eyes were cast down, watching my arm as it moved. And when Tiffany gasped as my fingertip trailed farther down to the seam of her neckline, I lowered my head. Just enough so she could feel my heat and I could smell her beauty.

"Say it again."

My hand reached back, pulling the band that held her braid together, and dropped it on the floor. She lifted her hand, but I stopped her before she could shake out this thick, sensual mane. That was my job.

I took one hand and tilted her head back by her chin. While the other hand curled and mussed that fucking sexy hair.

"Jagger."

When she said it this time, her eyes were wide, like bottomless pits I never wanted to end. Tiffany was soft and warm, and I could feel how she vibrated from my touch.

"Tiffany," I said just before my lips landed on hers.

With a swift swipe of my tongue to the seam of her mouth, she opened so I could take the kiss I had been dreaming about for weeks.

She tasted like coffee and honey, and I didn't think I could get enough. And when she whimpered my skin vibrated with anticipation. My hands fell from her head. One landed on that perfectly round ass as I squeezed.

The other hand took it upon himself to lift her shirt, tug at the cup of her bra, and pinch. No slow swirl of my fingers through dips and over mounds. A slow, chaste touch was for teenagers that only had curiosity and hormones directing their thoughts.

That tantalizing nipple needed my attention. I wasn't about to waste our time and not give Tiffany what she required.

Her head fell back as she groaned. Not only did she sound like I was giving her the perfect attention, but her hips kept grinding into my growing cock.

That's until the worst cockblocker that had ever been invented made itself known. Her cell phone went off.

Tiffany pushed me off her so fast, I was still making kissing movements with my lips to the air in front of me. When I stopped, realizing she had disappeared, I glanced up to see her adjust her shirt as she lifted the phone to her ear.

"Hello, David? Are you okay?" she said.

Still in a carnal fog, I blinked, pressing my hand against my achingly hard cock.

"Okay. Well, I'll come get you. Be there in about ten minutes," she said just before she put down the phone.

She turned and it was as if the last five minutes never happened. That she hadn't made me want to fall to my feet and wonder if kissing her lips was like tasting anything else on her body.

"I have to go pick up David now. Do you think you're well enough to go home?"

What was happening? Even more confusing, she came over and placed her hand on my arm like some friend doing their best to cheer someone up but not really wanting to put any effort into it.

"I guess," I said before she pulled me along with her.

"I'll walk you out. Let me know if you need anything," she said as she closed and locked the door behind us.

Once we were on the street, she didn't kiss me or hug me or even shake my hand. Tiffany waved goodbye, and turned her back on me as if her lips on mine just minutes ago hadn't turned me into a devastated mess.

SEVENTEEN

Tiffany

"Damn, that's cold," Morgana said as she lifted the teacup to her lips.

"I know, right. Even I wouldn't be that harsh," Aria said taking a bite from a small pastry with a strawberry on it.

"What about you, Evaleen? Am I that terrible?" I asked knowing Evaleen would have my back.

It had been two days since I'd left Jagger on the sidewalk outside my building to get my son from his sleepover. I knew how I reacted to that kiss wasn't right.

Ahh, that kiss. It was even better than I fantasized it would be. And I had imagined Jagger's lips on me a lot over the last few weeks. That man knew what to do with his mouth. And the way he untangled my hair . . . I thought I was going to orgasm right then and there.

Who knew taking out a braid could cause all the blood to race down to my vagina waiting for action?

"Did he say something bad to you after the kiss?" Evaleen asked as she nibbled on a chocolate chai scone.

"No. He only said something when I asked if he was feeling well enough to go home." I reached over and took the delicate white teacup with a brown design covering the top half, and took a sip.

"Hmm," Evaleen said as she sat back in the creamy upholstered seat. "What did he say?"

"I guess," I said before lifting the tea to my lips again and wondering how long she was going to stare at me. How long they all were going to stare at me.

"You guess what?" Aria asked.

"No, that's what Jagger said, 'I guess.'"

"Oh," they all chimed in at the same time.

"Then what do you think, Evaleen?" I asked noticing how much she wasn't looking at me now.

Evaleen went through a range of facial expressions. Some I had never seen on her before. She finally settled on one—pity.

"You should have at least asked if you could talk to him later. Even if it was to let him down."

Darn it to heck.

I felt bad with how I reacted to Jagger. There had barely been a free moment of time that I hadn't gone over my lack of response, or the kiss before it, in my head. I was hoping when I came to Morgana's bridal shower at The Lemington for afternoon tea today that my friends would tell me I did the right thing. Even lie if they had to.

"Ugh, I knew it. I got worried."

"About a kiss? Or was there something wrong with David? That would explain why you ran off," Aria asked after she swallowed the last bite of her pastry. "You know what? These are really good." It was hard to understand her with her mouth full of confection.

"No, not about the kiss. And, there was nothing wrong with David. He only needed to be picked up from the sleepover. I guess it was about everything. How long it's been for me and he's a government agent," I said.

"Was. *Was* a government agent. He's a free player now." Evaleen winked at me.

Everyone went silent at the table.

"Evaleen, did you just wink at Tiffany?" Morgana asked.

"Yes. There's nothing wrong with winking at someone," she said picking some pieces off her scone and popping them in her mouth.

"Edgar is rubbing off on you." Morgana chuckled.

"Anyway, Drake. Where's your mom and grandmother? I thought for sure they'd be joining us," Evaleen said.

Morgana shook her head. "Mom said she's too busy giving the baker specific instructions and tutorials about my upcoming wedding cake."

She shook her head laughing before growing serious. "Grandma's RVing again. She's in the Upper Peninsula now. She promised she would be back for the wedding and told me she had a big surprise for me she wants to give me before the wedding."

"Let me guess, a female blowup doll?" Aria chuckled.

Morgana's grandmother, despite much evidence to the contrary, believed Morgana was a lesbian. Actually, it wasn't so much belief, more like intense desperation. She wanted Morgana to be a lesbian so she could prove to her knitting group that she had a diverse family. There was some fierce competition in that knitting group.

"I don't know. I just hope she doesn't interrupt the wedding when the minister asks if there is anyone that has reasons why the bride and groom should not be married to speak now or forever hold their peace," Morgana said as she grabbed a scone.

"I'm sure it will be a nice gift. She does love you," I said having met the woman at a dinner Henrik had a few weeks after their engagement.

"Enough about me, how about that kiss," Morgana said wiggling her eyebrows.

"It was just a kiss," I said and it felt like the biggest lie of my life.

It wasn't just a kiss. When he touched my lips, my toes curled and heat crawled into crevices I never imagined I had. The potency burned and his tongue had yet to leave his mouth. I felt sure that kiss had the capacity to produce an orgasm. Because if David hadn't called, I might have climaxed, standing half on my gray rug and half on the wood floor. I relished every second of that off-kilter kiss.

"Whatever you need to tell yourself, Blackburn. But understand that safety is fine, but risk is the only thing that will bring reward," Evaleen said.

There was silence again.

"Edgar *has* been rubbing off on you. Either that or this pregnancy has changed you," Morgana said.

"And how have I changed?" Evaleen narrowed her eyes at Morgana making me believe there was plenty of the old Evaleen around.

"You're more . . . uh, how do I say this without sounding like a jerk?" Morgana tapped her chin.

"You're squishier," Aria added.

"What?" Evaleen said before snorting.

"You know, softer . . . with emotion. I think you're still badass, but your kickass-ness has some suppleness to it." Aria nodded, satisfied with her response.

"Now that's settled. Blackburn, you need to talk to him. Even if it's to say goodbye." Evaleen reached over and placed her hand on mine.

"You're right. It had been so long since a kiss happened to me. Afterward, I thought, well, I thought a million different things. None of them good. And in any of my thoughts, not once did he let me know that he wanted me. That he might want more."

Aria growled and everyone sitting at the table, and a few others nearby, turned to look at her.

She lifted her finger and pointed at me. "No. No, you don't. Tiffany, you are gorgeous. You are stronger than any of us. Sorry, Evaleen, you might be badass, but Tiffany has the inner strength of twenty buffalo."

Evaleen nodded. "It's true. As Dixon pointed out earlier, I'm squishy. But seriously, Blackburn, how you managed to handle losing your husband the same night you almost lost your son, it's humbling that you made it through without losing your mind. And on top of that, you have spent the last decade being your son's body, his voice, his caregiver, and his only parent. I'm nothing compared to that."

She squeezed my hand as the tears began to roll down my cheeks.

"I hated you when I first met you," Morgana said, and I glanced up to find her reaching for my other hand.

"You were beautiful and nice and were hanging on the arm of the man I wanted. I'm ashamed to say it, but I took my anger for how Henrik ran from me and directed it to you. But it took less than an hour when I sat with you during one of our first SWIM Meets to realize I could never hate you. You're the person every woman wants to be."

I knew my face was a mess with tears and I had to let go of Evaleen and Morgana's hands to grab a tissue in my purse.

"I thought this was Morgana's day?" I said in between sobs.

"No, Tiffany, it's *our* day. I wanted my bridal shower to be us ladies. You three have been here with me through all the ups and downs with Henrik. It wouldn't feel like a bridal shower if I wasn't celebrating my ladies!" Morgana said and then stood. She started to shake her hips as if something more contemporary than Mozart was playing.

"I'm afraid there's no dancing here, miss." A server rushed over and spoke directly to Morgana, "If you insist on dancing, I must ask you to leave."

Morgana turned toward the short man with matching red hair. "Fine. We'll just take it to my room. Send your best champagne to the Eternity Suite."

The man's eyes widened as he stood a little taller. "Of course. Right away."

"You got a room?" Evaleen asked as she stood from her chair, grabbing the gift bag for Morgana she brought to the bridal shower.

"Actually, Alex got us a room. He wanted all of us to have fun for the day," Aria said with a smirk. "And we are going to have so much fun. In fact, there might be a surprise waiting in the room."

Aria clapped her hands and headed toward the elevators. In her enthusiasm, she forgot about the rest of us.

She ended up in the elevator before us and we finally met up on the twelfth floor.

"You ready, ladies?" Aria asked in front of the door to the room.

"Yes," Morgana said as Evaleen and I nodded our heads.

Aria knocked on the door.

"Don't you have the key—" Evaleen was cut off when the door opened and standing there was a gorgeous, half-naked man. All he wore were jeans. No shoes, no socks, and definitely no shirt.

"Please, ladies, come in. Your room is ready."

We walked through the large entryway with marble tile floor and a round glass table with a beautiful flower arrangement on it filled with lilies. Putting our purses and Morgana's presents down on the table, we walked in awe into the next room which was a huge living room with a wall of windows overlooking the Chicago River.

"Oh my God! Is that a yellow grand piano?" Morgana shrieked before turning toward us. "Quick, does anyone here know how to play piano?"

"I know chopsticks," Evaleen said.

Morgana turned to Aria. "Where is the surprise? I mean, other than this amazing room, but Alex got us that. You said you had something."

Right at that moment, a different tall man, ripped with muscles, only in jeans came up to Morgana. "May I offer you some cake?"

He was British.

"Here is your gift, Morgana. He will be your personal servant all night, and that includes overnight. So—" Aria said before Morgana cut her off.

"If I wake up in the middle of the night and want cake, he would be there to serve it to me?" Morgana said with a tremble in her voice as a lonely tear slipped out of the corner of her eye.

"Yes," Aria said and was instantly seized by Morgana in a bear hug.

"This is my dream come true," Morgana said in a half sob.

I smiled and was thankful Henrik said he would look after David tonight. I think he was going to invite Edgar over, make it a guy's night.

The man who opened the door and two more men, all dressed only in jeans, came into the room.

"Tiffany, meet Lagi. He will be your server for the evening." Aria brought over a tall man with thick, curly dark brown hair and deep caramel skin. He looked like a model who would be advertising the islands of the South Pacific.

I blushed and gave a small wave. "Hi."

Aria said with a sly smile, "Why don't you two stand next to each other so I can take a picture."

This was weird and exciting and uncomfortable. I wasn't used to being waited on and to have half-naked men paraded around in front of me didn't feel right. But, if it made Morgana happy, I would try my best to have fun.

I scooted closer to Lagi as he wrapped his thick arm around me. His touch was soft, gentle, as if he knew I wasn't comfortable with all this.

"Now smile." Aria held up her phone and the flash went off. "Perfect. I'm totally posting this."

Aria tapped at her phone a few times and just before she turned to Morgana to take her picture, she leaned toward me. "My followers are so used to me posting my art. But, I'm sure they won't mind seeing some man candy." Aria winked at me.

EIGHTEEN

Jagger

"He's killed her," I said as I stared at the image on the screen.

The past few days hadn't been good. No, actually, they had been some of the worst days of my life. I'd rather be tied to a chair in an abandoned warehouse in the desert with ten large men taking turns using me for boxing practice, than dealing with Tiffany acting like our kiss never happened.

And then I saw the picture. That's when I imagined every worst possible outcome. In each of them, I'm too late and she's dead.

"You shouldn't be calling me, Jagger," Tenn said over the phone.

I called him this morning in desperation. There had to be some way Tenn could look up this guy Tiffany was standing next to. He seemed seedy, suspicious, and must have been a criminal.

"What could I do? He's probably going to hurt her. She's not safe. I need your help."

I heard Tenn groan in the background. "Fine, what's his name?"

"I don't know."

There was silence for several moments.

"You don't know? Then how am I going to help you?"

"Don't you have access to the ITA's face recognition software?"

"Yes, but—"

"Tenn, please. If this were reversed and you were the one desperate for my help, I wouldn't think twice about it. I would be there for you no matter what."

When I saw that picture on Aria's site, it felt like my heart was being fed into a shredder. I wanted to reach through my phone and pull her out of there. Away from his arms and into mine.

It's not like I had been stalking her or her friends on social media, or anywhere on the Internet. Maybe a little. But I had to make sure Tiffany was safe. That nothing out of the ordinary was happening to her. Specifically, any risk that she experienced from getting to know me, and of course, marrying me.

I knew how to deduce where she was based on what was in the photograph. The furniture and, even better, the view from the window behind them, gave me everything I needed. Tiffany was downtown, in the Eternity room at The Lemington.

I tried calling her, several times, but she didn't answer. What could I do? I grabbed my keys, intending to head down to the hotel and make up a story about being a federal agent and needing access to the twelfth-floor rooms. But when I was about to open the door to my tiny apartment that backed up to the red line, I stopped.

That was why I didn't deserve Tiffany. I would lie to everyone just to get near her. Something was very wrong with that. My career went into the gutter because of what I would do to be near her.

That's why I needed Tenn. He could do all that for me.

"Fine. But just this once. Send me the image and I'll get back to you. But don't call me anymore. I can't be talking to you," Tenn said, his voice hushed and I assumed Katlin was probably nearby.

He hung up and I pushed send on the image I already had waiting for him.

Then I waited. My foot bounced up and down. Glancing at my phone, I swiped the screen back on. He hadn't responded yet. I put the phone down and started to bounce my foot again.

Standing, I went to the kitchen to see if there was anything to eat in the refrigerator. Glancing at the clock on the microwave, it stated it was eleven thirty. Only one minute had passed since I had gotten off the phone with Tenn.

"Fuck," I said slamming the refrigerator door. I could hear something fall inside but I didn't care.

I needed to get out. Take a walk. The fresh, late summer air might help clear my mind. Maybe I'll take a walk to the lake.

Doing just that, within minutes I was out the door and walking the three blocks to the park. Once I went through the tunnel under Lake Shore Drive, I was there. Among the dog walkers, baby strollers, rollerbladers, and the evil squirrels. There was something about the squirrels in Chicago. I think they were tougher than the mobsters.

Without thinking, I headed south. Did I do that on purpose, I don't know, but I ended up not far from Tiffany's building. I like to think it was subconscious but I know it wasn't.

A refreshing walk turned into a twenty-minute dash to Tiffany's place.

I turned away from the park and back onto the city sidewalks. Since her building faced the lake, there weren't that many people on her side of the street. Therefore, I couldn't help but notice her as I grew closer. She was half a block from her building heading north and I was a block away, heading south.

Just as she glanced up from digging into her purse, she saw me. I braced for the worst. Pretending she didn't see me or making a U-turn and disappearing.

But something much worse happened. When she lifted her hand to wave at me, some guy ran up and grabbed her purse. She tugged back, and my heart pumped so fast I thought it might give me superpowers.

I don't even remember crossing the street as I ran to her.

"Let the fuck go, bitch. Don't make me take out my knife." The mugger let a hand go and started to reach into his pocket. But, this happened right when I got there.

Tiffany fell back, letting go of her purse. The thief had officially stolen her purse and threatened violence, which made it okay for me to rough him up. I would have tossed him around anyway, but at least I can tell the police I was afraid he would take out his knife and did everything in my power to stop him.

The idiot didn't count on a highly trained former secret agent to be directly behind him as he lifted the blade from his pocket. The moron turned which made it almost too easy to grab his knife-wielding arm— which I did. I wrapped my other fist so tight around his greasy ponytail I thought his scalp might bleed.

"Going somewhere, motherfucker?" I said and let go of his hair so I could punch him in the face. And the stomach. Just for good measure, I kneed him in the balls too.

The knife fell and I kicked it away, into the street.

He couldn't run anywhere, even if I let him out of the hold I had him in. I pinned him to the ground and forced his hands behind his back. When I gazed up I found Tiffany standing there, her ponytail askew and a few other people around her.

"I called the police. Man, that was a cool takedown. Are you a cop?" One of the guy's in a bike helmet asked.

"Something like that," I said but focused on Tiffany, looking for any signs of injury. "You okay?"

"I'm fine. Just a scrape on my elbow," she said but most of the color had drained from her face.

The police arrived shortly after and we explained what had happened. I informed the police that there were security cameras outside the building if they needed security footage.

Once we were done, I insisted Tiffany go to the hospital but she refused. Instead, I guided her to her apartment. Once we were inside, I told her to lie down in her room. I found her first-aid kit and cleaned up her elbow.

"What if it's broken. I may have ninja moves but I'm no doctor," I said with a chuckle trying to lighten her spirits.

She had been quiet coming up to her place. I was worried there was more damage than she was letting on and Tiffany might be in shock. Checking her pupils, I saw they weren't dilated. Perhaps it was just taking a while for the situation to settle in for her.

"Thank you, Jagger. For saving me," Tiffany said lying back on her light blue- and green-patterned bedspread.

"No need to thank me."

Placing the first-aid kit on her small, wooden bedside table, I turned back to put my hand on hers. She was shivering. I grabbed a navy throw at the end of her bed and pulled it over her.

"What will happen?" she asked as her eyes stared at the ceiling and tears ran down her cheeks.

"They'll lock him up. Then—"

"No, I mean here? With David?"

"What do you mean? Is he about to come home? Do you want me to tell him?"

Because I would do anything for you.

Her face crumpled as she gritted her teeth. Tiffany covered her eyes with her hand and sobbed. "I don't know what to do? He's everything to me. What will happen when I'm gone?"

I crawled onto the bed and pulled her into me, squeezing her trembling body.

"That's so long from now. Don't worry about that. Shh. It's all right. I'm here."

She turned and buried her face into my chest. Her arms tightened, and every tear she shed onto my black T-shirt felt like a stab to my heart. That bastard was going to pay for hurting Tiffany like this.

After a few minutes, she pulled back and looked up at me. Her face was streaked with tears and possibly some snot, so I reached over to the other bedside table and grabbed a tissue for her. She sounded like a fog horn as she blew her nose.

I chuckled a bit, but the laughter soon died as a few tears continued to stream down her face.

"What can I do?" I pushed strands of hair that had stuck to her face behind her ears. Her ponytail holder had long since disappeared, falling out somewhere in all this. Tiffany's hair was wild, her cheeks flushed, and her whimpers were subsiding.

"I don't care anymore," she said as she reached up and curled her fingers into my hair. "I'm so beaten down. I'm not brave. My friends, they think I'm strong but I'm not."

I lifted her chin. "Yes, you are."

"Not like you. All I could do was pull on my purse and in the end, I wasn't even strong enough to hold onto it. What happens when someone stronger than me wants more than my purse? I don't care about myself but what about David? What will happen to him?"

My eyes began to burn as I cradled the back of her neck with my fingers. "No, don't say that. Please, don't. I care about you."

"Then make me forget," she said as she took my hand from her neck and pushed it down until it was between her thighs. "I want your fingers to stroke and push and pinch away all the uncertainties. Even if it's only for today."

Twisted trepidation swirled in my head as I tried to figure out what to do. She lifted her head toward me until her lips dusted my ears. "I don't want to be Tiffany Blackburn today. I just want to be yours."

"I don't know if we should do this right now with what you just went through," I said but didn't remove my hand.

My cock was throbbing. It was so hard, and she knew because that's where her hand had drifted to when it left my hair.

"Tiffany—" I groaned, and I meant to say more but words failed me as she cupped and stroked me over my jeans.

"I'm sorry for walking away the other day after our kiss," she said as her fingers tugged at my button until it gave way. "I was scared. It had been so long."

"How, uh, how long?" I shook my head so I could see straight.

"Over a decade. And this," she slowly pulled at my zipper until the large bulge of my black boxer briefs poked out, "I haven't gotten to touch anything good like this in just as long."

Four things happened all at once—she yanked down my briefs, her eyes widened, and she licked her lips. And I tried my damnedest not to come.

NINETEEN

Tiffany

"You're so big," I said and didn't even mask the surprise in my voice.

I don't know what I was going to expect when I pulled out Jagger's dick, but I didn't think large cucumber. Except he wasn't green. Jagger's was a normal pinkish tan hue.

Perhaps my husband was small and Jagger was about average. I had watched porn before and my husband didn't appear small compared to those men.

"Is this unusual?" I asked in case he had an abnormality because he really was quite large.

"No, my cock isn't unusual. At least, I don't think so. Haven't really compared it to other guys before." He stared down and curled his fingers around the base, giving one tug.

Watching him do that it was like a dam burst open and heat bloomed between my legs. Crazy sexy.

"Do that again."

"What? This?" Jagger proceeded to give himself another pump, but this time his fingers drifted over the tip to spread a drop of precum that had formed.

"Yeah, that. Can I taste you?" I tore my gaze from his thick cock and watched his darkening green eyes.

His nose flared and for a moment and he said nothing.

"Please. Unless, you know, there's something wrong with . . ." I said as I pointed to his throbbing dick.

"No, there's nothing wrong. I get tested regularly but are you sure this is what you want?" His hand never stopped moving on his cock.

It's funny what you miss when you haven't had sex in a long time. Sure, I yearned for a man to go down on me and, of course, for sex itself, but what I fantasized about a lot was a man filling my mouth. The salty flavor and how lost a guy got by what I was doing to him.

Maybe it was the thought of being filled. Maybe it was the taste I pined for, but I wanted Jagger just like this.

I smiled as I watched him war with himself. He was trying to take care of me, and that was sweet. But I'm done with sweet. I needed something hard and rough, and I wanted it to make me scream.

I ran my finger around the edge of the tip as he pulled back causing him to stop. "I very much want this. Just a small taste. It's been so long."

He groaned as my hand replaced his. Jagger let go and moved his fingers into my hair. I lowered my head, my mouth watering as I inhaled his scent—a mixture of sweat and something uniquely him.

Just before I slid my tongue out, I looked up. "Is this okay?"

"Yes," he said as his mouth sagged open.

Was it gentle kindness or urgent need when he gathered up my hair and held it for me? I started at the base and licked my way up. Jagger whimpered, and I wanted to do something special for that melodic gift. When I got to the tip, I gave a kiss. Not a little peck, but deep with my tongue. I swirled and lapped for Jagger tasted better than any lollipop.

"Oh God," he said and I knew he wasn't going to stop me from getting what I wanted.

His eyes rolled back into his head. Jagger was too far gone to get out of this fervid hole I dug him into.

The corners of my lips burned as I opened my mouth fully to suck him inside, yet he was too thick to go any farther than halfway. I had to use my hand to make up the difference and push and pull him from me.

I wondered how I managed to go so long without this in my life—the taste of him, the toe-curling sounds he made, my body reacting to everything he did. This moment was bringing me more pleasure than I had in a decade.

A blissful ache twisted my belly as I sucked his cock. It was as if I was getting more satisfaction out of this than he was. When his hips rotated, pushing him deeper down my throat, I thought that would cause a problem. That I would start to choke or gag or something embarrassing, but only a moan rumbled up my throat vibrating over his cock.

He was slick, my hand was coated, even a few strands of hair tickled my nose, but nothing would keep me from tasting Jagger.

"Fuck, you're so good at this," Jagger said, his voice gruff and breathless.

I reached my hand back and cupped my hand over his as he held my hair back, guiding him to what I wanted. Because I wanted that bit of pain as he started to take control. Sex was always nice and pleasant with my husband, but over the years, since his death, I fantasized about sex with an edge. An experience that wasn't always sweet, but definitely full of pleasure.

"Is that what you want, Tiffany? You want me to shove my cock down your throat?" he asked and when I lifted my eyes to his, they were round and darker than I had ever seen.

With much reluctance, I took him from my lips. "Yes. Please."

His closed his eyes and a visible shiver ran down his body. When he gazed at me again, something had changed. He pushed me back so I was lying on the bed, and he pinned me in place by putting either knee by each of my shoulders.

Jagger stroked his cock and brushed my lips with his tip. He paused just before he pushed himself inside my mouth. "If you need me to stop, just pinch my thigh and I'll immediately get off you."

I nodded and flicked my tongue out to give him a quick lick.

"You are so fucking sexy, Tiffany."

His cock entered my mouth slowly and I realized he was taking it easy on me. I reached my hand up and realized I couldn't do much by the way he had his legs on either side of me. But I managed to slide my fingers around his balls and just a little back so I could press the precise spot I knew he would enjoy.

It worked, and he jerked into my face. My eyes began to water with his cock pushed farther down my throat.

"I'm not going to last much longer," he said, which I already knew. His cock thickened in my mouth and it was time to show him how much I was enjoying this.

I pinched his thigh and he pulled back, but just before he could move completely away, I sat up and wrapped my hand around his hard cock, stroking. My face was right there and when he mumbled he was coming, I opened my mouth, sticking out my tongue.

I gazed up to watch his glassy eyes with his mouth hanging open as his cum squirted onto my lips, my tongue, and deep into my mouth.

Smiling when the last drop was spent, I swiped my tongue around my mouth. As much as I enjoyed that, my body was still humming and fully heated with what had happened. I expected Jagger to fall back on the bed, exhausted with what we did.

But that's not what happened. He crouched down and his hand cradled my neck, gazing into my eyes. It was as if he wanted to say something, but he never spoke a word. His lips crashed onto mine, his tongue moving past my swollen lips.

Pushing me back on the bed, he climbed on top of me as we kissed. But soon he broke free and kissed down my body. His jeans still hung off one leg, and I was fully clothed, but that didn't make a difference. This was still the hottest sexual encounter I had ever had.

Jagger pulled up my shirt and tugged down my bra cups before filling his hands with my tits. His thumbs flicked over my spiked nipples, and I arched my back as a gnawing ache flooded me.

"Look at them. They're so stiff. That must have been torture watching me come and you had to just take it," he said as deviousness filled his eyes.

I squirmed even more but he wouldn't continue. Jagger watched me struggle with a fascination that made everything damp between my legs.

"I bet you want me to lick them or maybe even give them a little bite to relieve the pressure."

I nodded as the corner of his mouth curled.

He slipped his lips over my nipple and sucked, flicking his tongue. It was a relief and torture at the same time. Even when he did it to my other breast, I only wanted more.

As if Jagger read my mind, he began to kiss down my body again. He yanked at my jeans, unbuttoning and unzipping them within seconds. I lifted my hips, and he peeled them off me along with my panties. My body was humming for his touch, and when he did give me what I wanted, it was like a feather trying to satisfy an itch.

Jagger pulled my legs up and out so I was spread wide.

"It's worse down here. You're so wet, so swollen." He bit his lip before his eyes found mine. "How can I let something so beautiful be in so much agony?"

I lifted myself up on my one elbow, as my other was still in pain from the mugging, and watched as Jagger lowered his head in between my thighs. His tongue taking its time along the outside of my lips, nowhere close to where I needed him to be.

I'm not ashamed to say I whimpered because this man was such a tease. But how he did it only made me want him more. Like when he slipped one finger inside me, pulling in and out, but nothing more. Jagger sat up and watched as the small effort he was putting forth caused my greatest want.

"I want to hear you, Tiffany."

"Please," I said, almost panting as I begged.

He added one more finger, but it still wasn't enough. I gave him everything with that blow job, but he was barely moving for me.

"Don't you want me? Just one little please?" He frowned. "That makes me think you really don't want what I have to give."

He was evil. I narrowed my eyes gathering as much strength as I could to fight back. To tell him to give it to me because I knew he wanted to.

"Please, Jagger. Make me come. Do what you want to me."

Any backbone I once had dissolved, and I felt no shame.

He nodded and lowered his head. "With pleasure."

Whatever he was doing between my thighs was working. His tongue and lips and fingers were performing like some orgasm-inducing machine. My fingers curled into his hair and I couldn't stop myself from grinding on him.

Jagger seemed to like it as he groaned in response. It could have been I was suffocating him, but I was too far gone to stop. When he curled his finger inside me, that's when I lost it.

My head flew back and I screamed out his name, my body convulsing with the best orgasm of my life. As he pulled away, his lips and chin dripping and eyes hazy, all I could do was lie there limp with a huge smile on my face.

He grinned too. Jagger moved over me, and I noticed he was hard once more. He halted when he heard the sound of a door closing.

"Tiffany! We're here." The distinct voice of Henrik echoed through my apartment.

TWENTY

Tiffany

"Fiddlesticks. Get off," I said as I pushed Jagger away and scrambled to find my clothes.

"Tell me how you really feel," Jagger said, his voice coated with sarcasm.

Finding my lace undies and pulling them on I stared at him. "What?"

Jagger, while dragging up his briefs and jeans, shook his head. "Nothing."

Ugh, men. I gave him a perfectly good orgasm and now he's cranky.

"Not nothing. What's wrong?" I put on my jeans and secured them before readjusting my bra and top.

He shrugged and refused to lift his eyes to mine. But before I could say anything, there was a knock at the bedroom door.

"Tiffany? Is it okay for me to come in?" Henrik's asked on the other side of the door.

I stared at Jagger waiting for him to give me something. Anything that would help me understand why he was upset with me.

Did he normally turn into an asshole after an orgasm? If so, I might have to look elsewhere for satisfaction. Like my dildo and vibrator collection. I didn't go years and years without sex and not have something to keep me going.

"Fine." I threw my hands in the air. I turned and walked over to open the door.

Jagger folded his arms and stared at my green and gray rug.

I found Henrik standing on the other side of the door with a smile on his face but it soon fell. He noticed the bandage on my arm and then glanced behind me at Jagger.

I knew Henrik. He was a man of few words and easily assumed the worst. He's a lot better now, which I believed was due to Morgana softening his edges. But on occasion, the old Henrik reared his bitter head.

"What did you do to her?" Henrik almost knocked me back as he plowed past me.

"What?" Jagger said with the same angry glare directed at Henrik.

"You heard me." Henrik grabbed Jagger by the shoulders and pushed him back against the wall.

I raced over and tried to pull Henrik off Jagger but he was like a boulder of muscle.

"Henrik, stop it. Jagger didn't do anything . . . well, he didn't hurt me." I couldn't help the blush that bloomed on my cheeks.

Henrik turned his head, his eyes wide. "What?" His eyes drifted down my body as the realization of what happened sunk in.

His grip relaxed but he still wouldn't let Jagger go.

"I suggest you release me," Jagger said with a growing smirk on his face.

Henrik turned his head back to Jagger, narrowing his eyes. "Fuck. You son of a bit—"

"Language!" I shouted as I put my hands on my hips.

"Yeah, only I can use words like that on her. And only when we're alone," Jagger said as his grin grew.

Henrik's jaw tightened and I could tell he was about to explode but before he could, Jagger grabbed Henrik's pinky finger from his shoulder. With what seemed liked very little effort, Jagger pulled back his finger.

Henrik cried out and he fell to his knees. Jagger moved in a flash and had Henrik pinned to the ground.

"I told you to release me." Jagger's knee was digging into Henrik's back.

"Let him go," I said.

With a smile, Jagger turned his attention from Henrik to me. The grin didn't last as he sighed and released Henrik, getting up.

"Fine." Jagger lifted his hands in the air as if to surrender.

Henrik slowly rose from the floor and I thought he was hurt, but based on the red of his cheeks I realized it was only his ego that took a hit.

"You two act like boys, not men," I said and turned to leave the bedroom when I saw David standing just inside my room.

"David. How was your night with the guys?" I went over to give him a hug but he stiffened as I came near. "What's wrong?" I asked as I pulled away from him.

"What's going on in here? What happened to you?" David touched my arm.

I closed my eyes and sighed. As shaken up as I was from the attack, I was more worried at how I would explain it to David. The way he was glaring at Jagger, I knew I had to explain what happened right away. I didn't want David to think anything bad about the man who saved me.

"I was mugged."

"No," David yelled as his eyes began to water.

He stuffed his hand into his pocket and took something small and black out, rubbing it like it would help will away the tears. I couldn't tell what the object was, perhaps one of his little ninja action figures he collects.

"What?" I heard Henrik from behind.

I turned but kept my hand on David's shoulder. "I'm fine. Just got a scratch on my arm. Luckily, Jagger was nearby and saw what was happening."

All eyes turned toward Jagger as he stood by the back wall.

"He stopped the guy, and the police arrested the attacker. Jagger saved me."

Henrik's hands ran through his hair as he shook his head. He turned to Jagger. "I'm sorry. When I saw that she was hurt and you were here, I thought the worst. Thank you for helping Tiffany. We'd be lost without her."

I heard a gasp and turned to find my son with tears streaming down his face. Pulling him into an embrace, I held him as tight as I could.

"I'm fine, David. It's okay." I ran my fingers through his soft wavy hair and kissed the top of his head.

He was growing and becoming stronger every day, but David was always sensitive to other's feelings. I remember him as a toddler watching cartoons, and anytime the characters started to cry, he did too.

"You need to leave this neighborhood." Henrik put on his demanding voice.

"This is my home. Even if we did move out, our lease isn't even up until the late autumn. Besides, this building has an elevator."

"But you don't need an elevator anymore," Henrik added.

"But what about—" I stopped myself as I pulled away from David and stared at him.

"About me? I can walk now, remember?" David said fisting the object in his hand and shoving it back into his pocket.

That was true, but it wasn't like he was running up and down stairs. His gait was still slow and he needed to continue to build his core for balance.

"I don't know," I said watching David with unease.

It was surprising how quickly David went from sad to irritated, but I should get used to it. He was a teenager now.

"Really? You know I'm not crippled anymore, right?" David raised his voice.

"David! Don't say that. Don't you ever say that. We don't use that word here." I pushed my hands on my hips.

"You don't think I heard what everyone called me?" David turned to leave the doorway and walked toward his bedroom.

"Who called you that? Because no one that cares about you would say that. Ever." I followed him as anger pulsed through me in increasing speed.

He turned to face me at his bedroom, gripping the doorframe. "It doesn't matter who said that because they don't anymore. People treat me like a regular kid now. All the good and all the bad that goes with it."

Even if David had to take his time speaking, it didn't make his words any less impactful. "I like that. It was fine when those kids tried to steal my skateboard earlier this month because they thought I was like any of the kids there. But you . . ."

He swallowed as he got himself under control. "Mom, you still treat me like the boy with a body that didn't work. Why can't you see that I'm average? I'm just an average teenager and I love that."

Tears were streaming down his face as he slammed the door. When I went to open his door, it was locked, so I knocked.

"David. Please, open the door."

"Go away." His muffled voice slipped through the cracks.

My hand slipped from the brass doorknob and I stared at his plain white door. Nothing decorated it and with a heartbreaking realization, I knew there wasn't much décor in his room either. No posters or paint or colorful curtains. The most interesting, unique thing in his room was his red sheets. And I didn't even know if he still liked red. David enjoyed the color when he was five, but I haven't asked him since.

He was right. I treated him like he was just someone to take care of. That he had no thoughts or desires of his own. I only focused on what would keep him safe and healthy.

"I'm a terrible mother," I said and thought I had whispered to myself but someone was behind me.

"No, you're not." Jagger's hand came to my shoulder. It was warm and exactly what I needed so I turned into him. I let his arms wrap around me.

"Let me talk to him. He was up late and probably a little cranky from the lack of sleep and the mugging bombshell," Henrik said as he placed his hand on my back.

I let Jagger walk me to the living room and we sat on the couch.

I thought about every time I lost my temper or told David I needed to use the bathroom instead of reading his favorite book for the tenth time or any number of things that would nominate me for the worst mother of the year award.

"Stop it," Jagger said, placing his hand on mine.

"Stop what?"

"Beating yourself up. Mothers and sons fight all the time. It's a rite of passage for a kid to slam their bedroom door in anger." He smirked.

"But he's right," I said.

There was silence, and I raised my brow expecting Jagger to disagree with me.

That's what people do when they are trying to reassure someone who is feeling bad about themselves. They tell them things like, "no, you're gorgeous," or "no, you were the best girlfriend he ever had," or "no, you are the best mom ever." Especially that last one. He really should be saying that one to me.

"Yes, David was right."

I pulled back from his hand, frowning. My face burned as I stumbled and tried to stand. Jagger stood to help me but I waved him away.

"Don't." I took a breath as I straightened. "I may have coddled him a bit. And I may have been overwhelmed with having to take care of him alone. The only parent for the last decade. All the doctors and therapists and nurses that he required for ten years, I made the appointments and took him. I'm the one that spent hours and hours on the phone with the insurance company when they couldn't fathom a child might need physical therapy or that he used up his oxygen supply for the year in July. Oxygen, to breath, to live."

I took another breath trying to calm down. "That may have been my focus for ten years. But that's all I know. He gained freedom with that surgery in January, and I couldn't be happier for him but where does that leave me? I can't just flip a switch and let him walk out that door when just six months ago he couldn't even feed himself."

Jagger took a step forward. "I understand, I do, but—"

"You do? That's funny because last I checked, the one thing I do know about you is that you're alone. Are you the sole caregiver for a person, young or old?" I raised my brows waiting for an answer but he looked away.

"I didn't think so. I may not be a perfect mother, but I'm trying." I took a breath and walked over to the front door, opening it. "I think I need to speak with my son, alone."

TWENTY-ONE

Jagger

"Tiffany was right," I said as I tore apart a paper napkin. "Everyone was right."

I slammed my fist on the round table causing it to wobble and my coffee to spill a few drops.

"Why am I here?" Edgar asked, sitting across the booth from me at Wake Up Joe's with wide eyes.

Taking a deep breath, I chuckled in that way a person does when they know their life is shit.

"Who am I to think I know better than a mother that has spent almost her entire kid's life working hard to keep him healthy. To keep him alive. I've witnessed some terrible stuff as an agent and in my family. Things that would make you give up on humanity. Some things that parents do to their children, I still have nightmares about, but Tiffany is the opposite of that."

It had been two days since Tiffany kicked me out of her place after telling her that she needed to give her son more freedom. I'm such an ass. She'll probably run back into the arms of that shirtless guy that she was in the picture with. He probably doesn't judge her.

I still hadn't heard back from Tenn about anything he might have found out about that guy. Tenn probably didn't even look into it. I really am alone.

"Evaleen said you had something to tell me so I agreed to sit down to talk. Now if you don't mind, I need to get back to my pregnant girlfriend who happens to be craving scones. Lots of scones." Edgar got out of the booth, but I grabbed his arm and stared up into his gray eyes.

"But I need your help."

Edgar's eyes crinkled in satisfaction as he removed my hand from his arm like he was picking off a spider. He folded his arms and towered over me as I stayed seated. "Well, well, well, it seems the tables have turned. The big, thuggish agent now needs help from my tiny balls."

He glanced around realizing that a few people heard him. Edgar slid back into the booth. "Don't think I forgot what you did to me."

"You mean when I saved you, your girlfriend, and her mom from impending death?" I sat back staring at him.

Edgar cleared his throat. "That was your job, which you don't even have any more from what I hear."

I held up my hands in surrender. "Look, I'm sorry I kneed you in your balls in the alleyway that one time. You were right, I didn't have to do it."

"Then, why did you?"

"You were there and you wouldn't shut up. Asking all those questions about your supposed cousin, who wasn't your cousin at all." I tilted my head at him because he wasn't as innocent in all this as he made himself out to be.

"I thought you would take sympathy on me if I said Ashton was my cousin . . . that you might tell me something."

"I did take sympathy on you since I know what it was like to lose a cousin in a terrible way. You're lucky I didn't do more than knee you after I found out he wasn't your cousin and who you really were." I pointed at Edgar.

My shoulders fell as I leaned back in my seat. "I do a lot of things I wouldn't or couldn't normally do when I'm undercover. Some things I shouldn't do, like kneeing you in your junk. Some things are fun little perks like staying in a big suite in Las Vegas a few months back because Emma Hawthorne rented out the floor of the hotel."

"Fine. I guess we're even. I lied to you to get information and you kneed me in the balls. What is the help you need from me? If it's to lie to Tiffany, that's not going to happen. She's a sweet and a thoughtful woman, and I'm not about to deceive her."

She's not as sweet as you think. There's a wicked side to her that's just as addictive.

"I don't want you to lie to her. I want you to give her this letter." I reached into my back pocket and pulled out the slightly wrinkled envelope. "I get the feeling if I mailed it to her, she'd only throw it in the trash."

He took the envelope from my hand. "Fine but I don't think I'll have a chance to see Tiffany until the rehearsal dinner next week. With work, getting everything ready for Henrik's bachelor night, and dealing with Evaleen's unique cravings, I got a lot on my plate."

I nodded. "That's fine. It was time for me to be honest with her. The good and the bad. If she hates me I wanted it to be for the truth and not because she thinks I believe she's a bad mother. If anything, she's better than most parents I have come in contact with."

"Wow, she must hate you. Did you really tell her she was a bad mom?" Edgar leaned forward.

"No, I didn't. I just agreed with her son when they were having a fight—"

"Oh no. You don't ever do that. Look, I'm going to let you in on something. I may not be a parent or, obviously a woman," he waved a hand across his chest, "but I do know how women think. No matter what the woman says, you agree with her. She is *always* right. As for David, he has friends that he can complain to about his mom. It's what all kids do, but Tiffany, she needs her friends to back her up. You understand?"

"Not really. What happens when Tiffany is wrong about something. Say hypothetically, it's life-threatening. That her wrong decision will cost the life of someone. Then I really shouldn't agree with her."

I realized where Edgar was going with this, but I still felt that if Tiffany wanted to be the best mom she could be and loved David, then she needed to hear the truth no matter how much it hurt.

"That's when you let a doctor handle it. Tell her you both need to ask an expert, obviously. But, with anything else, I would go along with whatever she says. Remember, David isn't your son, and Tiffany isn't your wife or even your girlfriend."

He had a point.

"Okay, I still think she deserves the truth but if Evaleen trusts you, then I guess you know what you're talking about."

I had spent some time with Evaleen before I was fired, as she finally agreed to train to become an agent. I wondered if she told Edgar. She said she didn't want to be a field agent, which was a relief considering she had a baby on the way. But, she was very interested in our Intelligence Analysis department. She would analyze the intelligence gathered and help our agents predict possible outcomes in the field, like the next move a criminal we were watching might take.

Edgar nodded. "Now that's settled. I have to take this bag of scones back to Evaleen before she sends out a search party."

Just before he turned to leave I said, "Has Evaleen told you yet?"

I had to ask to see if she told him yet, wondering how Edgar would handle that.

His brow creased. "Told me what?"

I shook my head. "Nothing."

Edgar leaned forward wanting to know more so I pointed to his bag. "Better get those back to Evaleen before she comes looking for you."

His eyes widened and he turned his head, looking out the café window. He grabbed the paper bag that was on the table and my letter before rushing out the door.

I decided it was time to head out of here and sulk in my crappy apartment. Taking a few last sips of coffee, I threw it in the trash before I left.

It took a bus ride and a ten-minute walk, but I made it to my place. Just as I entered my apartment door and threw my keys on the television console that was three feet from the door, my buzzer rang.

Groaning, I pressed the talk button expecting to hear a food delivery guy that got the wrong apartment number. It happened on occasion here. But the voice I heard crackling back from the speaker surprised me.

"Hi. It's Tiffany. Can I talk to you?"

I hit the open button for the door and wondered how she got my address. Opening the door to my apartment, I waited for her to appear at the top of the stairs. When she did, my heart picked up its pace as if I was the one winded from climbing the stairs.

"Top floor?" she said pulling at the collar of her pink dress, letting a light breeze underneath.

"Nothing but the best." I smirked, stepping inside my place and holding the door as she walked past.

"It's uh, quaint." Her eyes surveyed my small living room and the window that gave a sprawling view of the train tracks.

I waved her over to my brown leather couch which took up half the length of the room. She sat giving me a small smile. Her thick, gorgeous hair was pulled back into a braid and the loosened pieces that fell stuck to her face.

"Would you like some ice water?" I asked.

"Yes, please. Don't you have air-conditioning?"

I got up and went behind the wall to my small galley kitchen to retrieve a glass. "Yes. I have wall units, but when I turn them on, it's too loud to hear anything so I save it for the night when I'm sleeping."

After I filled her cup with ice and water, I came back giving her the refreshing drink. She took a few gulps before pressing the glass to her forehead.

"It doesn't bother you when you sleep? The noise?"

"I got used to it. Besides, being an agent, I never spent much time here. When I used to be one, anyway." I shrugged.

Her eyes glanced around and it gave me a chance to study her. Even with the muggy heat of the apartment and how uncomfortable she was, Tiffany never let on she was unhappy. In fact, she smiled every chance she could.

That's what I kept my eyes on, her lips. Her grin did something to me. The curve of her lips was more than just a turn on, it was life-giving. Her smile could light the way at night, and still have me refreshed by morning.

"I wanted to say I'm sorry," she said as the light in her face died with her grin.

"What? Why?"

"Because you were honest with me when discussing David and I yelled at you for it. And, you were right." She sighed putting the glass down on the small oval coffee table. "I think that's why I got so defensive."

"You are a great mom to that boy. Please don't doubt that. If that's what you thought I meant, it's not."

Tiffany turned to the side, raising her knee on the couch. "I don't know anymore. I used to think I was good but maybe I only know how to take care of a boy whose body has rendered him helpless. Now that he's not vulnerable and can do most things by himself, I'm the one left feeling helpless."

"That doesn't stop you from being his mom. He may not need you to help him as much, but he still needs you." I took her cool hand in mine, giving it a squeeze.

"But I worry so much, still. That there will be that one moment, when I'm not there, and everything will go wrong." Her eyes became glassy as she turned her head from me.

"Then worry. Or better yet, let someone help distract you." I glanced down at her lips.

TWENTY-TWO

Jagger

"But, I'm alone. It's not like I have anyone there with me when all the bad thoughts come creeping into my head," Tiffany said as she looked up at me.

"I'll be there. I mean, I want to be there." I struggled to find the right words to tell her how I felt. "How we met, it was fucked up and the time since hasn't exactly gone to plan."

I shook my head at the last month with her.

"You could say that again. I remember when you showed up for the PT appointment the first time I thought you were the worst. I was itching to call the physical therapy center and get another person." She laughed as she edged closer, leaning back against the couch.

I loved her laugh. It was throaty and sensual and the world felt lighter.

"Little did you know I was married to you," I said causing joyous tears to stream down her face as her laughter grew.

"Ugh, and you still didn't say anything."

I covered my face with my hand. "Don't remind me." I shook my head letting my hand fall. "I guess I forgot how beautiful you were. I didn't really mind being married to you."

While there was a part of me that didn't want to tell her that, I felt like she needed to hear it. All these lies I had been living almost my whole life, it was time to change that.

Her smile faded along with her laughter. "Jagger, I didn't realize. I thought you felt sorry for me. The poor struggling single mom, which only made me mad at you."

"How could I ever feel sorry for you? You have everything I wish I had. I wanted to stay married to you, even in secret, because I wanted to pretend that I had a family like yours."

"I had no idea."

"I'm kind of glad I got fired from the agency. It was time for me to get a life. I know I was drunk when I came over to your place last week, but I remember telling you I had no one in my life. It's true."

She reached over and rubbed my arm and it was nice. I sounded like the most pathetic person on earth. Glancing around my place, I realized my life matched my apartment.

Something needed to change.

"Let's move in together," I said.

Tiffany's eyes widened and she sat up. "What?"

"I really need to find a new place, and you need to get out of that neighborhood." I scooted closer as she moved back on the cushion.

"Yeah, but I don't know if moving in together would solve anything. Besides, you don't even have a job."

"I've been toying around with starting my own business which I think your son might be able to help with."

Tiffany stood holding out her hands. "Whoa! You want to move in with me and use my son for your business venture? No, thank you."

I got off the couch and moved closer to her. "I'm not going to use him. If anything, he's already a part of it. As you can see, I don't spend a lot on living expenses."

"Obviously," she said rolling her eyes.

I chuckled. "But I was paid well enough by the government so I shoved most of it away in savings. I was thinking of buying a studio and starting my own ninja training business."

"That actually sounds like a good idea."

I came over to her, putting my hands on her upper arms. They remained folded as her eyes stayed weary. "So, we can move in together?"

"No, I never said yes to that. Only that the ninja thing was a good idea." Her arms drifted down, and I edged closer until I could feel her breath flutter over my skin.

Tiffany's eyes were like saucers of chocolate milk and her neck, like creamy butter. I lowered my head for the promise of a taste and when my tongue lapped at her sweet cream, I didn't stop until I reached her earlobe. "I bet I can make you change your mind."

Her fingers curled, and as they dug into my arms thoughts of her clinging to me as she rode my cock sent a bolt straight between my legs.

"Are you seriously going to use sex to get me to move in with you?" Tiffany said with challenge, with surprise, and with a deepening tone.

"Maybe. Will it work?" With one finger, which turned into two and then four, I twisted her braid around my hand, tugging so I could nibble on more of her skin.

"No, it won't." Her defiant attitude refuted as she raised her leg, curling it around my hip.

Lifting my head, I stared down and watched her chest rise and fall with a quickening pace. My fingers drifted, her damp skin puckering under my touch, until I found her tit. "We'll see what you say when I'm done making you come."

As Tiffany bit her lip, she was chewing pieces of my willpower like I was eggs for breakfast. My neck burned and my fingers itched to push her back on that couch and show her what she did to me.

But just as I was about to cave, she fluttered her lashes as she gazed up at my face. "Jagger, I've gone without sex for ten years. When we're done, you won't even have words left to give."

My ears were ringing from the blood in my veins rushing for her touch. My hand found her thigh, and I ran my fingers up until my palm was full of her ass. I gave her a squeeze letting her know how perfect she was.

"Is that a threat?" I asked licking my lips.

She pushed her fingers under my shirt scratching at my stomach as I let go of her braid. "No, that's a promise."

I thought I might fall over, sink into the floor, wrapping my arms around her and never letting go. But I found my strength and picked her up, pushing her legs until both were wrapped around me.

Her skin was slick from the heat, and I knew I was sweaty but I didn't care. If anything, it made this better. I wanted to slip and slide and move over her until we couldn't be peeled apart.

Turning the fan on overhead as we entered the bedroom did little to ease the heat. And I knew more sweat would drip and the heat would rise as I threw Tiffany on my bed. Her mouth opened in surprise as she fell back against the white sheets.

But she recovered and began to peel away her clothes. I followed, refusing to look away as I stripped off my shirt, my khaki shorts, and boxer briefs.

The Mona Lisa was art, a Porsche 356 Speedster was sleek on wheels, but Tiffany naked, sprawled out on my bed, was sublime.

"What are you waiting for?" she asked lifting her arms above her.

"You're so beautiful. I don't even know where to begin."

Tiffany spread her legs and moved her hands to her glistening pussy. When she pushed her fingers to her lips, spreading herself for me, I almost lost it.

"Why don't you start right here."

I groaned barely able to remain upright. "Tiffany, you have got to stop teasing me like this."

"How am I teasing you? If anything, you are teasing me. I tell you what to do, and you stand there." She lifted up onto her elbow, and I realized she no longer had a bandage on her other arm, only a healing scab remained.

All thought evaporated out the window as I fell to my knees. My fingers twisted and curled to watch her bend. Arousal leaked from my hand and hammered at my cock. I forgot, no that's not right, I didn't want to believe that Tiffany tasted this good. Like peach pie melting on my tongue. I savored her heavenly flavor.

She tightened as my fingers smoothed over that small rough patch inside her, waiting so long to be played with. I sucked on her clit and savored her as her body struggled under my touch. She screamed a few sounds of agreement and worshiped the almighty but when she finally gave in, I knew I was done seeking anyone else. When I nibbled and pumped that climax from her, she admitted only one name that could make her feel this way.

"Jagger!" she cried out as her back arched.

I lifted my head, her swollen pussy still twitching around my fingers. When I finally pulled out, I grabbed a condom from my side table, figuring a world record was broken for condom placement speed.

Her chest was rising and falling fast, but easing its pace as I settled between her legs.

"You still want this?"

There was a moment, as tiny as a millisecond, that I thought I saw doubt ghost her face, but when she moved her hands to my ass and squeezed, I knew I was wrong.

"Yes. I want your abnormally large penis inside me right now."

"That was your final warning," I said before I cupped her tit, pinching her spiked nipple.

My lips fell onto her mouth as my cock pushed inside her. She wanted to pull away from my mouth but I wouldn't let her. My other hand cradled the back of her neck as I kissed her lips and rocked into her tight pussy.

If she wanted this, then I was giving her everything. Her legs tightened around my hips, lifting herself to move with me. I plunged my tongue into her mouth as my cock plundered. If I could, I would fall inside her and never come out.

Finally, I lifted my head and gulped the air. Her hair was wild. I gazed into her hooded eyes and wondered if her heart stumbled in her chest like mine.

Her nails trailed down my back as she threw back her head. "You feel so good, Jagger."

That wasn't nearly enough. I wanted to give her laughter and smiles and everything wonderful in one moment. I needed the world to explode behind her eyes and drift warmly over her slick body.

I rolled off her and turned her onto her side, pulling up behind her. Lifting her leg, I pushed back inside, between her thighs, while my hand pulled at her braid.

"Do you like that?" I asked.

"Yes, God, yes."

I reached over with my free hand grazing my finger over her clit. She tightened and we both groaned. I wanted her to come again, but I didn't know how much longer I was going to last.

"Jagger. Oh, yeah, I'm coming," Tiffany moaned.

I let go of her hair as I curled around her body, my own orgasm causing me to shudder. Burying my head in the back of her neck, the waves kept coming.

We stayed like that for a minute before I finally rolled away. I got up and went into the bathroom to remove the condom and clean up. When I came back out, I had a damp cloth.

I settled between her thighs and started to wipe. I may have kissed the side of her knees a few times before I was done. After I tossed the cloth toward my dirty clothes hamper in the corner of the room, I relaxed back next to Tiffany.

She curled around me. "You didn't have to do that."

"What? Wash you?" I asked.

"Yeah. I could have gotten up and done it myself after you came out of the bathroom."

I turned to face her, trailing my finger down her cheek. "But I wanted to take care of you. I will always want to take care of you." My finger made it to her lips and I smirked. "Unless I fuck you. Then I only want to ruin you."

TWENTY-THREE

Tiffany

"They are beautiful," I said as stared at the bouquet in Morgana's hand.

"I picked out the flowers. These pink ones are peony rose, and the purple are hydrangeas, with uh, what are these again?" Morgana asked as she turned to the florist.

"Lamb's ear. It gives a little greenery to the bouquet," the woman in the green apron with silver hair said.

Morgana nodded. "Right, lamb's ear. And, of course, the blue ribbon to tie it all together."

I tilted my head. "Blue?"

"You know, *something old, something new, something borrowed, something blue.*"

"Oh, right. Of course. Well, I love it."

The florist smiled at Morgana. "It's not the final one. This is just a sample to give you an idea of what it'll look like. Yours will be much bigger for the wedding in three days."

It had been a week since I *finally* had sex. I thought my vagina might fall out if I didn't get something soon. It was so worth it. The wait. And, his cock.

I smiled and strolled around the small shop called The Bloom Room, running my fingers over the tips of petals. Their soft texture reminded me of Jagger's big dick.

Just about everything was reminding me of his cock.

Like when Evaleen took me to Chuck's Sausage Shack for lunch on Friday . . . Or when I went to the grocery store and passed the cucumbers. Then I stopped and gazed at the cucumbers. After which I grabbed a couple so I could lie next to one in bed at night and dream about Jagger's cock.

"I bet I know what's on your mind?" Morgana said as she slid beside me.

"What?" I felt my face heat, knowing she could see the blush on my cheeks.

Then I snorted.

"The cake. Well, it's a surprise. But let me tell you, it will be the best thing you ever tasted." Her eyes glazed over as she stared off into the distance.

"I've already tasted the best thing," I mumbled.

"Huh?" Morgana said coming out of her cake fantasy.

"Nothing. I bet it will be delicious."

The bell over the door rang and when I looked up, the current jacked up porn scene that was playing in my head appeared to be coming to life.

"Jagger," I said with too much enthusiasm to be dismissed as a simple surprise.

We met up again Saturday night after David went to bed but I didn't want Jagger to spend the night. This was just sex, I didn't want David to think the thing between Jagger and me was more than friendship.

But that's the last time we were together. We had been sexting each other the past several nights as he's been busy trying to make his ninja studio happen. I've been busy with doctor appointments, David starting school, a few client meetings over logo changes, and any last-minute wedding freak outs that Morgana's been having. All these things foiled any of our attempts to see each other.

"Tiffany." His eyes darkened as they traveled my body.

When he said he was free today and wanted to see me, I mentioned I had to go to the florist with Morgana in the morning but was free the rest of the day. Even David was hanging out at Diego's place. I had met his parents and they loved David. And, since Diego had a basement with a big screen TV and a PlayStation, the boys spent more time there than at our apartment.

"Oh, hey, Jagger. Funny running into you here." Morgana creased her brow walking toward him.

Jagger's eyes flipped between Morgana and me. I hadn't told my friends that Jagger had, with too many orgasms to count and sex in every room in his cramped apartment, ended my dry spell. Maybe dry spell doesn't best describe it. It was more like an arid desert, so vast it made the Sahara look like a patch of sand by a river.

"I asked him to meet me here. I wanted to thank him for, uh, some great advice he gave me." Heat traveled up my neck as I stared at him.

"I usually don't like to gloat, but that advice was really good. I couldn't stop thinking about it, it was fantastic," he said, his voice deepening as he inched toward me.

"And the way you, um, said it. So many different ways. I never realized I could see things like that. You really have a knack for advice." I bit my lip and took a quick peek at his jeans zipper, but was more interested in what was behind the zipper.

"Huh, I never knew you were so good at giving advice, Jagger? Maybe you can help convince Tiffany to let David be in the wedding."

That cooled me down like a bucket of ice directed at my vagina.

"I already gave you my answer on that, Morgana. Yes, David has made a lot of progress, even in the weeks since you asked, but I don't—"

Morgana turned to me with her hands on her hips. "The ceremony isn't even that long."

I glanced up at Jagger and could tell he was holding back whatever he was thinking.

I waved my hand at Jagger. "Out with it. I *know* you have an opinion on this."

"Screw Edgar," Jagger mumbled before turning his eyes up to mine. "I think Morgana's right. Have you even asked David?"

I slid my tongue over my teeth as I plucked up a rose from a vase. "No, but that doesn't mean—"

"Give him a chance." Jagger walked over and placed his hand on my shoulder.

He was right. This was exactly what David yelled at me about the other week. As much as I feared it would be too much for David, I had to at least ask if he wanted to be a groomsman. This was his decision, not mine.

"I should . . . I mean, I will." I turned to Morgana as a smile took over her face. "I'm sorry, David may be getting bigger and stronger with each day, but I can't help but still worry about him. I'll ask him tonight when he gets home from Diego's house."

Morgana jumped up and down, clapping her hand.

"Yay! I promise that we will have a chair nearby if he needs to take a rest. Oh, Henrik will be so happy." Morgana wrapped her arms around me for a big squeeze.

"What are you two doing right now? We should celebrate. Everything is going to be perfect at this wedding. The cake, the flowers," she gave the florist a smile, "the groomsman. Everything. I just wish Henrik would tell me where it's taking place."

I sucked in my lips so I wouldn't let my smile show. Henrik wanted the wedding location to be a surprise, and I knew Morgana would love it. It was going to be an intimate affair at her favorite bakery, Got Cake. Where right after they say I do, they feed each other a piece of cake.

She really was having the best wedding.

"Actually, I wanted to show Jagger something back at my place."

"Okay, we'll all head over there and then I'll take you both to lunch. My treat." Morgana's eyes bounced between us.

I gazed at Jagger. He wasn't happy. With a tightening jaw, I knew what he wanted me to say, but I didn't really want to tell everyone yet.

It was just sex. What if it got back to David? He cared for Jagger. It would break his heart if the thing between us fizzled out.

"I really need to show Jagger in private." I frowned unable to come up with a better excuse.

"That's weird. Why would you need to show him something in private?" Morgana said before chuckling.

"Because what she wants to show me is in her panties, and I would like to show her what I have under my clothes, too," Jagger said.

My eyes widened as Morgana's mouth dropped open. I could hear the muffled giggle from the florist behind us.

My cheeks heated and I narrowed my eyes at him. "Jagger!"

"Oh, I get it now," Morgana said.

I rolled my eyes. Morgana was nice and a bit goofy, but sometimes it took her a while to process things.

"What?" Jagger said, challenging me.

"They're my friends. If I want to tell them we're," I lowered my voice, "*having sex,* then I'll do it myself."

"Fine. I forgot how embarrassed you are of me," Jagger said before turning and walking out the door.

"Men are the worst," I growled as I balled my hands at my side. "Excuse me, Morgana. I'll take a raincheck on that lunch celebration."

"Of course," I heard Morgana say as I marched out the door.

When I was outside the shop, I noticed he was about to step into a taxi. I scurried over before he could close the door.

"Jagger. Where are you going?" I said slightly winded.

"To your place." He turned to me with the door between us.

"Without me?"

"I figured you would end up there. We need to talk, and I'm not about to do that in a flower shop." He pushed the door open to allow me to climb inside.

I turned to him once we were seated and he gave the address to the driver. "Okay, so let's talk."

His eyes remained focused on the driver. "Okay, so let's talk."

"Okay," I said through clenched teeth.

It was a silent and stuffy trip back to my building. What was only a ten-minute drive felt like hours with Jagger's irritable silence.

When we finally made it inside my apartment and I shut the door, all the words Jagger had pent up came rushing out. I was endangered of being knocked down by a tidal wave of sound.

"What is it about me that you find so repulsive? Is it that I'm not rich like every guy your friends date?" He paused.

My mouth fell open and as I was about to respond he continued, "Maybe it's that I'm currently jobless. Or you're ashamed of that night in Vegas. Which I can promise you nothing happened." He pointed his finger in the air as if that statement alone made him some sort of saint.

"Except we got married, and I have no recollection of that night." I folded my arms as we stood in the entranceway of my apartment. The man didn't even let me put down my purse.

He cleared his throat, his eyes taking a break from trying to burn me alive. "Except for that, yes. If I had known you wouldn't remember anything, I probably wouldn't have married you."

"Probably?" I took a step closer, throwing my purse on the kitchen counter beside us.

"Most likely. Not. No, I would not have married you."

And that's when I faltered. Something stuck in my throat, and I had to take a moment before I could speak.

"Then you regret it?" I asked.

He rubbed the back of his neck and shook his head. "No. I don't regret marrying you. I don't think I regretted it even when I stepped out of the hotel bathroom the next day and found you weren't there."

My eyes burned, and I couldn't tell if my heart wanted to jump out of my chest or melt into oblivion.

"How about you, Tiffany? Do you regret marrying me?"

Of all the uncertainty I had about Jagger, this was the one answer I knew for certain.

"Yes," I said.

TWENTY-FOUR

Jagger

"Our marriage ended," I said before I took a hefty sip of the whiskey sour in front of me, "with a stroke of a pen."

"That's usually how they end," the bartender said as he wiped down the bar around me.

"It's funny but I never thought I would get married. And I really never thought I would be fired as a secret government spy because I went rogue and started to plant cameras in a person's home that I didn't have the authority to spy on." I chuckled as I lifted my glass.

The bartender stopped cleaning and stared at me.

"Uh, were you supposed to tell me that?"

"No, probably not. But fuck it. What are they going to do to me?" I made air quotes with my fingers, spilling some of my drink. "Make me disappear?"

I laughed again but stopped as I found my answer. "Actually, they might. Best I not tell you any more."

I winked at him, and the bartender started to walk backward until he was at the end of the bar where he stayed.

Alone once more. Perhaps I was meant to be alone. No friends. No family. I should get a plant. Something that doesn't require a lot of water because I really don't like hanging out in my apartment.

After Tiffany took my heart and slashed it into a thousand parts and then pissed on it yesterday, I left. I may be a lying, lonely jerk but I don't hang around where I'm not wanted.

I spent the night barely sleeping and then most of the day trying to write a business proposal so I could ask the bank for a loan. I gave up an hour ago and came to this bar. It was filled with people just getting off work, lucky bastards.

I felt a slap on my back and without much thought as adrenaline kicked in, I grabbed the hand, turned, and twisted the man's arm until he was pinned to the bar.

"Oh, Henrik. It's you. How's it going?" I asked.

"Fine," he moaned, and I realized I still had him pushed against the bar so I let him go.

"Sorry, you surprised me."

He rubbed his arm and nodded. "I could tell."

"Where's Morgana?" I asked as my eyes scanned the room.

I zeroed in on two other guys I recognized, Edgar and Alexander. They were seated at a table. Edgar pretended he didn't see me while Alex smiled and waved.

"She's having her bachelorette party. So, I decided tonight was a good night to do the bachelor night with the guys." He glanced at my glass. "Is that a whiskey sour?"

I frowned. "Yeah."

We stood there in silence for a minute. It was nice to drink in peace and not feel like I had to talk. But just as I was getting used to Henrik being there, he opened his mouth.

"You want to join us? I don't think the guys would mind."

I turned back to look at the table Henrik was pointing toward. The table was small, seated four at most. There was a candle in the middle as if it was meant for a romantic evening and not for a bunch of guys wanting to get drunk.

I nodded at Alex who began to wave again. As I was about to turn Henrik down, I saw Edgar putting his hand to his face, trying to hide from me.

"Sounds good. I'd be happy to join you." I slapped Henrik on his shoulder.

He winced and rubbed where I had touched him, but led the way to the table.

"Hey, guys, look who I ran into," Henrik announced.

Edgar's eyes slid to me before he glanced back at Henrik. "He might steal your fiancée and make her do dangerous stuff for the government."

Evaleen must have told Edgar about her new job. No wonder he's acting extra icy toward me.

"What?" Henrik tilted his head trying to make sense of his friend.

"Nothing." Edgar glared at me before turning back toward Henrik. "Did you order the drinks?"

"Crap, I forgot," Henrik said.

"That's okay, it's your night. I'll go order." Edgar almost jumped off the stool and made his way to the bar.

"Hey, Jagger. Glad you could join us." Alex gave me a smile.

I liked Alex. He may have more money than I could possibly imagine and appeared to be a cross between a bear and an ancient god, but he was the most down-to-earth guy I knew.

"Aria told me she ran into you a couple of times. I don't know if she thanked you, but we are very grateful for you helping us," Alex said as I took Edgar's vacant stool.

"I'm sorry I had to take down your mom, Alex." I was unsure how he was handling that.

Emma Hawthorne was an evil and cunning person, but she was still his mom.

"I'm not." He shook his head. "She was worse than I ever imagined. All those years I thought she was just trying to control my life and then to find out she wanted to control everyone else's lives too. She was like some villain in a movie, but she was the woman who raised me."

We were all silent for a moment.

"You don't have to worry about her anymore. She's on tape admitting everything. There isn't a judge in this country that would let her get off." I slapped his back.

Edgar arrived with a tray filled with a pitcher of beer and three glasses.

"Help yourselves, gentlemen. Except for you, Jagger. I assumed you had your own drink." Edgar stared at my almost empty tumbler.

I stood and grabbed my glass. "You're right, Edgar. I'll go grab a refill and then we can all get to know each other a little better. Maybe talk about how we all met."

The color drained from Edgar's face and he was about to say something when Henrik spoke up, "Sounds like a great idea. I'd love to hear how everyone met Jagger."

With a chuckle still on my lips, I moved toward the bar. As I waited for the bartender to finish with someone else, I felt a vibration on my ass. Reaching back, I pulled my phone out of my back pocket.

"Hello?"

"Jagger, it's Tenn."

I put the glass down on the bar. I was surprised to hear from him since I was no longer an agent. Then I remembered asking him to look into that guy Tiffany was in that picture with.

"Did you find out about the man in the photo?" I asked.

"What? Oh, not yet. Other things have come up so I haven't had time to look him up."

How quickly Tenn forgot I worked with him for two years. His "too busy at work" excuse was code for not going to happen. Any belief that Tenn might have my back was gone. I was nobody to him now.

"Then why are you calling? I've got things to do," I said as I tried to keep the bitterness out of my voice.

"It's the Jewel."

"What about Emma Hawthorne?" I said before sighing.

I guess I'm not such a nobody now that he needed some questions answered about the case. Tenn went on and on this past month about how ready he was to head a big case and now that he's in charge, who does he call? Me, that's who. The nobody.

"She's escaped. We have no idea where she is," Tenn said right as the bartender appeared.

"Another whiskey sour?" the bartender asked, but I waved him away and turned my back.

"What? How did something like that happen?" I moved quickly past the guys at the table and out the front door of the bar. Once I was on the sidewalk, I moved around the corner to a darkened alley to hear better.

"I was hoping you might know something," Tenn said with a resolve I wasn't used to.

"Why would I know anything? I'm not an agent anymore, remember?"

My eyes watched the people walk by the alley, most unaware I was only a few feet from them. A few glanced my way when they heard me talk but the lack of light shaded me.

"You were fired for a reason—"

"Which was because you told Katlin about me spying on Tiffany." I was ready to reach through the phone and strangle him.

It was stupid of me to spy on her, but Tenn promised not to say anything. I told him I pulled the equipment, that I kept my word to stop spying on her, but he told Katlin anyway.

Maybe this was his plan all along? He wanted me fired and had the perfect excuse to make that happen.

"I never told Katlin anything. She only said you were let go because of something involving the Jewel case. Since Emma Hawthorne started to accuse you of framing her, I thought there might be some truth to that."

This was why I was in charge of missions. Tenn was great at putting agents and equipment in place, but he wasn't the best at keeping his mouth shut.

"I can see why you would believe that, but it's not true. You've known me for years, when have I ever helped a criminal?"

"The way you've been acting for the last few months, I wondered if I really knew you."

He was right. Tenn didn't know me. No one knew me. Not even Tiffany. Maybe that's why she regretted marrying me.

"As I said, it's not true what Emma Hawthorne was saying about me. But if it was true, Tenn, you just revealed everything to me. If I'm a suspect, why did you tell me all that?" I shook my head worrying what would happen to this case with Tenn heading it.

"Fuck. You're right."

"Did you put into place some ops on her old contacts?" I asked.

"I was going to do that but I wanted to call you first."

"This is so messed up. Get people tailing anyone she had contact with. Even me, if you have to. But, I have to warn you, I'll figure out who's tailing me before they even get a chance to put their car in park outside my building."

"I know," Tenn said, and I heard a loud sigh from the other end. "I wish you still worked here."

For the first time, I realized I was happy not being an agent.

"Well, I don't. You wanted to head a mission? You got it. Find the Jewel."

"Right. Who do you think told Katlin about you spying on Tiffany?"

"I don't know. But while you find Emma Hawthorne, I'm going to figure out who is spying on me."

Someone must have seen me because Tenn was the only one that I told. Obviously, I told Dr. Randy but he's required to keep everything confidential. He will give opinions to the department head if he believes an agent is a danger to themselves or others.

Maybe he thought I was a danger? He could have easily called Katlin after I left his office. It would have been a short conversation as it only took me a few minutes until I was outside her office.

I hung up the phone as the realization hit me. Emma could be coming after Aria. Aria was at the bachelorette party. Tiffany was at that party. I had to get to them right away.

Once I made it back inside the bar, I ran up to Henrik's table.

"You need to tell me where the ladies are?"

"I don't think they want you spying on them, Jagger," Edgar mumbled loud enough for me to hear as he lifted his beer to his lips.

"They might be in danger. I need to get to them," I said glancing at the men.

TWENTY-FIVE

Tiffany

"It's really loud," Morgana yelled as Aria and Morgana's mom guided her to our table.

The place had more lighting than I expected but Morgana was right, it was loud. She still didn't know where we were as her grandma insisted on keeping her blindfolded.

"Just one more step. There, you can take your blindfold off," Morgana's mom said as she let go of her daughter's hand.

Morgana slipped off the pink bandana and glanced around. Her brow furrowed. "There's a stage. Is this one of those dinner theaters?"

Her grandmother took her seat on the long white couch and waved over a shirtless man wearing leather pants and a bowtie.

"In a way. Except we already had dinner. This is more drinks with a show. And they do show everything here. Don't they, sweetie?" Her grandmother's hand slid over the man's bicep before drifting down his arm.

"Yes, tonight is the Full Monty show. Now, what drinks would you like to start with?" he asked.

I knew when I saw the sign out front that it was a strip club. Who would mistake Hunk O-Rama Male Revue as anything other than a male strip club?

Any other time I would be a little thrilled to come to a place like this. Something different and fun. But, looking around at the half-naked men made me miss Jagger. Especially, his chest. He had a better chest then all these men.

The first thought I had when I saw the strip club was making Jagger put on a show of his own for me.

Then I frowned as I remembered how brooding and silent he was when he left yesterday. When I tried to call him later and earlier today, it went directly to voicemail. I haven't heard from him since.

No Jagger show for me.

I wish he had let me explain what I meant when I said I regretted marrying him.

"Three shots a piece of tequila with some lime wedges. Oh, and bring out a basket of your curly fries," Morgana's grandmother said.

"Since you ladies have the VIP table, you get complimentary champagne," he said.

"Fine, bring that as well." Her grandmother waved the guy off.

"That's a lot of alcohol. Maybe we should just start with the champagne and then—" Morgana's mom said, taking her seat next to Morgana's grandma.

"It's a bachelorette party, Annette. Live a little." She rolled her eyes at Morgana's mom before turning toward her granddaughter. "What do you think?"

Morgana, with eyes so round I wondered if they might fall out of her head, glanced around the room. We were seated on a large, leather, U-shaped couch that hugged a low white table. The room was dark, with dark wood floors and black walls. Green lighting poured down from the ceiling against the walls to make it appear like a green waterfall.

"It's a bachelorette party all right," Morgana said with a frown on her face.

"I love it. Great idea, Mrs. Austin," Aria said reaching over to pat Morgana's grandma on the back.

"Please, call me Denise. I'm just one of the ladies tonight, and if I'm lucky enough, I'll be hanging with the guys after!" She wiggled her brows as Aria high fived her.

The waiter came back with the drinks and additional glasses of water. I slowly sipped my champagne and passed off my shots to Aria. Evaleen sipped on water next to me.

I snacked on a few fries and was surprised at how good they were. After we had been there about twenty minutes, the white lights lowered and colorful strobe lights began to wildly flash around the stage.

"Welcome, ladies, to the special Full Monty show here at the Hunk O-Rama Male Revue! In a moment, some of our seasoned pros are sure to make you sweat with our pre-show. Right after the pre-show, you will be in for a treat. All the way from our New York venue, four of the hottest men will let you see it all!" the announcer said overhead.

It was fun to see the guys dance around the stage, taking off their clothes. They were quite talented, and I wondered if they were professional dancers during the day. Even the light show was impressive. When the limousine drove up to the strip club, I thought it was going to be seedy, but they put on an entertaining show.

Morgana's grandma got grabby with a few of the dancer and had to be led back to her seat.

After a while, the men left the stage and the lighting changed. I heard the announcer come back on. "You ladies ready for the Full Monty?"

The crowd, along with Aria, Morgana, Mrs. Austin, and Annette, shouted that they were indeed ready for the men to strip all their clothes off.

"Welcome to the stage . . ." There was a muffled sound where the announcer was asking for the guys' names. "I don't care if you're not really from New York. What are your names?"

Everyone at the table looked at each other in confusion.

The curtain swung open and I thought my mouth was going to hit the table.

"Welcome to the stage Alex, Edgar, Henrik, and Jagger!"

Mrs. Austin and Annette jumped to their feet and began waving dollar bills at the men. I glanced at Aria, Morgana, and Evaleen as they seemed to be in shock at seeing their men up on stage.

"Is this part of the surprise?" Morgana asked.

"No," Evaleen and Aria said at the same time.

The men stood in the middle of the stage, gazing out into the crowd wearing nothing but their jeans. Jagger was the only one who's head moved as his eyes drifted over the crowd.

"Help these guys feel welcome, ladies," the announcer said.

The crowd roared and Annette stopped jumping. Slowly, she sat back down as she must have recognized her future son-in-law.

"Don't we have a bride-to-be in the crowd? Let's get her up here so these men can take care of her." I could hear the frustration in the announcer's voice as the men didn't move.

Our waiter showed up and offered Morgana a hand. Still a bit stunned, she got up and let the waiter guide her to the stairs. Once on stage, Morgana sat on a single white chair in the middle of the stage.

"Okay, guys!" The announcer's voice was laced with irritation. "Show the lady a good time."

The men started to move toward Morgana, but Henrik widened his arms, stopping them in their tracks. It was like a car wreck. I knew what would unfold would be horrible, well, horribly embarrassing but I couldn't look away. And as I had a quick glance around the table, neither could any of the other ladies.

Henrik shifted his feet from side to side like he was line dancing.

"Oh God, I think I'm going to be sick," Evaleen mumbled beside me.

There were insults from the crowd. One woman shouted if he's going to dance that badly the least he could do was show everyone his dick.

"Come on, ladies, we have to save them." I finally came to my senses.

"You're right. Morgana can take care of her own man, but I'll be damned if these savages will be ogling Edgar." Evaleen stood and began to move in the direction of the three steps that led to the stairs.

"Aria? Are you going to let Alex strip for everyone?" I asked as I stood.

"Fine. I guess not," Aria said more disappointed than mad.

As we approached the stage, a large bald man with a black T-shirt that said security in big white letters on the front, stopped us.

"Where do you three think you're going?"

"Those are our boyfriends up there. There has been some sort of mistake," Evaleen said folding her arms over her chest.

"Lucky, you. The only way on to the stage is if you are a dancer or you paid for a dance," he said.

Evaleen leaned forward until she was whispering into the man's ear. His eyes widened after a few moments as she reached into her pocket, pulled something out, and showed it to him. He quickly moved to the side to let us pass.

"What did you say to him?" I asked Evaleen.

"Just that I could make one phone call and have this entire venue raided. I had a feeling there were a few things that weren't necessarily up to code. And I was right," Evaleen said.

I wanted to ask why he would believe her, as any woman could make that claim. I had a feeling it was what she showed him that had him changing his mind.

The ladies ran over to their men. Jagger strolled to me and we all ran off stage. Jagger pulled me toward the exit, and I thought everyone followed. When I glanced back, after hearing another uproar from the crowd as they realized we were taking the men, I saw Henrik still up on stage dancing for Morgana.

"What happened in there?" I asked Jagger once we were standing in the parking lot.

We were gathered in a group near a yellow Volkswagen Karmann Ghia.

"They mistook us for strippers." Jagger ran his hand through his disheveled hair.

With his mussed-up hair and naked chest, I couldn't help but stare at his body. Even out here, in the dark parking lot, Jagger looked hot.

"Obviously, but why did you come here anyway?" Evaleen asked glaring at Edgar. I thought she was mad but the way she stared at his chest, I realized the heat of her gaze wasn't anger.

I glanced over at Aria, who was already making out with Alex.

"Emma Hawthorne has escaped," Jagger said.

Aria and Alex stopped kissing.

"What? But how?" Aria said as she walked up to Jagger.

"I don't know. But, I got a call tonight from my old partner at the agency, and he said she had escaped. I was afraid you ladies might be in danger."

"Alex. I think you should stay with me tonight," Aria said as she slipped her fingers into his.

"Being her son, it's best you two lay low for a while." Jagger turned toward them.

"But the rehearsal dinner is tomorrow, and the wedding is the next day. That's impossible," Evaleen pointed out.

"Whatever needs to get done, I'll take over. Aria, Alex, you stay in your home as much as possible. Emma wouldn't come after me. I only met her once for about five minutes. She probably doesn't even remember who I am," I said.

Jagger's jaw ticked as he turned to me. "No. You and David should stay in a hotel room. I want everyone to lay low."

"But things have to get done for the wedding and Emma doesn't know, nor care about anything involving me. I can help out," I said pushing my hands onto my hips.

Jagger groaned, pinching the bridge of his nose. "She knows you, Tiffany. That woman knows everything about any person she has come in contact with, and even people she hasn't."

"Jagger's right. She's my mother, but I wouldn't put it past her to use you in some way. If she thinks you can help her, she will find your weakness and use it to her advantage," Alex said.

"Then what should we do? We can't postpone the wedding. There are relatives of Henrik's that are flying in from Baltimore tomorrow," I said.

"Let's ask Henrik if we can at least move the rehearsal dinner. If Emma was planning to show up there for her son, then we can buy some time by switching the location. Where's Henrik?" Jagger glanced around the parking lot.

"He's still inside with Morgana. I think Morgana's mom and grandma are in there too. I'll go get them," Aria said.

Everyone moved toward the limo while Aria went back into the club. It wasn't long before she was back out without Henrik, Morgana, Annette, and Morgana's grandma.

"Where are they?" Jagger asked.

Aria, with a smirk on her face, threw her thumb over her shoulder. "Henrik's done the full Monty. Morgana's mom is hiding in the bathroom and I don't think a crowbar will remove Morgana's grandma from watching the show."

TWENTY-SIX

Jagger

"That was awful," Tiffany said as she flopped back on the bed.

Only moments ago, we had come back from the club after collecting Henrik and Morgana. Tiffany and I took a detour to pick up David at Diego's place. He was upset that he couldn't spend the night with his friend like they planned, but Tiffany wanted to keep her son near.

Alex rented one of the upper floors of the Bluff Hotel on the Magnificent Mile for everyone. David even got his own room adjacent to Tiffany's.

I'm standing in her room willing myself to leave. Alex got me my own room, but as I watched Tiffany squirm around on that bed, I hesitated. Her dark, lush hair against the crisp white bedspread inspired lurid thoughts and compelled my eyes to travel her body.

"I don't think we were that bad," I said as I watched her roll to her side, propping her head in hand.

"I mean finding out Alex's mom escaped. How are Morgana and Henrik supposed to enjoy their day knowing a crazy woman is on the loose and gunning for their friends?"

I took a step closer. Tiffany hadn't noticed, as she was lost in thought. I inched farther until I was sitting on the edge of the bed.

"Emma Hawthorne is probably long gone by now. When criminals, especially rich and powerful ones like Alex's mom, escape from prison, they flee to another country. She's probably in Europe or somewhere in Asia by now."

Tiffany sat up and came to the edge of the bed next to me. She twisted and bit her bottom lip as I stared. "You're probably right. I just worry, you know?"

A small chuckle escaped my lips. "Yeah, I know. You care, Tiffany. I hope they know how lucky they are to have someone like you to care for them."

I would feel like the luckiest guy in the world if Tiffany saw me the way she saw her friends.

"Who? My friends?"

"Yes." I nodded as I dared to reach out to her thigh, placing my hand on the bit of skin that poked out from her pink skirt above her knee. "I wish I had someone who was as concerned about me the way you are for them."

"I care about you, Jagger."

Her hair had fallen, covering the side of her face so I lifted my fingers to pull it back, rolling a few strands between my thumb and finger. It's soft. She's soft.

I let the strands fall, along with my eyes.

"But you regret—"

"I regret marrying you, yes. But you left before I could explain myself."

When Tiffany turned her head, her eyes glittered with something that refused to let me go.

"I don't know you, Jagger. I regret marrying a man I didn't know. For risking my life, even my son's future, by doing something so foolish.

And even now as we sit here, I still don't understand who you really are."

She was right. I had spent much of my working life—first as a CIA agent and then as part of the ITA—keeping people away. Because if anyone got close, they would ask questions. And my job didn't allow me to answer them.

"Maybe I was afraid you wouldn't want to stick around when you found out who I really was."

Maybe I let my job protect me from letting people into my life. My skin tightened in the best way as Tiffany's fingers combed through my hair. Thoughts of wrapping myself around her and letting her warmth ease away reality filled my head. In the end, I settled for kicking off my shoes.

"Jagger, life is so much more beautiful and so much more terrible than most people can fathom. We can't help what it throws at us, but we can choose to stop running. I think I ran for a long time by declining any extra help. I don't know how many times my neighbor or Henrik, over the years, would ask to watch David so I could have some moments to myself. Almost every time I said no." Tiffany wiped away a tear.

"I felt guilty. That it should have been me in that car and not my husband. Or, I should have insisted he wait to get a Christmas tree when I was feeling better so we could go as a family. Or the millions of other arresting thoughts I had in the last ten years. All excuses for what a terrible mother, a terrible person, I was. I didn't deserve to be happy. I certainly don't deserve to have a man like you want to be with someone like me."

I grabbed her wrist and pushed the palm of her hand to my lips, I flicked my eyes to hers before brushing it with a kiss.

"You deserve so much, Tiffany. You are worthy of all that is good and sweet and body tingling and anything that can produce that beautiful smile." I pointed to her lips as they began to curl.

Sighing, I reached under my shirt and pulled the ring out from underneath, removing it from my neck.

"He was a coward. My father." I held up the ring but focused on Tiffany. "*Honor always. Protect fully. Love forever.* Was a lie he told my mother, me, his sister, and anyone he came in contact with. He used his position in the government to get what he wanted. If he desired a woman, he got her, whether she wanted him or not."

Bile rose in my throat but I swallowed it back. "He told me once that when a woman sees a man with power, they will always want him. Even if they say no, they mean yes. Unfortunately, he didn't like that my mother said no to him too many times."

My eyes never wavered as I said, "My mother died when I was six. She had a blood clot from an untreated concussion when she fell down the stairs. Fell or pushed, it was all the same to my father."

"Oh, Jagger. I'm so sorry." She cupped my cheek and I slipped my hand over hers.

"He even convinced his sister to use tough love on her son, like he did on me. My cousin, Ben, was David's age when he died of dehydration and malnutrition. My father insisted that Ben could do a lot of things, like walk and talk. That he was disrespectful and lazy. Ben had Cerebral Palsy."

The lump in my throat grew, and it took a minute for me to continue. I turned my head, unable to watch her tears. I never told anyone this, not even Dr. Randy.

"He couldn't walk or talk. He might have if my aunt had ignored my father and taken Ben to the right doctors and therapists. But she didn't. They threw her in jail, and my father dismissed it. Told the police he tried to help Ben, which was a lie. Then it all finally came out—what happened to my mother, to Ben, because of my father . . . The fucking coward died of a heart attack just before the trial."

I turned my body toward Tiffany, bringing my leg up on the bed. "That's why I started to work as an agent for the government. My father was protected, being high up in the government. But someone like me could help take him down. These sick people—like my dad, like Emma Hawthorne—truly believe what they are doing is right. They don't understand how many lives they've ruined to justify their view of the world."

"That was your father. You can't help who your father was," Tiffany said as she rested her forehead against mine.

"I was ten, but I could have taken Ben away from that."

"How? You were a child."

I pushed off the bed and stood over Tiffany. "He was almost half my weight. When the police walked in, they thought he was seven years old. He was twelve. I could have lifted him out of that bed and ran away with him."

My body began to shake. "I could have saved him." I shut my eyes for they burned. Everything was hot and consuming. I wanted to rip the world apart and never put it back together again.

And that's when Tiffany stopped me. She wrapped me in her arms and held on. No matter how much I trembled or what I said or how loud I yelled, she clung to me.

"I love you, Jagger. I want you to know that. Right here, in this spot, you are so loved. And your cousin Ben, he loves you too. Because you were the one person in his life that cared. Caring isn't always wanted or pretty, but it's forever needed."

We stayed like that for several minutes. My body eased as I listened to her breathing. The tension slipped away as exhaustion took over. And regret, so much regret. I fell into it.

My knees buckled, and I wrapped my arms around her legs. She was blurry from my tears as I gazed up at her, but even then, she was beautiful.

"I'm sorry. I'm so sorry," I whispered over and over.

Because I was. I was sorry that I cowered for so long, never letting anything go. I hid from the world in plain sight.

"Don't be sorry, Jagger." She slid her fingers through my hair.

"Then, thank you. Thank you." I got up and pulled her into my arms.

"No need to thank me, either. I meant everything I said." She took my hand and guided me to the bed. "Here, let's lie down. It's been a rough night. I think we've done enough talking for one day."

She pulled back the covers and we slid in next to each other. Tiffany put her back to me, curling into my body. This was all I needed. To feel her warmth, smell her sweet scent, and hear the soothing rhythm of her breath.

It didn't take long for the both of us to drift off to sleep. For the first time in many years, I fell into a deep, restful slumber.

TWENTY-SEVEN

Tiffany

"Love? Really, Tiffany?" I said to myself in the mirror of the hotel bathroom.

I was naked. Having just taken a shower, I felt it the perfect time to dissect the night before when I told Jagger that I loved him.

"You must have been high on strip club fumes," I said to the mirror as I grabbed the tiny complimentary toothbrush and swiped on some toothpaste.

Shoving the brush into my mouth, I pointed my finger in the air. "One, you have known him for just over a month."

I scrubbed my teeth before spitting and putting up another finger. "Two, he's jobless. Which, before that, he was a government agent that did classified stuff that involved taking down powerful criminals. Which is good for our country but bad when it comes to a safe, dependable mate."

After wiping my face and pulling a brush through my hair, I held up my third finger. "Jagger has lied to me in the past. While I can overlook the other things, as time would take care of number one and number two has been wiped out from him not working for the government anymore. Number three is sticky."

I walked over to the bathroom door to open it but turned to my reflection once more. "And I hate being sticky."

Jagger had gotten up early this morning and left. I knew because I heard him leave. I pretended to be asleep and listened to him stumble around trying to find his shoes. Once he was gone, I sat up in bed realizing I made a terrible mistake.

I never should have said I loved him. It's not that I didn't feel that for him, because I did. It may have been over ten years since I felt that twisty, heart thundering explosion that love for another man does to my body, but I could recognize it the moment it happened.

When he opened up last night, all I wanted to do was resurrect his father so I could punch him in the balls. I wanted to hold Jagger and kiss him and never stop. That's when I knew.

I stupidly got swept up in that moment, letting my heart spill it all for him. And maybe it helped him get through his grief last night. For that I am glad, but last night isn't today. What about tomorrow or all the days after?

It's out there, and I can't take it back. I can't unravel my heart and pick out the burgeoning love that thrives in his eyes as they sweep down my body. Or gain strength from his fingers as they curl into mine so I can push him away. And when Jagger says my name, it's as if I hadn't realized I wasn't breathing until that moment.

Just because I felt this way didn't mean it should happen.

Nothing about this was safe. Even the smallest risk could crack a life in two. My heart may suffer and yes, the guilt of telling him how I felt will eat away at me when I take it all back. But this can't go on. We can't go on.

I stepped out of the bathroom and came to a full stop when a pair of green eyes grew wide, darkened, and focused on my chest.

"Jagger. You came back," I said like an idiot who was naked and only a foot away from a fully clothed man.

The way his gaze swept my body held me captive. I should have turned around and ran back into the bathroom, but I didn't.

"Yes. I guess I should have called. I went home to change but wanted to return before you woke."

My nakedness was glaring. But we talked like two normal people where one happened to be without clothing.

"I might not have heard you if you were to call, as I was in the shower." I nodded and thought putting my hand on my hip would make the situation less awkward.

It didn't.

"Are you cold?" he asked.

Not at all. I thought I might pass out from the heat traveling up my neck. Worried that any moment I would move my arms and an ocean of sweat would flood the room.

"It's just that . . ." He stepped closer and brushed his finger across my intensely erect nipple.

I shook my head trying to ward off the flood of pleasure that came from his touch. When I opened my mouth to deny him, what escaped was a mistake. The moan that came out was so wrong.

I shouldn't be naked. My body needed to stop reacting to his fingers. And I had to start forming words. Words to stop this. Words to end us.

But I couldn't find them so I moved. My feet inched backward but the man followed.

"And you have goose bumps all over. You must be freezing." Jagger slipped his hands around my back, pulling me flush against his hard body preventing me from taking another step away from him.

God, everything about him was hard. I wanted to rub myself against all that was firm on him. Especially what was hiding beneath his pants.

No, Tiffany. Stay strong.

Holding up my hands, I tried to push away and I was successful. It felt like a gulf was between us and my spine straightened with the strength I had been seeking. But when I looked down there was barely an inch between us.

I should have kept my head down or turned and ran back into the bathroom. But my feet wouldn't move. So, I held up my hands to push him away again but this time my fingers curled into his shoulders, pulling him down. When Jagger's lips slid over mine, any fight I had was gone.

His fingers curled into my hair which made me do the same, but when he groaned, everything changed. I had forgotten why it was so important to stop him, to run away from him. As much as I feared it before, it all melted into a deep want.

But then he stopped. Jagger pulled away. I knew as he closed his eyes taking gulps of air, he was warring with himself, just as I had in the bathroom.

"I came back here to tell you something. And before this can go any further, I need to let it out." His eyes opened and reality began to fall back into place.

"I've been thinking about what you said to me last night."

"Jagger, you were in pain and I wanted to help you. Don't worry about—"

"No." He cupped my head and with a deep breath he continued, "I was in love."

Tears were prickling at the corner of my eyes, and I didn't know whether to push my lips back onto his or run back into the bathroom and lock the door.

"I had been falling for you from the first moment I met you, back in Vegas. Maybe that's why I didn't immediately track you down and get a divorce. The way you looked at me . . . it was different."

He stood a little taller and swallowed. "I wasn't the relationship type, and maybe women could sense that because I never had trouble finding a woman who wanted anything more from me than sex. And then you took my hand and we danced and you proposed."

He chuckled before continuing, "And I wanted that. I think I was lonely at first but the more we talked, the more you wanted me. I told you my real name that night. I even mentioned a few things about my father. But nothing I said stopped you from gazing at me as if you only wanted to know even more about me. You saw me as fascinating, and I saw you as the best thing that could have ever happened to me.

"Please, whatever happens, know that I love you," he said.

"I do. I love you," I whispered kissing his cheeks and his neck and pulling at his shirt.

It didn't take long for him to take his clothes off but it felt like forever. His fingers slipped between my legs after he pushed me back onto the bed and I wondered why we hadn't done this the moment I walked out of the bathroom.

When his head slipped down until I could only see his shaggy brown hair, I gasped and prayed David was sound asleep. My mouth was going to wake him, I knew it. I pressed my teeth onto my fist, fighting Jagger's tongue. That was his secret weapon.

That tongue, when it slipped and flicked my clit, while his fingers pumped into me, it had to be magic. Because I came. Was it seconds or minutes? I had no idea because time seemed to melt over on itself.

"I need you," I said as I sat up and pulled his arm.

He grabbed his jeans and managed to find a condom. But he was taking too long. I pushed him back and ripped that foil apart like a pro, even though it had been a long time since I opened one.

When I rolled the latex over his dripping cock, I pushed my legs to either side of him, ready to mount. Jagger's nails, as they gripped my hips, felt sharp and needy. I slowly eased my way onto him—rocking back and forth, inch by desperate inch.

Until I was lost. The sounds of grunts and skin slapping filled the air and I wondered if anything sounded sweeter. He captured my nipple in his mouth as I leaned forward. I thought it was all I needed until that sneaky spy slipped his finger down to brush my clit.

Over and over, his tongue, his finger, his thick cock. I was chasing some body-tingling wave and Jagger was helping.

He was *really* good at helping.

"I'm going to come," Jagger said as he released my breast.

His finger faltered so I replaced it with my own. I watched him come undone as I let my climax roll over me. Jagger cursed his undoing, and I begged for only him.

I collapsed on top of him, our bodies slippery and spent.

Even as he was regaining his breath and I could still feel the tremors between my legs, he pulled me to the side, turning to kiss me. The kisses were lazy but bursting with serenity.

"I'm glad you came back." My voice rough as I traced my fingers over his damp chest.

"I'm glad I married you," he said.

My lips curled. "Well, now that I know you, I'm glad I married you too."

He could hear the hesitation in my voice.

"Tiffany, you know I won't ever let anything happen to you or your son. I'm afraid you are stuck with the most well-trained ninja at your side for as long as you'll have me."

He was right. Anything could happen to David or me. That was glaringly obvious when a week and a half ago someone attacked me in broad daylight. Jagger saved me. He stopped the guy so he couldn't hurt anyone else.

I wanted a man that could protect my son, and well, it looks like I got my wish.

"Is that a promise?" I asked bringing my finger to his lips.

"It's more than a promise. It's a fact."

TWENTY-EIGHT

Jagger

Tiffany was beautiful when she had a bit of beef sliding down her chin.

"Is it there?" She pointed to the opposite side of her chin where no beef could be found.

"No, maybe I should lick it off. Seems a waste to wipe away perfectly good steak," I said dabbing my white cloth napkin to the corner of my mouth.

Her eyes widened as she glanced around the restaurant. We sat at the end of a long table. Next to us was Henrik's cousin and his wife. His wife leaned over to Tiffany.

"He does have a point. This meat is tender." The woman with the long black hair winked at Tiffany.

"Jos, maybe you let her decide," her husband said shaking his head.

"Pierce, I'm just helping with their problem. And the food is really good. When we visit Chicago in the future, we'll have to come back here."

The steak suffered the most in all this as Tiffany tackled it with a napkin to her chin.

"There, it's gone. Problem solved." Tiffany turned slightly in her chair, giving Jos more of her back.

And what a beautiful back it was. Creamy, and having licked it earlier today, I knew it was the perfect mix of sweet and salty.

Tiffany's jade dress was almost backless, giving everyone a view of her flawless skin.

"You're beautiful." I put my elbow on the table and rested my chin on my hand gazing over at her.

"The meat is now on your cheek," Jos said pointing to her own cheek for location.

"Excuse me." Tiffany got up and walked toward the restrooms in the back while cupping her cheek.

I watched her hips twist as she danced around the tables on her way toward the back.

"She's so graceful," I said.

"You're a lucky man," Jos said.

I smiled at the woman. "I am."

They seemed nice. We had talked earlier just before the food was served at the rehearsal dinner. Me, along with Alex, managed to find a restaurant in Humboldt Park. Alex arranged to close the restaurant for the night, and I scoped out the place until I was sure it was safe.

I glanced over at the table close to the door, where David sat with some little kids. One being Pierce and Jos's little boy. I thought David wouldn't want to hang with small kids, but he's having fun making them laugh.

It felt like for the first time in my life everything was falling into place. Even the white lie I told Tiffany this morning was for a surprise I wanted to show her on Monday.

I told her I went home to change, which was true, but I also had a meeting to sign a lease for a building I'm renting. It's perfect. There are two floors. The bottom floor has a large window facing the street which can be used for my ninja gym, and the top floor is a small two-bedroom apartment.

When I asked her to move in with me, I meant it. Even though we haven't known each other long, I can't imagine not being with Tiffany.

My phone vibrated in my pants pocket. Lifting it, I noticed it was from Tenn.

"Hey, Tenn. Any news on Emma?"

"I'm outside," he said.

"What?"

"The restaurant. I'm in the alley next to the restaurant you're in," he said.

How did he know I was here? Then I remembered that he still worked for ITA. I'm sure I was being followed from the moment I left that job.

"I'll be right there."

I ended the call, shoved the phone back into my pocket, and made my way toward the front door. As I passed one of the tables, I felt something sharp dig into my ass. Turning, I noticed Morgana's grandmother smirk at me.

"I had to check to see if the buns were warm." She winked.

The only reason the woman was getting away with that was because she's related to the bride.

I picked up my pace to get to Tenn quickly and away from lecherous hands. He was just on the other side of the building, leaning against the brick.

"She's here," Tenn said.

I turned around in a circle taking in our surroundings. "Where?"

"No, in the city. I thought Emma would have left Chicago. I'm surprised she didn't leave the country, but she's here."

"Why would she stay here?"

Tenn's jaw tightened.

"What aren't you telling me, Tenn?"

My throat tensed, my hands fisted, and I knew what Tenn was about to share wasn't going to put a smile on my face.

"She mentioned, when I asked her a few questions last week, something about a wedding. I thought she was talking about how she tried to force her son to marry that the Dorton woman. But, I think she might be talking about Payne's wedding." He pointed at the brick wall that separated us from the rehearsal dinner party inside.

Rubbing my forehead, I fought like hell to stop myself from punching that brick wall. Because that would be stupid, not to mention it would require a trip to the emergency room. But I felt like being stupid. I wanted to run around the city like a madman and search every crevasse for the deranged Emma Hawthorne.

"The venue will have to be changed," I said as I lowered my hands and leaned against the wall.

"Can you make that happen in such a short period of time?" Tenn crossed his arms, challenging me.

I may be a disgraced ex-agent, but I could still help take down a wanted criminal.

"Of course. I'll go back inside and get Henrik. He may not like this, but I don't think he would want to endanger his guests. It's either that or cancel the wedding."

My heart hammered in my ears, and I tried to suppress the bubbling excitement from showing on my face as I asked Henrik to follow me outside. This felt like old times. Perhaps I gave up the spy thing too easily. Maybe walking away from it for a short time was just what I needed.

"Where are you two going?" I heard Tiffany's voice from behind me.

Turning, I remembered why I wanted to stay away from the government. The one thing that was always missing from my life and made each day harder to do without was love.

I was lost in a sea of adventure. That can be dazzling although it can't last. But Tiffany? She would always be in my heart.

"I need to discuss the wedding tomorrow with Henrik, outside," I said and turned to go.

It wasn't until we were on the sidewalk that I realized Tiffany had followed me.

"I need to discuss this alone with Henrik."

Totally ignoring me, Tiffany pointed at Tenn. "Who's that?"

"My old partner. He has news about Emma. I'm afraid we need to discuss this—" I threw my arms in the air as I wondered why I even bothered to open my mouth.

Tiffany walked around me and stuck out her hand. "Hi, I'm Tiffany."

"Hello, Tiffany. It's nice to meet you. I'm Tenn. I used to work with Jagger."

She nodded and glanced at me for a second before turning back to Tenn. "Did you know about what he did? About the whole," she made a circular motion with her finger, "at my place."

Tenn's eyes flickered to me before gazing down at the ground. Did he know what she was talking about? Because I didn't.

"Yes, but I told him to get rid of the listening devices at your place. And, as I told Jagger, I didn't tell our boss that he spied on you. Someone else must have said something," Tenn said with a glimmer of something in his eyes.

Did he think he was helping with that? Because he wasn't.

My eyes widened and it was like slow motion. I tried to reach out for Tiffany and tell Tenn to shut up, but my body was too slow for me.

"Spy on me?" Tiffany turned, and it was painful to see the hurt and confusion that filled her eyes. "You actually planted spy equipment inside my apartment?"

"Oh, shit," Tenn said.

Oh, shit was right. When I was done groveling to Tiffany, I was going to kill Tenn.

I waved my hands around. "It was my fault."

"Damn right it was your fault." She pushed her hands onto her hips. "You're a flippin' spy for gosh darn sake. Even I know it's against the law to spy on someone without a warrant. Or, did you get that? Maybe made up another lie. Something about me being a bad mother and you needed to make sure I wasn't spreading my terrible parenting skills to the rest of the country."

"You are not a terrible mother." I took a deep breath as I prepared to put myself in a position to get thrown in jail. "And, no, I didn't have a warrant. What I did was completely illegal."

She stepped closer to me, and I could see the tears stream down her face like I had turned on a faucet that might never shut off. "I trusted you. Was that all a lie? Did you tell me those things because you heard me talk about how I wanted someone to love my son and me? That I wanted a man I would feel safe with. Did you spy on me to get that information and use it to have sex with me?"

"What?" Henrik said.

"No, Tiffany." I gazed around to see one man with guilt in his eyes and another with venom. "Can we go somewhere to discuss this in private?"

"Are you kidding me?" Tiffany said with an octave that could shatter glass. "I don't ever want to be alone with you again. How can I trust you? Don't come near me again."

My heart felt like a million knives were slicing away—sliver by agonizing sliver—as I watched the woman I love walk away. She stopped just before she turned out of the alley, gazing back with thunder in her eyes.

"I made a mistake with you. A scary mistake that once this divorce comes through, I will never repeat again." Within a second, she was gone.

I took a step forward but fingers curling around my shoulder stopped me.

"Don't," he said, and I was too far removed to know if it was Henrik or Tenn.

For I was floating, hovering with my senses so raw there was a hum. A vibration in my ears and my skin felt like it would fly away. Nothing made sense until something hard hit me on my jaw. I fell back to earth with a pain exploding up my face and into my eyes.

I looked over to find Henrik gritting his teeth and shaking out his hand. "You stay the fuck away from her."

"Come on, man. We have more important things to discuss like the safety of your wedding," Tenn said turning to Henrik and pushing him back.

I got up and shook off the hit knowing I deserved it. I almost wanted to thank Henrik. That blow finally made everything so clear.

"You do need to talk about the wedding. You need to focus on your fiancée and your guests. Talk to Tenn to figure out if you can come up with a different venue. Don't worry about me. You won't be seeing me anymore," I said and made my way up the alley, across the street, and toward the L-train to go home.

I was foolish to think that I deserved love. That I earned someone that was like a quake to my heart and shone brighter than any sun.

TWENTY-NINE

Tiffany

"What a view," Evaleen said standing next to me as we looked out over Lake Michigan. The water was a beautiful tropical blue and dotted with white sailboats.

I frowned. "Gorgeous. But, Henrik always did have great taste. Too bad he doesn't live here anymore."

"But Dixon does." She nudged my shoulder with hers.

I nodded. It should be a happy day, full of smiles yet everything felt like dry toast. Henrik managed to find another place for the wedding, which happened to be his old condo that had a spectacular view of Lake Michigan. Aria was more than happy to help out, as she was the one who currently owned his old place.

"Yup. She sure does. Kudos to her," I said leaning my head on the glass before taking a deep breath.

"Hey. What's wrong?" Evaleen's placed her hand on my back.

"Jagger. I made a mistake. He wasn't the man I thought he was."

Not that I knew much about him until two days ago. That should have been clue number one. A man who refuses to let you inside until after you've fooled around with him, that's not a good sign.

"I drunkenly married him in Vegas and he took a month and a half to inform me about it. Then he lied about being a physical therapist, taking advantage of me and my son. As if that wasn't enough, Jagger spied on me. Like, he actually planted listening devices inside of my apartment. All to gather information so he could lure me in to bed." I rubbed my neck.

Evaleen sighed. "You found out about him spying on you?"

With tremendous surprise, my breath caught and for a moment I couldn't speak.

I lifted my head, shaking out a cough. "You knew?"

She nodded. "I can't tell you much, but just know that I've spoken to his old partner a few times. Jagger is a good guy. He really is, but he fucked up. He knows it, I know it, and everyone can agree to that."

"What do you mean you can't tell me? Did he swear you to secrecy?" My ears burned with anger and wonder, that so many people, friends I trusted, were deceiving me.

"No, it's not that. He doesn't even know that I found out about it." She took a deep breath, glancing around the room before leaning into me, "I took a job recently. Nothing super-secret like Jagger, but it is with the government."

My head went back as I let her words sink in. "Does Edgar know?"

She nodded.

"Okay, I won't ask you anymore about it. But you are right about Jagger, he did fuck up," I groaned.

"Fear is a powerful thing. It can cloud judgment and make people do crazy things, believing that what they're doing is for the best." Evaleen stared out at the view for a moment as she pursed her lips.

"I guess that's true." A warmth crawled up my neck as memories of me trying to talk David out of the surgery that ultimately gave him the ability to walk and communicate with greater ability.

I was scared. There was a risk he wouldn't make it and I couldn't take losing him too. And when he fell into a coma after the surgery, I feared the worst. I said and did things during that time that I regret.

Glancing over at Edgar fixing Henrik's bowtie, I can't help but think how I almost ruined Henrik's chance with Morgana. All because my fear allowed me to assume the worst in everything.

"This is your life and you have David to think about, but I really wanted you to know that one bad action doesn't make the man," Evaleen said.

She was right, but Jagger went too far. What he did wasn't just creepy, it was an invasion of privacy. I was about to explain that to Evaleen when Aria came up behind us.

"I think Morgana needs you, Evaleen," Aria said.

They went off to the back bedroom where Morgana was finishing getting ready or as Aria put it, "being held."

I turned toward the guys and smiled at the skinny one with a mop of brown hair sitting on one of the white fold out chairs in the front row. His long fingers fidgeted with something in his hand.

The place was cleared of Aria's furniture and filled with people sitting in folding chairs, excited chatter, and flowers. Henrik, Edgar, and the minister stood in front of the massive stone fireplace that was in the corner of the room. I moved closer and sat next to David.

My breath caught in my throat at how handsome my son looked.

"What do you have there?" I asked and fought the urge to run my fingers through his hair to get it under control.

He was nervous about today. David wanted to make Henrik proud and not have to sit during the ceremony. I told him Henrik would be proud of him no matter what, but David insisted he do this. He also insisted on shaving despite not having a bit of scruff on his chin.

"Just something I found at home a few weeks ago. It must have fallen off that old blender you threw away. I've been keeping it in my pocket as something to fidget with. And it has a sleek design. I might draw it."

David sighed examining the small object. "I figured I'd need as much help today as possible. It's sort of soothing, at least for me, to play with it."

I still couldn't help but be impressed with how far he's come with communication. What he just said to me came out clear as day and without any delay. My mind wondered how he would be this time next year. Would he even need his therapists anymore?

"That would be cool. Maybe you could add it to your comic. Some special device the hero has to use to catch the bad guys."

David groaned, "Bad guys? Come on, Mom. I write about cyber mutated creatures that are both good and bad. It's the twenty-first century. Nothing is black and white anymore."

"Sorry. I was just trying to help. Oh wait . . ." I looked around as I heard the music begin. "I think the wedding's about to start. You better get up there."

I offered a hand to David, but he waved it away, determined to do everything by himself. Once he stood, he took his phone out of his pocket and my eyes widened.

"Shut that thing off. Here, give it to me." I tried to reach for it but he held it away.

"No. I'll shut it off, but I want to get pics after the ceremony."

"Fine. But put it away."

He shoved everything in his suit pockets. I was thankful for once that my boy was as skinny as a bean pole and his tuxedo trousers hung off him. At least all the stuff in his pockets wouldn't be obvious.

David got into place and I snuck out my phone from my clutch and snapped a few pictures of him standing proud next to Edgar and Henrik.

I turned in my seat and watched Aria and Evaleen in a tentative stride walk down the middle of the aisle of chairs. They looked beautiful in matching long, pale pink dresses.

But when Morgana entered, everyone went quiet. As she began to move with her arm intertwined with her father's, we all stood. Morgana looked radiant, and I placed my hand over my heart as I watched the smile on her face.

She glowed in that dress with its plunging V-neck and white lace ball gown. It seemed to be made for her and accentuated her beauty. She didn't wear a veil and I didn't blame her. It would have covered the pretty flowers in her striking red hair.

When I glanced up at Henrik, I had to hold back a giggle. He looked to be in some sort of trance as he watched her. They really were perfect for each other.

Once we sat, after Morgana kissed her father's cheek and took Henrik's arm, I watched as Morgana's big, burly dad wiped a tear from his eye.

The ceremony flew by and before I realized it, the minister was asking the crowd if anyone would object to Morgana and Henrik marrying.

"I do." A woman's deep voice rose from the crowd.

There were gasps and my eyes flew to Morgana's grandmother. In fact, everyone was looking at her.

"I swear I didn't say a word." Her grandmother held up her hands.

"It was me." I turned completely around, and toward the back row stood a woman with a wide light green hat with flowers flowing off the side. She seemed familiar and then I realized, too late, who she was.

She walked toward the front, but as the men stood to block her path down the center aisle, she turned and came up the side until she was standing next to my son.

"It's time for my son to finally get married to the right woman," Emma Hawthorne said.

I stood and tried to move toward David, but Emma Hawthorne had other plans. She took a gun from her purse and as she wrapped her arm around David, she pointed it to his head.

"No! No, please. Don't," I screamed and held out my hands.

"Stop this, Mother. If you want me to go with you, then here I am. Let the boy go." Alex's voice came from behind me but I refused to turn my attention away from my son.

"Of course, you'll come with me, Alex. But to make sure no one follows us, I'll be taking this kid as protection."

Alex leaned over and whispered in my ear, "I'll make sure nothing happens to him. I promise."

My body trembled as I helplessly watched the woman push my son down the aisle and toward the elevator in the back. I broke through the crowd to follow but stopped a few feet away.

"I would advise no one follow us. That includes you too, mommy dearest," Emma said turning toward me with my son in her arms.

Just as they got on the elevator my son looked up at me and said, "It's okay, Mom. Don't worry about me."

The doors closed and I crumbled to the ground. I think I screamed but everything felt like a horrible nightmare with parts missing. Cleaved from my soul because if I could feel everything, remember it all, it would destroy me.

I knew I was sobbing but I wasn't conscious of the words coming out of my mouth.

"Tiffany. Tiffany, let's get you up." Evaleen was helping me up onto a chair.

"We have to stop her. Where's Tenn?" I said as I glanced around the room.

"We're on this. Don't worry. I promise to get your son back safely," Evaleen said and glanced up at Edgar.

He came over to the other side, taking off his tuxedo jacket and wrapping it around my shoulders.

"But how can you help?" I reached out and grabbed her hands. "You're pregnant. It's not safe. Edgar, tell her it's not safe here."

"Tiffany is right. Once you make the call, I want you to leave, Evaleen. Who knows what that crazy woman has planned."

Evaleen stood and folded her arms. "I will go but I want to make sure everyone is here that can help."

I gazed around, only now realizing a wedding was ruined and other people were affected by that woman.

"Where's Aria?" I asked.

"Henrik took her back to one of the bedrooms and is helping her. I think Morgana's in the bathroom, probably grabbing tissues," Edgar said as he eyed the room.

"Jagger?" Evaleen asked and my eyes shot up to her as she held her phone to her ear.

"Where are you?" She paused for a moment. "You're needed here, at Aria's place. There's a wedding that's been interrupted by a Jewel. Yes, that Jewel."

I didn't realize I was squeezing Edgar's hands until I heard him groan.

"Sorry." I let go as he winced.

"I don't care if you aren't an agent anymore. You are needed here. Tenn obviously botched this up and she got in. Jagger, you have to come here. Yes, you are wanted."

I stood and took the phone away from Evaleen and pushed it to my ear. "Jagger, please. She took David."

It was all I could get out before my throat tightened and a sob took over. But I heard him before I dropped the phone.

THIRTY

Jagger

"Fuck the sun," I said just before I moved a thin sheet of plywood in front of the grimy window.

It was a bright day with low humidity. Some would say a flawless late summer Chicago day. People were out walking and enjoying the beautiful weather. A perfect day to crash a wedding.

I think I ended up coming home to my old apartment around three in the morning. I would have stayed out all night, walking each street until I found Emma Hawthorne, if I hadn't tripped and fallen. My knee hurt but not enough to quit. But the blood gushing from it made me realize it was wiser to start again once the sun came up—and after I bandaged up my leg.

When I got up this morning and had some coffee, punched a few holes in my old apartment's wall, I got my old tuxedo on with the full intention of inviting myself to Henrik and Morgana's wedding. If Emma was still in Chicago, I knew she would be near that ceremony and I wasn't about to let her get away.

But then I realized I didn't even know where the new location for the ceremony was being held. And, I had no way of finding out. I wasn't an agent anymore. Perhaps, I could head over to the original location of the ceremony to see if Emma Hawthorne was around. But first, I came to my new place to drop off a few boxes.

That's when Tiffany moved into my head and refused to leave. Seeing all those happy people walking on the sidewalk, especially the couples, just heightened the fact of how much I messed up.

I could be at that wedding with her, protecting her and watching David with pride. Instead, I let my fear plant little devices in her place which caused me to get fired and lose her.

I chuckled to myself, it's like I wanted to fuck up my life so bad that no one would be left in it. It's not like I could help my mom when I was little and I still had some guilt for Ben, maybe I wasn't worthy of anyone as wonderful as Tiffany and her son.

I moved to the floor, lying back. Perhaps the rigidity of the floorboards was what I needed. I didn't deserve comfort or warmth.

My pants vibrated and I reached in my pocket to take out my phone. I sighed but answered as I saw who was calling.

"Hi, Evaleen."

"Jagger. Where are you?"

I pushed up onto my elbows. "At my place, why?"

"You're needed here, at Aria's place. There's a wedding that's been interrupted by a Jewel," she said.

That got me to sit up. "What? You mean Emma."

"Yes, that Jewel."

I was ready to hop to my feet and run there when images of Tiffany telling me she never wanted to see me again flickered to light.

"I don't work for the ITA or anywhere in the government, remember?" I said.

"I don't care if you aren't an agent anymore. You are needed here. Tenn obviously botched this up and she got in. Jagger, you have to come here."

I gritted my teeth, refusing to jump just because she said so. "If Tenn fucked up, then that's on him. Everyone has made it quite clear that I'm not wanted."

"Yes, you are wanted."

I stood and began to walk around the room. "Did Katlin tell you to call me? Or maybe Tenn got scared and needed someone used to being in the field. Because I know that—"

There was a shuffling sound and then someone else got on. "Jagger, please. She took David."

I didn't even blink before responding to Tiffany. "I'm on my way."

Shoving the phone into my pocket, I ran out the door. Sweat rolled down my neck but I didn't care as I raced through the streets to find a cab. I offered to pay him more if he got to the wedding location in less than ten minutes.

By the time I made it to the building where Evaleen had texted me the address, only eight minutes had passed. I ran into Tenn just outside. He was also dressed up in a dark suit and tie.

"What happened?" I asked.

"What are you doing here?" he grumbled, and I knew he was beating himself up inside.

He was angry that Emma got through and was now taking it out on me.

"Evaleen called. Said Emma took David."

"Fuck." Tenn ran his fingers through his thick blond hair. "I know. She's still somewhere in there."

He pointed to the building.

"Where's Tiffany?"

Tenn pointed across the street to a coffee shop. I nodded and ran over in no time thanks to the government and police cars blocking the road.

When I opened the door, a bell sounded and everyone in the place looked my way. I only cared about the pair of caramel-colored eyes that held mine.

When I got to her, I fell to my knees. "What happened?"

She covered her face and I knew she was crying. The kind of sob that wracks a body so no sound can escape.

"She was seated at the wedding. In the back. No one noticed her," Edgar said from the other side of the table.

"They haven't left the building, Tiffany. Your boy is still in there. You have to tell me everything you remember from the moment you walked into that building until the moment she took him." I got up, taking the seat next to Tiffany.

The small, rectangular table wobbled as I leaned in. Edgar pushed a paper cup filled with black coffee toward me, but I waved it off. I had plenty of adrenaline to keep me going.

Tiffany started to tell me how she showed up early because David was excited to be the groomsman. She didn't notice anything unusual. The flowers were still being put in place when the first guests arrived. She recognized most of the people from the rehearsal dinner, except for one.

"Who didn't you recognize?" I asked.

"Grace's date. She mentioned she had a date a few weeks ago, but I didn't expect her to bring him to the wedding."

She went on to describe him and I made a mental note to tell Tenn to ask the guy questions.

"I think his name is Will," she said.

"Okay. Were there any items there that looked unusual? Even small things stuck to something. Specifically, small black plastic or metal objects that look like they fell off something or didn't belong."

I wondered if Emma or someone she hired had planted any devices that we might be able to get information from.

Tiffany creased her brow and started to shake her head. "No, I don't think . . . wait." Her eyes widened and she turned to me. "David was fiddling around with something small and black. He said he found it in our apartment though. He thought it fell off a blender I threw away."

"That wouldn't help," I said before the realization smacked me sideways and I had to smile. "No, that does help. I have to go."

I got up but turned before I opened the door. "Tiffany, I promise I will find your son and he will be safe."

She wasn't convinced and I didn't blame her. It's not like I proved to her with my past actions that I'm a trustworthy guy. But with this information, I think I could help get him back. I just hope nothing had happened to David since he was taken.

I ran out of the shop and up to Tenn. He was standing over the front of a car looking at the architectural layout of the building.

"I think I may be able to listen in on Emma," I said slightly out of breath.

He looked up and frowned. "How? We don't even know where she is in there."

I got out my cell and tapped it a few times. I took a deep breath before lifting the phone to my ear. There was silence.

"Fuck," I whispered.

I shook my head realizing I had made a mistake. Just as I was about to lower my phone, I heard it. Faint, but it was there. Sounds of people talking.

Holding the phone out, I handed it to Tenn. He took it and listened. His uncertain eyes began to widen with the realization I had figured out just minutes ago.

"You bugged them?"

"No. It's one of the listening devices I planted in Tiffany's apartment a month ago," I said with a smile.

Tenn straightened but still held the phone up to his ear. "So, they *have* escaped—"

I waved my hands. "No. When I went to sweep for the devices there was one I couldn't find. I had planted it in her kitchen. It must have fallen, and David found it. Tiffany just told me he was fiddling with it before the wedding."

Tenn shook his head. "Even your fuck-ups save people. Let's just hope someone mentions something that will give us a clue as to where they are."

I was itching to grab the phone back and listen, but this wasn't my case. I had to let Tenn take over. He yelled out for a headset and within a minute someone ran up with a pair. I hovered near him for what felt like hours but was probably a few minutes when he finally said something.

"They're in room twelve thirty-two."

I began to move toward the building entrance when a hand grabbed onto my arm. "Where do you think you're going?" Tenn asked.

"To get that kid."

"You don't work for ITA anymore. You know I can't let you inside," Tenn said as his eyes softened.

"I've got to do something, Tenn."

He held up my phone. "You have."

"No, that's not enough. I can't just stand down here and hope these guys don't fuck this up. Because if they do, I have to go over there," I pointed to the café across the street, "and tell a woman who has been through hell and back with her son, that he's gone. I can't do that."

Tenn looked down and wrinkled his forehead. After a few seconds, he shook his head. "There's a fire escape in the back of the building. It only goes to the second floor. But if you get caught—"

"Then I tell them you forbid me from coming in the building but I didn't listen. Like usual," I said with a wink before I took off.

The escape was old and rusted but once I made it down the alley to the back, it was easy to spot. I had to maneuver a dumpster under it to reach up, but once it opened, I made it to the second floor. The door was locked but I knew how to pick a lock from my years going undercover with criminals.

"Thanks, Jonsey," I said with a new appreciation for the best lock pick in the Midwest.

I got inside and immediately took off my coat and bowtie. Rolling up my sleeves, I knew it was going to be a workout making it to the twelfth floor. Especially since the stairwell wasn't air-conditioned.

Old buildings were the worst.

Racing up the stairs until I thought my legs would fall off, I stopped to catch my breath.

"I need to work out more," I wheezed.

When my breathing regulated, I stepped into the hall. Based on the numbers on the doors room 1232 was right around the corner. I moved along the wall and just as I was about to peer around to see if anyone else was there, something hard hit my head.

It felt like an explosion inside my brain and it seemed like I was falling. I saw a pair of black loafers just before I passed out.

THIRTY-ONE

Jagger

"Is he awake?" A woman's voice filled the room.

I tried to open my eyes, but they were heavy and damn, it felt like someone was attacking my head with a baseball bat from the inside.

"He's coming to," a male voice said.

I finally opened my eyes and saw I was in a living room, sparsely decorated with only a few chairs and a cheap white coffee table.

"What is . . ." I trailed off realizing it was harder to speak than open my eyes.

"Oh good. He is awake. Thank you, Will. You've been the most excellent of helpers today." Emma Hawthorne finally came into focus.

I glanced over at her as she handed the guy, Will, an envelope.

"Where's David? And Alex?"

She smiled and it seemed painful.

"I've had Will retrieve your tuxedo jacket and tie from the stairs. There will be a wedding today, just not the one you were invited to," she said.

I looked down and discovered I was once again, wearing my jacket and bowtie.

My head fell back because it was hard to hold it up, but I laughed. I fucked this all up. I wanted to save David and give Tiffany back her smile, and all I did was get myself caught. I wasn't in the building more than five minutes before Emma got me.

It's best I wasn't an agent anymore because apparently, I'm terrible.

"What's so funny about being tied up?" she asked.

I lifted my head and smirked. "Because you are so fucking crazy. You still want to marry your son off to that Dorton woman? Do you really believe he's going to get elected to any office with you as his mother?"

That woman was delusional. She wanted her son to marry into a political dynasty so he could one day become President and get back at the men who hurt her. She's like a crazy ex-girlfriend times a thousand.

"I've given up on the Dortons. Sure, they had some higher-ups in their family, but they're not what they once were. The future is tech. And that's why my son will be marrying a woman who will one day run a very powerful tech company. In fact, the bride is already dressed for her big day."

Shaking my head, I tried to get my brain to focus on anything Emma told ITA when she was caught back in June. Nothing came to mind. The only tech company she tried to mess with was Mimir. But, it's not like Mimir is the leader as an Internet retailer. They're only the third largest.

"Are you talking about Mimir?" I asked as my head wasn't working as quickly as I wanted it to.

"Of course. Now I know what you're thinking, it's not number one. But that's where you're wrong. They made a deal this past spring that happened to propel the company to number one throughout Europe. And, if their numbers are right, they should be the number one online retailer, package delivery service, and employer in almost every country in the world within ten years. Except for the United States. But, with my help, we'll make that happen too."

"But you have money. It's not like you need more."

She shook her head. "Jagger, you government people can't ever think outside the box. What influences the government the most?"

"Rules? Regulations?" I was seriously lost and knew if my head wasn't banged up I would have figured this out by now.

"Wrong. Wrong. Jagger, it's money. The more money a corporation or organization or association—basically, anything that ends with a *T-I-O-N*—has, then the more they can contribute to politicians. Even create special research foundations that make it look like it's trying to do good, but secretly, it's only existence is to influence government officials."

"But that's illegal," I said.

She waved her hand at me. "Not if you do it right. So many loopholes and red tape. People complain about it, but the government doesn't actually want to do anything to change it. I wonder why?" She put her finger on her chin.

"Money," I said with a groan.

"Maybe you aren't as stupid as I thought. With my money and this lady by my side," she waved her hand at Morgana being pulled into the room by Will, "I will make the world a better place. At least, a world where men like my father-in-law can't destroy lives anymore."

Tenn didn't tell me Morgana had been taken.

"You're going to force Morgana to marry Alex?"

Emma pursed her lips as she began fiddling with Morgana's hair. I watched as a woman, on what should have been the happiest day of her life, sobbed in despair.

"She can see her betrothed in secret if she wishes. It's not the 1500s where she'll have her head chopped off for adultery or whatever they did to women back then who didn't submit to men. It's the twenty-first century. It will be an open marriage. Alex can still see Aria and you, my dear," she cupped Morgana's chin, "can still see your Henry."

"Henrik," Morgana said with a hiccup.

"Doesn't matter. Anyway. We need the others brought in." Emma turned to Will.

Once Will left the room, I tried to pull my hands out of whatever I was tied up with. But I soon realized that whoever did it used plastic restraints. I may be good at picking locks, but I wasn't a magician.

Emma pushed Morgana down on the chair next to me.

"Now, wait here. I wouldn't think about escaping. Will isn't the only one I have helping me. As I said, money can pay for anything. Even government officials." She winked at me. "Even former partners."

"Tenn?" I said and shook my head as blood rushed to my ears.

"You didn't think he kept your little spying secret because he was your partner? The juicy tidbit was perfect. I knew once he told his boss what you did, I would no longer have to worry about you."

"But he told me where you were? Even let me get in the building to—"

"To save little David? Aww, how sweet you want to save your wife's son. He informed me the moment you ran for the fire escape to keep an eye out for you. Which was wonderful because now you won't be in our way anymore. And as for your wife, that was a fun twist I never expected to happen. But when you try to drug your son's girlfriend and her friends get drugged by accident, you just have to chalk it up to bad luck."

My brain was starting to work again as all the pieces were falling into place. No wonder Tiffany or Morgana didn't recognize me after Vegas. Emma was trying to drug Aria but got Morgana and Tiffany instead.

"That was you? But I checked those drinks with my special nail polish that can detect date rape drugs," Morgana said.

"Not all. Like I keep telling you both, money can buy lots of things. Even brand-new drugs that haven't gotten FDA approval yet." She patted Morgana on the cheek and then turned to walk down the hall.

I glanced over at Morgana as I heard her weep. "Morgana, can you see if there are any knives or scissors in that little kitchen?"

She lifted her head with a sniffle and nodded. Wiping her nose on her arm she said, "That bitch is going to pay for what she's doing."

Morgana raced over to open the drawers in the kitchen. Luckily, the kitchen was behind us so if anyone came strolling down the apartment hallway, they wouldn't see Morgana.

"It's to cut me loose. Don't try to go after Emma. She has too many people to help her. You wouldn't get very far. But if you get me out, I might be able to help."

"Fine," she said and I could hear the irritation in her voice.

After a minute, she came back with an old battery and a plastic bag.

"I'm not MacGyver," I said.

"There's nothing there. This is all I found."

Shit. I scanned the room and realized anything sharp or anything that could be broken to be used as a sharp object was removed from the room.

"I'll try to do something when the ceremony . . . Wait, your earrings," I said.

Her hands went up to the diamond studs that sparkled on her ears. "What about them?"

I shook my arms. "Try to poke a bunch of holes through the plastic at my wrists. Maybe you can make enough holes that I can pull the restraint apart."

She immediately took off her earrings and got behind me. I remained still as possible to listen for anyone coming down the hall.

"I think I almost got it," she said but when I pulled my wrists apart it still wouldn't break away.

Then I heard something.

"Get back up here. Someone's coming," I said.

Just as Morgana sat back in her seat, Emma strolled into the room with Alex and Will holding a gun to David's head.

"Let the boy go," I said through gritted teeth. A part of me was relieved David didn't appear hurt. The other part was pissed that I couldn't save him.

Emma pointed to David. "He's to make sure you don't try anything."

I felt helpless. No agents were coming to the rescue, Tenn would make sure of that. And I was trapped.

"It's time for the bride." Emma clapped her hands as another man walked into the room.

"The minister's here?" Morgana asked.

"They get paid, don't they?" Emma asked but I was guessing she didn't expect an answer.

Emma arranged her son and Morgana like dolls she was playing with. Will stood closer to the front door with his arm wrapped around David, fingers curled onto his shoulder—the gun never wavered.

I stared into David's eyes trying to will thoughts of comfort to him. He had the same helpless gaze that my cousin had days before his death. Anger welled up inside of me and I decided I couldn't do anything. I was trapped but if I was in David's position, I could easily get out of that hold.

And then I realized I had taught David one thing that could get him out of that hold during one of our sessions.

Emma was arguing with the minister when I nodded at David. He creased his brow, but I directed my eyes to where Will was grasping his shoulder. I held my breath, hoping David would know what I was trying to tell him.

David gazed around the room, but after a few seconds his eyes widened. He quickly reached up and grabbed Wills pinky finger, twisting it completely back. My mouth dropped open in shock and pride as I wondered if that boy had broken the man's finger.

Will screamed and fell to his knees. I don't know how it happened, but when I pulled my arms apart this time the restraint snapped. I jumped to my feet and ran over to David. But Emma was running too.

I dove for the gun and we wrestled. But she's a spoiled rich woman who probably hadn't lifted anything heavier than two pounds of caviar in her life. I easily took the gun from her. She made a break for the door and I shot.

What I hadn't realized was David was next to her. I thought he was behind me and I had pulled the trigger too soon. His eyes widened as I ran to him.

Both of them fell but I only cared about one. The young man that had blood on his shirt.

THIRTY-TWO

Tiffany

"Where are they?" I pleaded for answers for the twentieth time in the last hour.

I kept glancing back at the wall of windows that looked out onto the street. All I could see were police, men and women in suits, and cars parked along the side. No pedestrians and no one driving by. It had been like that for a while.

"I wish I knew," Evaleen said just as her phone buzzed.

She glanced down as her eyes widened. When her head lifted they were focused past me, out the window.

"You got something. What is it?" I asked, grabbing her wrist.

"It's nothing. Just something about a coworker. I'll be right back." She scurried off to the front of the café and I watched her put her phone to her ear.

Coworker? Evaleen worked for herself as an author. Did she recently hire an assistant?

"I'm going to go check on Henrik. Oh, I forgot to give this to you yesterday at the rehearsal dinner. Jagger gave it to me over a week ago, but I haven't had time pass it on." Edgar removed a wrinkled envelope from his tuxedo trouser pocket and slid it toward me before getting up.

"How's Henrik doing?" I took the envelope but stared up at Edgar.

Edgar frowned and shook his head before turning toward Henrik. I felt guilty. I was too lost in my thoughts and hadn't asked about Morgana.

Evaleen told me after she called Jagger that Morgana was missing. She tried to get as much information as possible from Tenn but was having a tough time. She wasn't happy about that and neither was I.

But when Evaleen set her mind to something, she made things happen.

Henrik was huddled in the corner, by himself, his fingers curled in his hair. As Edgar approached, Henrik seemed to shrink.

Sighing, I glanced down at the envelope and decided to open it. Much had changed in over a week and I wondered if what he had to say was even relevant anymore.

Dear Tiffany,

I know you hate me and I don't blame you. Even if you never want to see me again, I wanted you to know that you are a wonderful mother. David couldn't ask for a more caring mother that only had his best interest at heart.

I brought my hand to my mouth, forcing the cry back as I continued to read.

It's me that's a terrible friend. I assumed the worst in you when I first met you. I thought you would reveal all my secrets so I kept them hidden. I spied on you like a coward, assuming you needed me to protect you and your son when it's clear how intelligent and strong you already are.

The tears ran down my face as it was hard to believe he saw me this way. Would Jagger say the same right now, as I allowed a deranged woman to take my son at gun point? Probably not.

That's right, I spied on you. You see, I was too spineless to tell you that I planted listening devices in your apartment because you were the best person I had ever had the chance to fall in love with. I was afraid you would get hurt because I let you into my fucked-up world. And then I was too afraid to tell you I removed those devices.

If you are going to hate me I wanted you to know that I love you. I may not know how to give you my heart without breaking a few pieces first, but I wanted to write you so that if you should ever need some comfort, some help, and anyone to fall at your feet, then I will be there.

I promise to love you always. I will be there to protect you if you should ever give me the chance. And I will always admire your quiet strength.

Forever Yours,

Jagger Chance

I stared at the paper, rereading it a few times. He was admitting to me about the spying well before I found out. While that gave me some comfort, it wasn't enough to forgive him. He never should have done it to begin with. But it made me realize Jagger was as new to love as I was to letting my son be independent. We both stumbled and made mistakes.

I folded up the letter and put it into my purse. Looking around I saw Aria—standing alone in the front—staring out the window.

We should be together. I got up and went over to her.

"Hey. How are you doing?" I put my hand on her shoulder.

"I'm going to kill her. I've decided, if she hurts anyone, I will kill her," Aria said with a vacant stare in her eyes.

I took her hand in mine. "Come. Let's cheer Henrik up." I guided her toward the back where Henrik and Edgar were.

"May we sit?" I asked.

Henrik nodded but then turned his head to face the wall.

There was silence for a minute. The kind of quiet that feels like a boulder on your heart. That heaviness wasn't new to me, but it was to them. The waiting. The not knowing if the person you loved most in the world would be alive or dead when it was all done.

I had to guide them through this.

"Well, this sucks," I said.

That got their attention. Their eyes landed on me as if I just burp-sung the national anthem.

"You think?" Aria said.

"Don't, Tiffany. Whatever you are planning to do, just don't. I'd rather sit in my misery," Henrik said, knowing me too well.

"I was just remembering a few years ago when I took David to the Art Institute of Chicago." I smiled and noticed I still held their attention so I continued, "We were walking through one of the gallery sections and some people stared at him. He was in a wheelchair and I remember being angry that grown adults would stare at a child in a wheelchair. I remember one guy, who looked old enough to be a grandfather, pointed and laughed."

I took a breath, willing back the tears. "David had recently got his communication device. He commented that he was glad they were looking at art from all around the world. They needed it. They needed to see things that were different so they might begin to understand the world better. He would always say the wisest things, that boy."

"Did he realize the man was laughing at him?" Aria asked.

"I think so because as we passed by that guy David let out the biggest fart and then used his device to tell me who ever smelt it dealt it." I chuckled.

That brought some smiles and a few giggles to the table.

"Morgana farts in her sleep," Henrik said turning his body to face us, "a lot. And it's not just once in a while. I would say she does it most nights of the week."

"At least you can trap them in the covers. When Alex farts, he considers it a challenge to get me to smell them. He always wants a hug after he farts. Only I don't realize he has farted until I'm trapped in his arms and he won't let go."

We were laughing and enjoying our memories of the people trapped in that building. It wasn't that we weren't scared and desperate to know they were safe, but we needed to remind ourselves of the good too, not just the bad. Something to help us through.

That's when the door to the café opened. Aria stood, her eyes wide as she watched Alex walk into the room.

"Thank God," she whispered before she raced over to him. That huge man opened his arms and allowed her petite body to crush him with love.

Everyone in the café stood. Most of the customers who had been here when we invaded left long ago. A few remained to help bring us coffee and pastries. They stood as well as hope lined their faces.

Popping out from behind Alex the giant, was a little redhead in a disheveled wedding dress.

"Morgana," Henrik said and I had never heard such relief and love in one word.

He got up and ran to her, falling to his knees and wrapping his arms around her waist.

That's when I started to really see them. They each had blood on their clothes, yet none of them appeared to be wounded. Not even a scratch.

"Where's David?" I asked and couldn't help the tremble in my voice.

Right at that moment, Jagger came through the door. His face not like the others. Both Morgana and Alex looked tired, but appreciative to be there.

Jagger eyes were heavy, and he seemed to have a hard time bringing his gaze up to mine. And his shirt . . . it had the most blood. Alex and Morgana were staring at me, frowning.

I shook my head as Jagger stepped closer.

"No. No. Please, where's David?" I ran up to him, grabbing his arms, shaking him.

Jagger pulled me close. "I'm sorry, Tiffany, I never meant for this to happen."

Pulling away I forced the man to look at me, grabbing his chin and pulling it down. "What happened? Tell me."

"David was shot," he whispered.

And just like that, my world spun beneath my feet. The pounding in my ears grew until I couldn't hear what anyone was saying. I didn't even realize but Jagger had sat me back in a chair.

"How?" I kept repeating over and over again.

It was as if my brain was stuck and couldn't think past that one question.

"I didn't see him. I swear, I didn't see him," Jagger said as he knelt at my feet.

I shook my head. "What do you mean?"

He took a breath but held my gaze. "I shot him."

It took a few seconds for those words to sink in. But when they did, all the fear and sorrow I felt died, only to be replaced with anger. A fury so fierce, I couldn't control what my body did.

I pushed him over. "You piece of fucking shit."

The words flew from my mouth without thought as I stood. Jagger scurried to his feet and held up his hands. "Tiffany, I don't think—"

Then I punched him in the stomach. "You shot my son. The one thing in this world you knew I loved more than anything. You took him from me." My words wobbled with tears but deepened, being fed by anger.

I felt a hand on my shoulder but shrugged it off.

"Tiffany," Henrik said from behind.

"No. God damn it, no! You got the woman you love back. What do I have? I have nothing now. Well, fuck that."

"Tiffany, language," Henrik whispered.

"That doesn't matter anymore. I worked hard to raise that boy and even made sure no one cursed around him." I shook my head as a jagged laugh made it past the tears. "Jokes on me. All the hard work. All the not cursing and he's still dead."

"They don't know if—" Jagger tried to speak but he didn't deserve to say anything right now.

"Shut the fuck up. Haven't you done enough? You lie and you spy and now you take a little boy's life."

I was so busy screaming that I didn't hear the bell over the door chime as someone entered the café. It was only when a warm hand came to rest on my arm that I turned with total expectation to halt any sympathy someone wanted to send my way. I needed to be angry. It was time for me to have my say.

But when I turned, the fury, the sorrow, it melted into overwhelming relief. Like a thousand pounds had been lifted and I could breathe again.

"David," I choked out the word.

He didn't have time to respond as I pulled my boy into my arms. David lifted his arm to wrap around me. I held him even when he tried to pull away.

"No, just a little longer," I said and knew the blanket he was wrapped in was drenched with my tears.

"Please, Mom. I need to sit," he said and that was the only thing that took me away from my son, his comfort.

"Of course." I pulled out a chair and helped him into it.

"I thought you had been shot?" Henrik said as he took a seat next to David.

I pulled a chair to the other side of David and ran my fingers through his hair. I could see blood on his clothes that peeked out from beneath the blanket.

"Yeah, that was cool." David smiled and glanced over at Jagger.

"Not really cool when I thought you were dead." I didn't really gaze over at Jagger in the same admiring way as my son did. My look was more like throwing knives—most likely knives dipped in poison.

"I tried to tell you that the medics were out there looking at him to see how badly the wound was. I came in here to tell you so you could go to the hospital with him if need be. But you—"

"Didn't let you speak." I sighed and bit my lower lip. "How about next time you start your speech with my son is alive before you tell me he's been shot."

Jagger nodded. "Noted."

"So, if you'd been shot, shouldn't they be taking you to the hospital?" I asked and gazed around David's body trying to find the wound.

David pulled off the blanket and winced as it fell from his arm. There, on his left upper arm, the sleeve had been ripped off. A large, white bandage was taped to his upper forearm and shoulder. Streaks of dried blood ran down his arm.

"The bullet just grazed my skin. It only had to be cleaned out and bandaged. I don't think Emma Hawthorne was as lucky," David said as he glanced over at Alex.

"Yeah, they took my mother to the hospital," Alex said.

"I'm sorry, Alex," I said.

He shrugged. "She's still my mother and I don't want to see her hurt, but she kind of brought all this on herself."

Truer words had never been spoken.

"I think it's time to head home, David. It's been a long day," I said.

"Can Jagger come? He saved us," David said.

"I wouldn't have been able to do it without my ninja-in-training." Jagger smiled and put his hand on David's shoulder once David stood.

"Hey, Henrik. Can you walk David out? I need to discuss something with Jagger for a second." Henrik nodded and I watched the love of my life regale Henrik with all the tales of the day.

Once they were out the door, I turned to Jagger. He stood tall and I knew he was bracing himself for my wrath. I knew he wasn't going to like what he heard but I wasn't about to rip him apart.

"Thank you for helping everyone get away from that monster. I know it isn't your job, but I want to thank you anyway for coming when I asked."

His eyes softened and he took a step forward. "Anything for you, for David. I would do it again and again if it meant you two are safe."

I took a breath and chewed on his words for a bit. He was telling the truth. He had come to care for David and, in his own way, he really did love me.

"But, I don't think we can see you anymore. All that has happened today made me realize it's best to move forward. You helped me get past what lingering guilt I had about my husband, but I need more than that. You lied. You shot my son. It seems to me you do things with good intentions that can hurt people. And, as a mother, I can't have someone like that around my son. Goodbye, Jagger."

I clasped his hand, staring at his blood-stained fingers as they gripped mine. But then I let go. I turned and walked out, determined never to look back.

THIRTY-THREE

<u>Tiffany</u>

2 Months Later

"I liked it," I said as we stepped out of the petite apartment building and onto the street.

"That one was too small. Plus, it had a weird smell," David said as we turned the corner of the street and walked away from the fifth apartment we had looked at this past week.

It had been two months since the first time Henrik and Morgana tried to get married. They did it again a week later, but just a small affair at city hall. Then we all went out to dinner at a wonderful Italian restaurant where the owner—a small woman with rather large hips— kept fawning over Morgana.

Which Morgana didn't mind as the woman made her a special "bridal" cake. Just for her. I think if Henrik and Morgana ever divorce, Morgana had her eyes on the owner.

"You said the last one was too big, as if that should ever be a problem in a home. Now this one is too small." I shook my head at my very independent son who seemed to find something wrong with every place we went to. At this rate, we'll never move out of our current apartment and our lease was up at the end of the month.

"I'm just not feeling these apartments. We need something that says we're wise and know a thing or two about the world." David fanned his hands out as we walked by shops.

I rolled my eyes. The entire wedding event went straight to my son's head.

Since David was shot he felt the need to show the scar to everyone he met. His friends all thought he was the coolest person in the world. I had to finally put an end to it when he tried to show his scar to the checkout woman at the grocery store. I kept getting weird looks from adults, as they seemed to assume I was somehow involved with him being shot.

"What about this place?" David came to a stop and pointed at what looked like a gym.

There was a sign in the window that said apartment for rent. Before I had a chance to get a good look, David grabbed my hand and pulled me along. How could a boy grow so much and gain such strength in a matter of a few months? He was now taller than me.

David opened the door and we stepped inside. There were floor mats, a large punching bag that hung from the ceiling in the corner, and some things I recognized from what David had used in PT. I wondered what sort of gym this was.

"No one is here, David. It's noon. They're probably at lunch. We should go." I tried to tug my son back toward the door.

"Wouldn't they lock the place before leaving it. Come on, Mom." David gave me his perfected *I'm smarter than you because I'm a teenager* voice.

"That's true, but—" I stopped talking and perhaps, stopped breathing as a man walked through a door from the back and into the room.

"Jagger." I found my breath and voice once his green eyes found me.

He stopped the moment he saw me. The man hadn't changed. His body still firm and thick like a tree trunk. It suddenly seemed hot in the gym as I stared at the black T-shirt that hugged his chest. I had to take off my red scarf and navy wool coat for fear I might pass out.

"Tiffany. David. What are you two doing here?" he asked and I had to glance away at the flicker of hope I saw in his eyes.

"We're here for the apartment for rent," David said before I could stop him.

"Actually, I think we should look somewhere else." I turned to my son to indicate we were leaving. "David."

"I want to see it. I think it would be cool to live over a gym." David pulled away and stepped closer to Jagger.

Jagger's eyes bounced between me and my son. "Maybe your mom is right. I've told you before, David, your mom wouldn't like this."

"Before?" I tilted my head to my son—whose cheeks turned crimson and eyes fell to the floor. "What does he mean by that, David?"

"Uh, nothing." David shook his head and tried to walk toward the door before my arm reached out to stop him.

"No, it's something. Tell me."

"Ugh, fine." David's head fell back as he groaned. "I found out Jagger opened his ninja gym and I came here to sign up for classes."

My eyes widened, and I glanced over at Jagger. "You let him sign up for ninja lessons without me knowing about it?"

Jagger held up his hands. "No, absolutely not. I told him he had to get your permission first. There's even a form that requires a parent's signature. Which he tried to hand back with the worst forged signature I'd ever seen."

"David!" I said.

David turned to me and threw his hands in the air. "Come on, Mom. I just want to learn to be a ninja. This is, like, my dream. And Jagger is so cool, and you refuse to let me call him."

I stepped closer to my son and lowered my voice. "He shot you. Why would I let you near a man who could have cost you your life?"

"That was my fault," David yelled.

"David, don't blame yourself. I had been trained in what to do in that situation, and I knew to look first and then pull the trigger. Obviously, I didn't do that. It was my fault."

David shook his head. "I didn't say anything, even when the police questioned me. I'm sorry."

"Say what? That I shot you? David, they already know that," Jagger said.

"No, that I jumped from behind you to try and take down Emma Hawthorne. I thought . . ." David paused as he stared at the floor. "I thought since I was able to get away from that big guy, Will, that I could help you capture Emma. You thought I was behind you when you aimed at her and you were right. But, for some stupid reason, I thought I could leap around you and take her. I thought I could help you."

"Oh, David," I said and put my arms around my son. "I love you. You know that. But if you ever try to do something like that again you will be grounded for a year."

Jagger moved closer and put a hand on David's shoulder. "But you had been trained on what you did to Will. You hadn't been trained on tackling someone or dealing with anything involving guns. That stuff only works in Hollywood movies. In real life, situations with guns are very complicated. And even someone like me—someone who is highly trained—can make mistakes. Especially in a chaotic situation like that."

Jagger sighed and shook his head. "That's why you have to work on your skills before you ever use them. I appreciate you wanted to help, but make sure you know what you are doing next time."

"I'm sorry," he said barely above a whisper.

"My sweet boy, I'm proud of you. What Jagger said was right, you need to know what to do in a situation like that before you try and do it. But I'm proud that you wanted to help."

I glanced around the room and then gazed over at Jagger, hoping I wouldn't regret my decision. "I tell you what. How about I let Jagger keep training you? I'll sign you up for ninja lessons."

David pulled away and looked down at me with a big toothy grin. "Really? That would be *epic*."

He immediately scurried off to the punching bag and started to practice his ninja moves. I giggled watching my superhero.

"You have a great kid. I don't think I ever had the chance to tell you that," Jagger said coming to my side. "How are your friends? Evaleen, Morgana, and the gang?"

I sighed. "Morgana and Henrik are happily married and back to work. They finally got married and went on a wonderful honeymoon to Italy. Evaleen is uncomfortably pregnant and you know what that means for Edgar."

Jagger chuckled shaking his head. "That poor guy."

"Aria and Alex are living somewhat normal lives. As normal as you can get for being with a billionaire. As for Grace, that poor woman. She seemed to always date a bad guy. After Will from the wedding, I think she's sworn off men. She also plans to leave Mimir and move to the East Coast. I think Baltimore."

"At least Will's locked up behind bars. How does Alex feel about his mother in that maximum-security prison?" Jagger lifted his brow to me.

"I think he's disowned his mother. He wants nothing more to do with her." I shook my head as my heart ached for that poor rich man. "How about Tenn? I heard he's in a max prison too."

Jagger nodded. "Yeah. It was tough watching Katlin take him away in cuffs. But that guy fooled everyone."

"It was weird those guys from Morgana's bridal shower, the ones that waited on us in the Eternity suite, were also working for Emma. It's not like they could get much information from us as we celebrated her upcoming wedding? At least they were caught and are behind bars now." I shook my head.

"Weird." Jagger said and I thought I saw a slight twitch of his lips.

There were a few moments of quiet as we watched my son with smiles on our faces. Glad the bad people were locked up and the chaotic months of the summer were now a memory.

"You have a great gym. Congratulations."

Jagger turned to face me. My breath caught as the curve of his lips made my insides flutter.

"Thank you. I opened two weeks ago. Your son showed up last week, but I had to keep turning him away."

I nodded. "No wonder he wanted to look at the apartment. He knew you were here that little sneak."

The conversation lulled and as much as I wanted my feelings to fade for Jagger, they stubbornly held on. I thought about him often and sometimes it involved my vibrator. For that brief period when we were friends, and more than friends, it was satisfying. It was nice to be loved in that way again.

"I never really did eavesdrop on anything when I put those listening devices in your apartment," Jagger said as he rubbed the back of his neck.

"If that's true, why did you even put them in there to begin with?" I folded my arms and turned to him.

He sighed. "There isn't a day that goes by that I don't ask myself that. Right after that first ninja lesson with David and Diego, when you made that delicious pasta, I wondered what would happen if some criminal I was after found out about you and David. I worried they could get to you and I would never know. So, the next day I went out and bought some devices and came over with the excuse that I left my wallet behind and planted them."

I could see why he did what he did, but that didn't make it right. "If you were so worried, why didn't you walk away?"

"I did. Each time I came to your place I wanted to end it but seeing David's smile, and especially gazing at yours . . . it was too hard. That dinner made me realize you two were the family I always wanted but never had. Anyway, I felt guilty about planting the devices and decided three days later to take them down. And for the first time, I listened in to see if you were home. That's when I heard you talk about the date you were about to go on."

My eyes widened. "You knew I would be at that restaurant. You spied on my date."

He held up his hand. "Guilty. I admit I did come to that restaurant with the intention of interrupting your date."

I smacked him lightly on his upper arm. "You bastard."

"But I didn't have to do anything. He pulled a perfectly good Gregger, doing all the work for me." He chuckled.

I folded my arms and huffed but eventually a giggle made its way to my lip.

"He was a dumbass," I said and we both chuckled.

My heart felt a little empty since I said goodbye to him.

"I can show you the apartment if you want?" Jagger said.

Did I even want to? I was tired of looking at apartments for rent but there was a slight buzz in my chest—and definitely in between my legs—that wanted to be alone with him.

"Okay." I blushed as I said it and wanted to hide my face. Why did I feel like a schoolgirl going to see a boy's bedroom?

"David, Jagger's showing me the apartment. Are you coming?" I said.

David stopped punching the bag and was breathing heavy. "No. I'm sure it's cool. I'll be down here practicing."

I shook my head. "He was so picky with all the other places. Insisting he be there to look at the apartments and now he doesn't care. Go figure."

There was a door on the side of the wall that Jagger unlocked with a key. It led to a set of stairs. At the top, Jagger took another key to open the door to the apartment.

The inside was small. The living room had enough room for a tiny couch and coffee table, and that was it. Even the kitchen was back against the wall with only a refrigerator, oven, sink, and one small counter.

"This is a two bedroom?" I asked.

"Yes, but the rooms aren't that big. There's only one main bathroom and it's shared." He walked me back to the two tiny bedrooms, both had a view of the street below. And the bathroom had a stand-up shower that I wondered if anyone could actually fit inside.

"If David thought that last place was small, I'm sure he'll hate this place. No offense." I frowned.

"None taken. You can see why I want to rent it. Not only will it help with paying for the building, but even for me, it's tiny. I think my old place by the train tracks was bigger and it was a one bedroom."

"Can a person actually fit inside that?" I pointed to the shower.

"It's legal but I hadn't attempted it myself," he said.

I walked over and had to back up to open the glass door to the shower. Stepping inside, I was surprised that I could fit, but when I turned to step out, my sweater got caught on the entry.

"Here, let me help you." Jagger came over and tried to work the material out of the hinge.

It was awkward because of the tight space. He had to push his stomach to mine and lean over until his breath fell down my neck. I watched as the tiny wrinkles around his eyes deepened as he concentrated on the task.

"There. It's fixed," he said and turned his head, catching me watching him.

His smile fell and those creases by the corner of his eyes smoothed out. Jagger didn't move. He was an inch from my lips and as stuffy as this tight space became, I didn't want him to step away.

His eyes stayed on my mouth. "I miss you."

I bit my lip, willing myself not to lean toward him. But I couldn't stop from saying what I felt, "I miss you too. But?"

"No but, I just miss you."

The divorce papers had been finalized a month ago and I didn't think my heart would hurt as much as it did.

One blustery Thursday evening, I opened a thick piece of mail and there it was, all typed out, the end of my second marriage. Something in my chest tore. And I swear, it had yet to heal.

"I want to kiss you," he said as he grabbed my waist and pushed me back against the wall of the small shower, "but I want to say something first."

He searched my eyes for an answer. I wanted to give him that answer but as I opened my mouth, nothing came out but a moan.

"We aren't perfect, Tiffany," he said as he began to dot kisses over my cheeks, my throat, and into my hair. "I'm so rough around the edges, I should come with a warning sign. But you're sweet and so caring that you're like syrup—sugary and addictive and messy. Very messy."

He pushed my hair into his face or maybe it was he pushed his face into my head, it didn't matter. I only noticed that when he inhaled it was the sexiest thing I had ever heard.

"But I love that. Because when the both of us came together we weren't any of those things. We weren't rough or sweet, we were somewhere in between."

He lifted his head and gazed at me as if I was some fading dream. "What we have isn't pretty like a picture, it's the mountains and the valley and the sun that inspired the artist. We are forever like that rock and earth and ball of fire. We may be hot and cold, but we will always be solid because we are the eternal. You are what I had been looking for most in my life, even if I only just met you in June."

Then his lips devoured mine. And all his words melted into that kiss and I knew I would never let him go again.

EPILOGUE

<u>Jagger</u>

4 Months Later

She was mine.

I leaned my back against the wall as I tried to scale back my smile. It was becoming out of control. As Edgar mentioned a few days ago, it was bordering on creepy.

I chuckled as I thought about how Edgar and I first met. Now look at us, friends. Since his wife, Evaleen, started to work for ITA, I had gotten to know them better. Not that I ever went back to the government, but I came to find out that Evaleen had a little network of spies she liked to keep in case she needed information. I became part of her network.

"Can you get me a beer?" Tiffany yelled from the bedroom.

"Of course." I pushed off the wall and headed into her kitchen.

Evaleen was on maternity leave right now and Tiffany and I had gone over to help with Lucy, or little Lam as the proud parents have nicknamed her, a few times. Even David wanted to help. That boy got his caregiving side from his mother. I wouldn't be surprised if he grew up to be a nurse or teacher, instead of all his talk about being a ninja.

Evaleen insisted I didn't have to help her with the baby, but if there was any other woman besides Tiffany I would bend over backward for, it was Evaleen. She helped stop Tenn before he had time to run off after Henrik and Morgana's first wedding

I texted her, just after I shot Emma, with Will's phone as Tenn still had mine. I let Evaleen know that Tenn was working for the Jewel. She immediately contacted Katlin and ran over to tell the police sergeant who had been helping Tenn outside on the street. The sergeant distracted Tenn when Katlin and some agents showed up to take him down.

After finding only two beer bottles, I searched around what was left in the kitchen to find some red plastic cups. I poured the beer into two cups and decided they needed something extra.

I made my way back to her bedroom and held out a cup to her. With a smile that still made my heart stumble, she took it. "Thanks. Only a few more boxes and we can start loading the truck."

She was mine.

Tiffany and David were moving into my apartment and I felt like the luckiest guy in the world. I had found another, much bigger, two-bedroom closer to downtown just before I opened The Ninja Gym. It was quiet and in a great neighborhood. There were only two things missing—Tiffany and David.

Over New Years, I asked her to move in with me and she said yes. I wasn't sure if she was saying yes to the moving in or the fact that my mouth was between her legs and I was giving her an orgasm. But, she told me later after we left the bathroom and returned to the holiday party that she was saying yes to both.

Due to the terrible Chicago winters, I made them wait until it was closer to spring to move in.

I raised my cup to her. "Happy St. Patrick's Day."

She raised hers too and just before taking a sip, she stopped when she looked into the cup. "It's green."

I nodded. "Yeah, because it's St. Patrick's Day. They dye the river green."

I waved toward the window even though we were nowhere near the Chicago River.

Tiffany frowned. "You know Blackburn isn't my maiden name. It's Ryan."

"Okay," I said and took a sip from the cup.

"Dying things green doesn't mean it's Irish." She folded her arms in front of her chest, plumping up her tits. It caused me to stare. She was wearing a tank top, it would be impossible for me not to stare.

"Uh huh." I nodded not really listening to what she was saying anymore.

"I'll drink this beer because it's beer and I'm thirsty, but know I do it in protest." She pulled her hair back as she drank from the cup.

I watched her chest rise and fall in between sips.

She was so sexy, even drinking green beer while packing.

Tiffany drained the cup and let out a loud belch, slamming the cup down on the side table. She held up a finger and said, "One point."

I blamed her son. David and Henrik expanded on the fart game they made up to include burps. Tiffany told me she was grossed out at first by the game but was gassy one night and decided to play. She's been champion ever since.

"You know how sexy I find you when you release bodily gases," I said as I blinked at her.

She smirked. "You're just jealous because you can't beat me."

Tiffany picked up the tape dispenser. "David conveniently had to help his friend, Diego, with a class project. So, it's just you and me moving the boxes when we finish packing up."

"It might be more purposely, than conveniently." I put my cup on her dresser and stepped closer as she finished sliding the tape along the seam of a box.

She put down the tape dispenser on the table and turned to me with her hands on her hips.

"Did you tell David to stay away on moving day?"

"Possibly," I said slowly moving closer to her.

"Possibly?" Tiffany asked.

"Probably."

I reached over and slid my hands around her waist.

"Probably?" She tilted her chin up and curled the corner of her sexy mouth.

"Definitely," I said as I watched her eyes darken.

"Definit—" I cut her off as my hand cupped her neck and my mouth brushed over hers.

She tasted like madness and as my fingers slid over her skin, her shudder felt like the sweetest indulgence. I pushed her back onto the bed and dropped to my knees.

"You're so easy," I said as my fingers crawled slowly, but intently, until my hands had completely unbutton, unzipped, and pulled off her jeans.

Then I spread her legs.

"I like these." I hooked my finger through her green lace panties and rubbed the back of my finger over her drenched pussy.

"I wore them the night I met you." Tiffany's voice had lowered and her eyes were like pools of chocolate.

"I remember. Now take them off."

She pulled them down and flicked them away with her foot before spreading her legs again. I pushed one finger inside her, desperate to hear her gasp. She didn't disappoint. When I hooked my finger and twisted my hand, she added an extra moan.

"I could listen to you forever. You sound better than any song ever sung," I said.

Reaching into my pocket with my free hand I grabbed the thing I put there just for this moment. I placed it on the ground next to me.

It had to wait a little bit so I could hear more of my love's song. I lowered my tongue to between her thighs, lapping up Tiffany's sweet flavor.

Working my fingers over her slippery folds, she sung some more. The melody sweet but guttural. I lifted my eyes and found she was watching. Fuck, I loved it when she watched me devour her.

Her lips soft and puffy and her cheeks flushed, I added another finger for her to ride.

"Oh, Jagger." Her head fell back as her hips swayed toward me.

My tongue swirled around her clit and I knew she wanted more. Her face desperate as she lifted her head and reached for my head.

Her fingers tugged and pulled at my hair. I closed my eyes at the pain as I focused on her pleasure.

"I'm coming," she said but I already knew.

Her pussy tightened around my fingers, convulsing in a frenzy. I sucked on her clit and her eyes widened, knowing another longer wave started as the first orgasm waned.

"Fuck," she said.

I did that to her. I smiled knowing she never used to curse before me. When we first had sex, she was pretty quiet. But now, she talked as dirty as a sailor.

She had been leaning on her elbows but she fell back, her chest rapidly moving up and down. Her hands curled into her hair and I stood over her, watching her lazy smile.

Glancing down on the floor at what I had taken out of my pocket before, I hesitated. Maybe that could wait just a little longer. Reaching over to the bedside table and thankful she hadn't packed up the condoms yet, I took one out of the drawer.

When I pulled off my jeans and boxer briefs, I quickly rolled on the condom. I pushed up her tank top and was so fucking happy nothing was underneath. I cupped her tit and could feel her muscles still giving slight tremors.

I pushed back her thigh with my other hand and pushed my cock to just outside her opening.

"You want me to fuck you?" I asked but knew the answer.

"Yes." She pulled her other leg up, rising to me, showing me everything.

"Look how horny you are for me." I trailed my finger over her drenched folds and back just before I got to her puckered little hole.

I watched her lift her ass toward me, gnawing on her lower lip and whimpering.

"You're so fucking dirty. I bet you want me to completely fill you. I bet you need it all," I said trying to hold back from pushing inside her.

Tiffany, over the course of the last few months, was like a flower opening for the first time to the sun in the bedroom. If I had known that the more time you spent with a woman in the bedroom the more open she became to doing things, I would have given up being a spy a long time ago to have a girlfriend.

I finally gave Tiffany what she wanted. I pushed my finger inside her and then my cock. My hips gyrated, and she trembled as I pumped into her. She was more stunning than a cool, breathless night filled with stars winking with wonder. It didn't take long for her to begin orgasming again. And as she did, I felt my climax creep up and hit me. I collapsed over her, clutching her body.

She was everything I had ever dreamed of in a woman, and I couldn't imagine being with anyone else. As I rolled off her and we both lay there sweaty and gasping for breath, I knew it was time.

I got up and went to the bathroom in the hall and washed up. Coming back, I brought a wet cloth and got down on my knees on the floor, opening her legs. I gently wiped her and then threw the rag aside.

"Come on up here," she said, lifting to her elbows to glance down at me.

"I have something for you." I lifted the box and placed it on the bed.

Her eyes crinkled with confusion. "What's this?"

"Something I promised you."

She shrugged and took the box to open it. At first, she tilted her head and I knew she had no idea what to make of it.

"Put it on," I said.

"Okay." Laughter laced her voice.

She removed it from the package and slid it down her finger.

"Doesn't quite fit. I think it's made for smaller hands. But what do you think?" She held out her hand.

"It looks beautiful on you," I said.

Tiffany lifted it to her lips and swirled her tongue around it. "Mmm. It's cherry. Ring Pops are the best."

I smiled and couldn't wait for our life together to begin. She didn't know this yet, but I planned to replace that ring with a real one in May, on her birthday.

"It's perfect. Pretty and sweet. Just like you."

THE END

BEHIND THE SCENES

This is the part of the book where I tell you little factoids about different parts of the story and/or why I wrote the book. As I write, I throw in things that have happened to me, to people I know, or stuff I witnessed in life. Some of it is crazy and some is dorky, but that's me – crazy and dorky.

Let's get started!

In Chapter 7 Tiffany mentions when she was pregnant with David that The Beatles songs made her nauseas. That was based on my pregnancy with my first son. The only music I could listen to was Led Zeppelin and Classical. Everything else made me nauseas. I remember walking down the street and someone drove by with their window rolled down and a Beatles song blasted out. I instantly became nauseas. Once the car was gone and I couldn't hear the music anymore, the nausea went away.

In Chapter 8 in the middle of trying to figure out if Tiffany and Morgana were drugged, Tiffany ends up going off on a tangent about Evaleen being pregnant in Vegas. This was inspired by me. I wanted to show Tiffany's frustrating side. I knew, from the many times my husband had pointed out that nothing I said made sense. My husband rarely understands what I'm talking about either because I mumble or I made a 90 degree turn in the middle of a conversation.

In chapter 18 Jagger mentioned the evil squirrels in Chicago. This was based on my experience with the squirrels in the park along Lake Michigan. I was once walking my dog (who was large enough to make grown men cross to the other side of the street when they saw him coming toward them) and a squirrel followed us. Jumping from tree to tree. It was kind of creepy so I waved my hand at it and my dog began to bark at it, which just made the squirrel more daring. The squirrel kept lunging toward us and making crazy noises. I immediately pulled my dog back and ran away. Those are some tough squirrels.

In Chapter 22 Tiffany remembered taking David to the Art Institute of Chicago. She mentioned a man old enough to be a grandfather laughing at her son in a wheelchair. That was inspired by something that happened to my son. He has Cerebral Palsy and when he was 3 years old he got a medical walker. He had freedom for the first time and to celebrate that weekend we, as a family, walked around the mall. He had only ever been in the mall in a stroller. With the biggest smile on his face, he raced around and I walked with him, guiding him so he didn't bump into people.

We got a lot of stares but it was the older man that stopped walking, turned to my son, pointed and started to laugh that I'll never forget. I was thankful my son hadn't noticed him because I immediately put my body between him and the man to block his view. But I knew I wouldn't be able to shield him forever from the ignorance and hurtful nature of some people. That man was old enough to know better.

The character of David was very loosely based on my youngest son. While David was 12 and turned 13 in the book, my son was 5 years old at the time of writing this. But, when I first created David, three years ago, my son was two, the same age David had his accident that left him disabled.

My son wasn't in a car accident but he has a physical disability, Cerebral Palsy. In the book David had an operation that gave him the ability to walk, talk, and start to feed and get dressed by himself. I did that because these were all the things my son's learning to do with his limitations. He still can't get dressed by himself and has trouble feeding himself, but he can now walk (with help) and has limited speech.

I think David and Tiffany were a way for me to process all the ups and downs that go along with being a parent of a kid with special needs. It wasn't easy to write these characters and many times I broke down in tears because what Tiffany was feeling I had felt so many times.

I hope I did the characters justice and you got a chance to fall in love with them, as I have.

ABOUT THE AUTHOR

Elizabeth Lynx was a printer. She was also a graphic designer, photographer, actress, comedic improviser, merchandiser, and now she is adding author to that extensive list of professions.

She has written an erotic romance called Her Night with Him. Since she spent a lot of time training and moved halfway across the country to pursue comedy (much to her husband's chagrin) only to change her mind and take up writing, Elizabeth decided to write a romantic comedy series called Cake Love.

Follow Elizabeth Lynx:

Website: www.elizabeth-lynx.com

Fan Group on Facebook: Elizabeth Lynx's SWIM Meet

Newsletter: http://bit.ly/NwsltrDHinspire

THANK YOU

There was so much I wanted to say, but I didn't think there was enough space to thank you without turning the book into a 500-page novel. That you read to the very last page of my book and spent your hard-earned money to read what I wrote, means the world to me. Thank you so much!

To think, the humble beginnings of the Cake Love characters started on my website as a character blog. And now, many novels and years later, it's finished (or is it?). I had spent so much of my time in the Cake Love world that writing new characters for a new series, won't be easy.

I'd like to thank Silvia & Marla. If you two hadn't told me the harsh truth I never would have been able to turn this series from a piece of flaming poo into a beautiful piece of cake.

Thank you to Becky, Monique, Melissa, Phala, Nikki, Athena, Gina, Tina, Desiree, and all of SWIM Meet. You bring a smile to my face every day. Your support, honesty, and friendship mean everything to me.

Special thanks for the tremendous help I received from the Inkers, ASN, and the RomCom ladies. I felt like I finally found a group of peers that are supportive and so very helpful. I learned so much from you all.

Finally, thank you to my family. To my mom and dad, who were nothing but supportive when they found out I wrote romance, you know, the kind with sex in it (LOL). To my boys who know mommy writes but only understands it's for adults. Thanks for not expecting me to read my stories to you. And to my husband, thanks for volunteering your body for research and pretending you care when I go on and on about my latest plot twist.

www.ingramcontent.com/pod-product-compliance
Lightning Source LLC
Chambersburg PA
CBHW071901220626
47052CB00002B/161